Lion in the Heather

The Longleigh Chronicles, Book Six

Lynn Shurr

A Wings ePress, Inc.
Historical Romance Novel

Wings
Press, Inc.

Wings ePress, Inc.

Edited by: Jeanne Smith
Copy Edited by: Christie Kraemer
Executive Editor: Jeanne Smith
Cover Artist: Trisha FitzGerald-Jung

Wings ePress Books
www.wingsepress.com

Copyright © 2022 by: Lynn Shurr
ISBN-13: 978-1-61309-516-4
ISBN-10: 1-61309-516-3

Published In the United States Of America

Wings ePress Inc.
3000 N. Rock Road
Newton, KS 67114

What They Are Saying About
Lion in the Heather

"Shurr is a wonderful storyteller."

—The Romance Studio

"Very easy read, well written, combined with conflict, believable plot and secondary character that make the story come alive."

—Jane Lange, *Romances, Reads and Reviews*

"I love the picture the author paints of the town and the way of life, and the characters are strong and interesting.

—Joan Conning Afman
Author of *The Cheetah Princess*

"Lynn Shurr breathes life into the characters and allows each turn of the page to lead up to a pleasurable ending."

—Cherokee
Coffee Time Romance and More

"I love how deep and well-written the characters are."

—Juliette Brandt
Paperbacks and Frosting

"You can count on Lynn Shurr to deliver interesting characters and great romance."

—A.C. Mason
Author of *Deadly Bayou*

Dedication

For my editor, Jeanne Rubba Smith.
Thanks for the encouragement.

* * *

One

London, August 1814

"Of course, you shall have an invitation for the autumn grouse hunt," Pearce Longleigh, Duke of Bellevue, bellowed at the two young men on horseback. By the tone of his voice and the raising of his brawny arm as he gestured them away, the words seemed more of a threat than a cordial promise. "Off with you! Cease imploring my daughter and upsetting the carriage horses."

Inside the ducal coach, Lady Euphemia Longleigh neatly added the small nosegay and the box of bonbons her admirers had proffered to the heap of tokens others had left. The stack on the seat beside her unbalanced, and a few wilting floral tributes toppled over onto the dark skirts of her sister, Pandora, who brushed them to the floor. Both young women resumed reading—Phemie, the latest novel that was the talk of the ton, *Waverley* by an anonymous author, and Panny, yet another of her abolition tracts.

Sitting opposite, their mother, Lady Flora, Duchess of Bellevue, beamed over the success of her youngest daughter's first London season. Not since her eldest daughter, Thalia, had come out had she been so pleased with the result of her efforts to rear a perfect, lady-like female child. Considering that Euphemia was the last of six daughters, this said a great deal about her other attempts. Her most colossal failure glanced up as if reading her mother's mind. Not that Pandora was ugly, certainly not.

She possessed a severe beauty. Never allowing a single lock of her shining, straight black hair to be frizzled into curls, Panny preferred to draw it up into a simple knot hidden under the plainest of bonnets, while Phemie's natural dark curls frothed about her lovely face. The younger sister's wide brown eyes shone with joy, and sometimes mischief, while Pandora's dark glance burned under slim, black brows. True, she had inherited more of her grandmother's Shawnee Indian coloring than Phemie, and was rather dark-complexioned because of it, but she had also gotten fine, high cheekbones, and a straight English nose. If only Pandora would not compress her lips into such a severe line and instead, let her smile bloom into a sweet bow as her sister did.

The duchess put these thoughts aside and returned to more pleasant matters. "Phemie, do you not favor any of your suitors?'

Barely taking her eyes from her book, she replied, "No, Mama. They are all pleasant enough, and I did enjoy their company, the dancing, and my new gowns. I did not weary of the season as Panny said I would, but none has won my heart. They do not compare to Papa or any of my brothers. I shall need an exceptional man to stand up to them."

"Well, there is nothing wrong with taking one's time and having a second season to decide, is there, Pandora?"

"If you mean to foist a third season upon me, I decline." She rattled her tract in an annoyed manner.

"Phemie so generously shared her dancing partners with you, I thought you might have considered one of them for a husband," the duchess replied with too much hope in her voice.

"*I* thought if I heard Phemie say one more time, 'My card is full but please allow my sister Pandora to honor you with a dance,' I would puke into the floral arrangements. The only reason she has so many beaux is that she hides her true nature, while I do not. If those young men knew she can do equations in her head and fix a broken watch as well, they would have fled the ballroom. Instead, she chose to play the empty-headed heiress."

Her curls shaking, Phemie slapped her book shut. "For the fun of it! While ending slavery and gaining women's equity are great causes, we need not give up enjoying life for them. You will not free one slave or gain a vote in Parliament even if I were to give up dancing forever, so no harm done."

Pandora's smoldering eyes lit. Her mama shut her own gray eyes, knowing the battle was on.

"I see you plan to rot your brain with that romantic rubbish all the way to Bellevue Hall. None of your suitors are around. Here, read one of my tracts and improve your intellect."

Pandora thrust a pamphlet embellished with a woodcut of a naked, dark-skinned woman in chains at her sister. Phemie shoved it back.

"I have my own reading, thank you. I'll have you know I've learned a great deal about Scottish customs, religion, politics, and history from *Waverley*. You see, it tells a tale of the great uprising of the clans sixty years ago. The author is anonymous," she added, as if that made the story all the more thrilling.

The duchess opened her eyes again. "Everyone knows the poet, Walter Scott, wrote it to pay off his debts. No secret there."

"You see, even the author is ashamed to own it. So is Waverley some gothic mansion or the pure, puerile hero who rescues a damsel because she cannot rescue herself?"

Phemie's usually sweet, full lips compressed. "Waverley is the hero, and I do admit he is rather immature and foolish. But oh, the portraits Mr. Scott paints of the mighty Fergus Mac-Ivor and his valiant sister, Flora, more than make up for him."

Seeing a chance to steer the conversation away from conflict, the duchess said, "You do know Flora MacDonald, not Mac-Ivor, was a true heroine of the rebellion. She aided Bonnie Prince Charlie's escape, and our government imprisoned her in the Tower of London for her efforts. So brave and gentle-mannered was she that she soon won her release and gained permission to live in the city. Dr. Johnson admired her greatly. I sometimes fancy I might have been named for her, as my mother made her acquaintance, but being the wife of a good Whig, she would never own up to that."

"Oh, Mama, you would have made a fierce Scottish Jacobite, I suspect." Knowing their mother's weakness for compliments about her spirited nature, the girls exchanged small smiles and set their quarrel aside.

"I would have! Pandora, here's a bit you would enjoy. Flora MacDonald wed a soldier and went to the American colonies with him during that rebellion. After many adventures, she tried to return home to Scotland, only to have her ship attacked by a privateer. She refused to leave the deck, took part in fending the scoundrels off, and was wounded in the process. She died at a ripe age not all that long ago when I was a young woman bearing my babies. Her tomb is engraved with the words, *courage,* and *fidelity.* I've been to the Isle of Skye to see it."

"A heroine after my own heart, Mama. Still, I'd rather read a biography of her than have her story serve a novelist."

"We shall write the bookseller to search for one and read it aloud to each other during the long winter evenings at Bellevue Hall." Peace restored, the duchess opened her fan and stirred some breeze. "Stuffy in here." She called out the open carriage door to her beloved husband, "Dearest, when will we be leaving for the north?"

"We wait for Jason, my love. I know our son has a watch, because I gave it to him myself. If only he would use it. Drat! Here come three more smitten young men with enough flowers to cover a bier."

He closed the door abruptly and intercepted them. "As you can see, we are about to depart, gentlemen. Yes, I will see Phemie gets your offerings. Of course, you will receive an invitation to visit Bellevue Hall at some time." Blocking their view of his daughter with his stalwart form, he eventually encouraged the suitors to move along.

Opening the door again, the duke heaved himself inside. The carriage listed a bit on that side as he sat. Always a large man, he had thickened some with the years, but his bulk still consisted more of muscle than of fat. While he waited for his errant third son, a footman held the reins of the black horse, huge enough to carry a full-armored knight into battle, that he intended to ride on the journey.

"Might as well sit for a while." He added the bouquets to his daughter's pile of booty but held back a net of Jordan almonds. "At least, these will be of some use on the journey."

Placing the sweets in the large pocket of the greatcoat he wore, though vastly out of style, the duke asked Phemie her preference. "Do you have a liking for any of these lads, or must I trot them out before you at Bellevue, one by one, like young stallions at a horse fair so you can make up your mind?"

"You needn't for my sake, Papa. I believe I will require a second season to reach a decision."

"I will see you get it. Lest any of your suitors try to carry you off to Gretna Green for a quick marriage, I have stationed some of the Armstrong boys in that town. You shall be stopped before you reach the anvil and the blacksmith says his words over you. Pandora? Any young gentleman you would wish me to invite for the grouse season?"

"Let them all rot in London."

"I see. Never fear, Panny. Once Phemie has made her choice and wed, we shall up the ante on your dowry and get you a husband."

The duchess folded her fan and rapped her husband on the forearm. "What a dreadful thing to say. Our daughter is not for sale."

"Yes, I am. Quite a few men would have me for the twenty-thousand pounds you already offer, but I would not have them." Pandora's perpetual scowl returned.

"Indeed." Trying to put a good face on her comment, the duke continued. "Never fear, every family needs one maiden lady to care for the parents in old age."

This earned him a double rap of the fan. The duchess did enjoy reprimanding her husband in this manner, an old custom between them. "Pandora will find a man to love and have a felicitous marriage just as we do. If only she would not stare so fiercely and speak of her causes at the dinner table."

The duke rubbed his arm. His deep, black eyes were alight and focused on his wife. The sisters shared a dismayed look. Whenever Mama began chastising with her fan, their father felt the need to retaliate in the most amorous fashion to defend his manhood.

"Is all packed for the removal to Bellevue? The sheets, the bedding?"

Lady Flora's color rose. "I am not certain, my love. Perhaps we should go upstairs and be sure."

The duke exited the carriage and helped his petite wife down by circling her still small waist with his large hands. Their daughters watched his iron gray queue and their mother's eagerly bobbing curls, which still retained a hint of gold, disappear into the townhouse.

"There, you've set them off again, Panny. The baggage train left hours ago while we took our breakfast. How long do you think they will be?" Phemie rarely quarreled with her closest sister, but she was more than ready to abandon London for the estate that lay so near to Scotland. Perhaps dear papa would take them for a jaunt to Castle Laughlin, one of their holdings in that country if she begged sweetly.

"I will bet you a pound on twenty minutes."

"More likely thirty."

Pandora consulted the small watch she had pinned to her bodice and noted the time. "And thank you for repairing this for me. You know how I detest always having to ask the time of a man. I don't care if the weight of the instrument ruins my gown."

"Simply a broken spring. I do hope they hurry."

"We still must wait for Jason. I wish Kate had come along and taken his seat so we needn't suffer his lame verses all the way home."

"Panny, we can only be happy for our sister-in-law. Now that she is finally *enceinte*, naturally, she would rather be closer to her mother at the Grange and do her lying-in there."

"Ha! Kate much prefers our mother's liberal attitude, but Greenway Grange is only a day's ride from London, and she wants to be nearer to Joshua toiling away in the city to make his mark as a barrister. In my opinion, it is our second brother's fault that she did not conceive sooner. And why can't we simply say 'pregnant?' Why must all words concerning birth be coated with honey and spoken in French, I ask you?" Pandora crushed her tract with her gloved hand as she spoke, another of her complaints against society.

"You know our mother does not mince words among the family, but even she glosses the subject when out in polite society. Kate felt her terrible physical ordeal kept her from catching for more than a year, so why blame Josh?"

"Yes, fault the woman when there is no child. I suspect men might have their problems, too, in making one. But in our brother's case, I believe he applied himself more to his career than to Kate in his eagerness to prove he could support a family. He did not do the job in hand or rather, out of hand."

"Panny, you are scandalous!"

"We have four brothers. You know what nasty creatures boys can be."

"Here comes one now."

Jason Longleigh flung himself inside the carriage and, taking up far too much room with his long legs, lounged back against the squabs. He wore a deep green velveteen jacket spewing lace at the neck and cuffs, dark pantaloons, and shining boots. His inky hair in need of barbering curled into his coat collar, and it seemed he had forgotten to shave that morning. Phemie assessed how gallant he might look in a kilt, though he had not a warlike bone in his aristocratic body. Generations back, there had been a drop of Scottish blood added to the Bellevue line, however, contributed by a bride named Rose.

Placing his high-crowned hat on the seat and closing shadowed eyes of the same shade as his siblings, he said in explanation, "Late night. Are we ready to leave, then? Did my boxes arrive in time for transport?"

"Yes, to your boxes. No, to our departure time. Mama rapped Papa with her fan and off they went to make sure all the linens were packed. How long has it been now?" Phemie answered.

"Fifteen minutes," Pandora replied. "I've bet a pound they will be twenty minutes gone, and Phemie has chosen thirty. Are you in, brother?"

"Of course. I can use the blunt. I'll say twenty-five. To think that Papa criticizes me for dallying with older women, when he is the only man I know who still desires his wife after so many years of marriage. I do wish they would be more circumspect in public."

"Don't we all?" Panny answered.

"Still, when Cupid's arrow finally pierces my throbbing heart, I do hope I am smitten by a woman I can adore for all of time. What are you reading, Phemie? It seems a mighty tome."

"*Waverley.* Would you like to have it after me?"

"Ah yes, I heard the esteemed poet of *The Lady of the Lake* is the author. Poor sod that he had to prostitute his muse and write a novel to pay his debts."

Pandora answered wryly, "That will not be your problem as long as Papa continues your allowance while you study to be a barrister like Josh. How goes the career?'

"Poorly and dully. That is why I am in need of country air, a bit of fishing and shooting. Besides, with Kate being the brooding hen, and Josh afraid I might upset her with what he calls my antics, I thought it best to make my residence elsewhere for a while. Life was so much easier when we shared that house as carefree bachelors. Three truly does make a crowd, especially if one is a woman."

Phemie sorted through her gifts and finally tore the ribbon off the box of bonbons. Seeing the sweets were melting about the edges from the warmth of the day, she peeled off a glove, and selected one for herself. Jason reached out with his long, naked, poet's fingers and snatched away two.

"No gloves, Jason?" Pandora asked.

"No breakfast. I thought I might jot down a few verses as we go along, and gloves impede me."

"It will be a long journey," Panny sighed.

"Here, you will need all your strength for patience. Let me sweeten the way." Phemie popped the last chocolate into her sister's mouth.

The door of the townhouse opened. Waving away the assistance of his footmen, the duke escorted his wife down the steps and lifted her into the carriage. Lady Flora's chest and cheeks showed the flush of a woman well-pleased. She settled herself next to Jason and resumed fanning.

"Here at last, son," the duke remarked.

"I seem to be right on *time*," Jason replied, with an emphasis on the last word.

"Twenty-eight minutes," Pandora murmured. "I appear to be the only loser." She opened a small reticule and tossed a pound note each to her brother and sister.

"Whatever is going on amongst you?" the duchess asked.

"Only a silly game to make the minutes pass, Mama." Phemie sat the empty candy box aside.

"And so, onward, onward, 'crosst hill and dale, the Longleighs go, knowing not what 'ventures wait," Jason intoned.

"Hmmm," said the duke. "I believe I shall ride my horse this morning as I planned."

Two

Bellevue Hall, North England, August 1814

"Did ye read the book? Have ye considered my plan to restore the glory of the McLaughlins?"

Leonidas McLaughlin towered over the fanatical old man gnarled with age, but still quite spry of body and mind, as they moved along the garden path. "Yes, I've read *Waverley*. It seemed verbose to me. And no, I would never consider such a cracked-brain scheme. As the title said, '*Tis Sixty Years Since*' the McLaughlins lost their lands to the Dukes of Bellevue in that great folly to restore the throne to King James' line. Let it go, Uncle Duncan."

"I ken ye are no soldier, Leo, but an over-educated physician. Still, I thought the perfect bloodless coup might appeal to ye. Look about ye. See all the Duke of Bellevue owns while the McLaughlins have naught. Surely, the great man can spare that small holding in Scotland he treats as a hunting lodge."

They crunched along the gravel on the right side of the fabulous fountain of Triton—the side that did not spray a visitor with water when the hidden trap was triggered. The sound of its waters drowned out their words for a moment until they passed.

Leonidas shook his head. "I do imagine the Duke might miss the income from the grazing of sheep, the quarry and the fisheries, however. Besides, his eldest son holds the title Viscount of Laughlin."

"That lad rarely shows his face about the place. Gone to more foreign lands, he is. To give Lord Bellevue his due, he does come to inspect twice a year—during the salmon run, and when the grouse are plumpest."

They turned off the main path and started down a side track going past the Indian wigwam set within a patch of maize, beans, and pumpkins, a folly built to please the duke by the duchess, Duncan had told him.

"Castle Laughlin is more habitable now than it has been in a hundred years."

"Aye, that's Lady Flora's doing as well. Tapestries on the walls, and Turkey carpets underfoot. Chimneys that dinna smoke, and garderobes that dinna stink. Featherbeds to lie upon when a good plaid on the floor before the fire is all a real Scotsman needs."

"What would you know of that? You were born the year of the uprising same as my grandfather and have lived here since your fifteenth year."

"Aye, forty and five years, I've toiled on this land, first as an apprentice, then under-gardener, then head gardener because of my gift with growing things. I been here so long all have forgotten I'm a McLaughlin and call me Duncan Gardener. Started under the vera duke who laid claim to our lands after the Battle of Culloden because some ancient kin o' his carried away Rose o' Laughlin and married her. Ye see the fairness of my plan, don't ye, laddie?"

"Bride stealing. You expect me to abduct the duke's daughter and marry her in order to regain our lands."

"It's a time-honored Highland tradition, Leo. Why the immortal Flora MacDonald's own mother was a stolen bride. Ye'd be doing the duke a favor as Lady Pandora has ended her second season without an offer, I'm told."

"What is wrong with her? I understand she has a dowry of twenty-thousand, and still no man will have her."

"Dinna think of her that way. Why, she is a beauty if a bit tart-mouthed. Spirited, though, and full of opinions a woman ought not to have. Her body is womanly with hips to bear the start of a whole new clan of McLaughlins, and the breasts to feed them. Her skin is a trifle brown, but nay more than many Scottish lassies who spend their time outdoors."

Great-uncle and nephew turned off the trail and onto a narrow footpath leading back into the wildwood. The old man paused in a patch of sunlight filtering through the trees, Leo thought to catch his breath, but he was wrong. Duncan regarded his kin's physique with the keen eye of a livestock dealer.

"Aye, Lady Pandora is likely to fight, but ye have the height and strength to handle her. Ye simply throw her over your saddle and escape the way we rode yesterday, taking all the back roads into Scotland and then to Gretna Green."

"To think I believed we'd merely gone on a pleasant excursion as part of my holiday at Bellevue Hall when it was all part of a plot."

"Aye." Duncan's blue eyes so like his own glittered in a lined, tanned face like watery lochs set amongst the crags of the Highlands.

"You are mad. I'd have to drag her bound and gagged before the preacher."

"Wouldna be the first time in history a marriage began that way. Once ye overpower and seduce her, all will be well. The duke will drop her dowry into your pocket and offer Castle Laughlin, too, out of sheer gratitude."

"Why do I doubt this? Uncle, I am a man of science, not of romance. I've enjoyed staying with you and viewing the grandeur of Bellevue Hall and the gardens under your care, but must return to my patients and my inventions shortly."

"Aye, and who do ye have to thank for the roof over your head and the use of the duke's dungeon at Castle Laughlin for your wee contraptions but me."

Leo felt his face flame, the curse of a fair-skinned man. "I earn my keep by giving free treatment to all the servants and tenants. Why, I could leave at any time and set up practice anywhere in Scotland or England."

"And have nay time to dally with your machines, nor the space. Not to mention if the duke knew the last laird of the McLaughlins had taken up residence in his castle, ye'd be out on your ear, lad, and those devices ye love more than your heritage broken into rubbish. He wouldna do that to his son-in-law, however."

"Desist! Let us enjoy our last evening together, Uncle, with a more pleasant conversation and a bit of that fine Scottish whisky I brought for a gift."

Their path ended in a glade, home to a thatched cottage that looked as if it had grown out of the earth like a large brown mushroom, shaggy topped. Enough trees had been cleared away to allow the sun to shine down on a barrier of bramble roses that fenced the yard and discouraged the deer from invading, not that Duncan Gardener kept his own vegetable plot. He had all he wanted from the duke's kitchen garden. The space consisted of beaten earth swept clean by the broom near the door.

"Home, sweet home," Duncan said as he opened a gate in the thorny hedge.

For the first time in a long time, Leonidas set foot in the place allotted to the head gardener of the Bellevue estate. Being a physician who'd seen to a few minor ills among the staff during his stay, the housekeeper had provided a comfortable, but not luxurious, bedchamber for him at the Hall. He had taken his meals with his uncle and the other higher servants, though that good woman had clucked and fussed, saying he should eat his food apart, being an educated man and a step above them. He thanked her for her bountiful meals, but claimed he was not proud and preferred company when he dined.

Tonight, he would stay with his uncle as he had when a child in the enchanted cottage in the wood. He'd listen to the old Highland tales again, but sip Scotch whisky instead of warm milk. He'd sleep before a wood fire topped with a few turves of peat, just for the scent of it, his uncle said, since the head gardener was welcome to gather all the deadfall he wished and had a ration of coal for the winter, too.

The plaid he'd wrap around himself, moth-eaten as it was, bore the McLaughlin colors of sea blue and forest green with a stripe of brown for the good earth.

His great-uncle went easily under the low frame of the cottage door. Leo paused before bending down to enter without bumping his head. He regarded the roses, heavy with hips this time of year, ringing the yard. A few late summer blooms adorned the thorny canes. They were white roses, of course, the flower of the Jacobite cause, same as those always shown tucked into Flora MacDonald's hair in her likenesses. He'd never noticed before. Laughing, he bent his long body and passed into the dark interior of Duncan's lair.

Three

The small fire they'd lit more for light than heat on this summer eve burned down to coals, and the level of the Scotch whisky lowered in the bottle. The last of the peat-scented smoke escaped through the thatch as Duncan McLaughlin corked the vessel sitting on the crude table between himself and Leonidas, putting it safely away in a small cabinet. He brought out a cheese and a tin of crackers to replace it.

"I thank ye for bringing the water of life, nephew, as good as any spirits the duke possesses. Just as ye are good enough for his daughter. Ye have a proud heritage and a pedigree as ancient as Longleigh's own. Lord Lyon King of Arms in Scotland acknowledges ye as laird of the McLaughlins, your coat of arms—two rampant lions or, flanking a tower gules, on a field of vert.

"Not again. My sainted English mother always cautioned me not to take your stories to heart." Leo shook a head, slightly fuddled with drink, and noted his hair had grown past his jacket collar again. A golden red and vigorous, it always seemed in need of a shearing. He brushed it away from his face and accepted an offering of cheese and crackers "to settle the wame for the night," as his uncle recommended.

"My father did not think of himself as a laird. He'd had enough of that during his upbringing in France and was pleased to find an

English merchant's daughter who would bring him a small fortune and embrace Presbyterianism for his sake. As it was, that religion, and the Mc in front of my surname, kept me out of Oxford, and I had to conduct my medical studies elsewhere."

"Thanks be to the body snatchers of Scotland, then, for the corpses they brought ye and your fine education. Still, it pains me ye've dropped the *a* from that Mc."

"Simply more economical when I sign my name."

"Aye, 'tis all about economy and cutting up the dead now."

Duncan stirred the coals and added enough fuel to bring a kettle to the boil for tea. He brought the conversation round to more pleasant memories. "Your mother was a good woman in her way, letting ye visit me as a wee lad when the duke took his family off to London. But to think a McLaughlin laird married a Briton and his son has become one of them."

"Happy chance that he did and chose to dwell in England, with both my grandparents and uncles perishing in the French Revolution because of their association with the court."

"Aye, the year ye were born, so ye never heard the family tales from their lips."

"My father said he'd had enough of those delusions in his youth, with none of them worth a penny and always having to scrabble for cash."

"Pity his removal to England dinna prevent his being run down by a carriage in the streets of London when ye were but fifteen."

"The lairds of Laughlin do seem to have poor luck."

"Aye, they do and for a reason. I'll come to that later."

Indifferent to tales of ancient curses, the man of science did not urge his uncle to tell now. Duncan poured the boiling water into a chipped brown teapot. The aroma of citrus rose into the air.

Leonidas inhaled the scent. "Rose hips?"

"That, and orange peel from the conservatory to cover the taste of the more bitter herbs that will help ye to sleep. I had the receipt from an old healer woman at Castle Laughlin many years ago. The new young physicians like ye discount the power of plants harvested at their peak by the full moon, but I know their strength. Ye will snore soundly on the floor, even though ye've grown accustomed to a featherbed."

"Uncle, I'm sorry I haven't visited more since I was sent away to school and then medical college. I was not so far away in Glasgow. You have taken the place of a grandfather in my life, and I am grateful."

Old Duncan's eyes took on a glitter. "Will ye humor me, lad, and put on those clothes in the trunk, then?"

While waiting for the tea to cool enough to drink, Leo opened the indicated box and laughed as he drew out the first garment. "Heaven help us, what are these?"

"Tartan trews. Drop your breeches and put them on. I'll wager you another bottle of Scotch whisky they fit like a glove."

Leo held the absurd checkered pants to his waist. They did seem the right length.

"Ye can keep on your doctor garb above. Though rather plain, a short black jacket and waistcoat and that simple white stock will do."

Feeling he'd neglected the old man during adolescence and after, Leo turned his back and did as his substitute grandfather requested. The trews fit tightly to his calves and thighs—and his backside for that matter. He noticed a moth hole or two as well.

"Now a true laird's Highland bonnet," Duncan requested.

He donned the flat blue cap with the feathers of a golden eagle and a white cockade yellowing with age pinned to the side. "Wrap yourself in the plaid at the bottom," his uncle prompted again. Leo removed the same plaid he'd nestled in as a small child.

"As I thought. Ye are the image of the chieftain, Ian McLaughlin, who fell at Culloden—minus his breastplate and claymore, of course," said Duncan.

"Well, I feel quite the fool as if I might be going to a costume ball. How would you know about Ian McLaughlin? You were a babe at the time."

"I've seen his portrait in the storage room at the castle, all covered up behind boxes of rubbish. It's there I found the trews and bonnet on my last visit some years ago to see my ailing brother, still steward of the place. As he dinna die, he was willing to take ye in, young Leo, and hide ye from the duke since ye be the true laird o' the castle. But back then, fearing he was on his deathbed, my brother told me once more what he'd witnessed at Culloden. Sit, lad, sit, drink your tea and listen to the tale again." Duncan poured the brew into a fine porcelain cup of blue and white with the handle half broken off.

"Aren't you having any?" Leo asked, as he raised his fragrant, steaming cup to his lips.

"Nay, at my age, I'll be up all the night at the pisspot if I partake. Enjoy it and finish the lot. So, reading *Waverley* did not stir ye?"

"Not at all. In truth, *Waverley* goes back to being a good Hanoverian and subject to King George in the end, and the author lauds this as the right course, one which brought progress to Scotland."

"Och, I dinna agree with him there. It's all roads a'building and letting the fields turn to scenery now. Hard times after the clans dispersed. I wouldna know how to read his book, with no money to be had for proper schooling, if my brother hadna taught me. The author dinna touch on the final glory of the clans at Culloden so as not to distress his female readers, nay doubt. He told not the tale I will tell ye now. Have a second cup and listen."

"Sander, the eldest of my brothers, and twelve at the time, lit out from his school in Inverness to lie in the heather with his friends the night before the battle. There they stayed hidden past noon the next day as the clans formed up behind their chieftains on Drummossie Moor by Culloden house, and the scarlet-coated British ordered themselves into lines not five-hundred yards away. The weather turned ugly, great boiling clouds out of the west pelting the soldiers with rain. Still, the war pipes screamed their battle songs, special to each clan. The British answered with a drum roll and a volley of cannon straight into the Highland ranks. Our warriors cried out the names of their ancestors. Our chieftains stood before their clansmen, waiting for the command to charge, while the English officers hung back behind their ranks as is their way. Men in tartan dropped, cut down, and still Prince Charles Edward did not utter *Claidheamh Mor*! Do ye hear me, lad?"

"Yes, aye, *Claidheamh Mor*!"

"Good. Have more tea."

Obediently, Leo filled his cup and drank. Least he could do to please the old man, but he grew so drowsy his great-uncle's words began to flow over him like the sweet peat smoke. His head lolled back against the chair.

Duncan noted the glazing of the deep blue McLaughlin eyes and his nephew's impulse to obey. The formula to bend a person's will to one's own still worked, though he'd used it scantily over the years and regretted having to use it now. Pity Leonidas had a stubborn streak.

"His ancient breastplate and drawn claymore nay more than a dull pewter gleam in the downpour, your great-grandfather in his tartan riding trews sat a horseback before his kin. His hair so bright like yours, Leo, was drawn back in a tight braided queue and darkened by the rain, my brother said. Grim-faced, Ian McLaughlin could wait nay longer as the cannon shot savaged his men. He led the charge across the sodden heath into the thick red ranks before him and took down many bloody Britons as he went. Alas, alack! Old armor and a blue bonnet are scant protection from cannon fire and a well-placed musket ball. Shot between the eyes he was. As Ian fell, his most loyal tacksman took up his leader's sword, snatched his bonnet, and retreated because his chieftain lay dead and needed him no longer. All about, the clansmen retired, overrunning their camp where the same man found the plaid his chief had slept in but a night before the battle."

"Are these his trews?" asked Leo, regarding his long, outstretched plaid-covered legs with wonder. Had he been in his right mind, the young man would have made a joke of it, Duncan knew.

"Nay, nay, there wasna time to strip him down, though I am sure some Brit stole the breastplate. Possibly ye wear an extra pair he left at home."

"Oh, good. I'd rather not wear a dead man's breeches."

"Have more tea and forget it. Back to our story. The tacksman fled clear 'crosst Scotland to Castle Laughlin, where Lady Ellen waited with her babe in arms."

"There is always a babe in arms," Leo remarked dreamily.

"Ye should be glad, or ye wouldna be here. Now hush, lad. Let me finish."

"Go on."

"The loyal clansman brought news he was but a day or so ahead of rapine and plundering by the British troops. We'd given no quarter at Preston and Falkirk, and they gave us none. My brother and those lads in the heather were flushed from their hiding place by a dragoon and nearly run down, but not before they witnessed every wounded Scot on the battlefield put to the sword. In their bloodlust, the victors slew innocent wayfarers on nearby roads and despoiled the women of Inverness. Such a fate awaited Lady Ellen. She wished to defend her husband's lands by holing up in the old keep, but wiser heads prevailed. She took ship for Ireland with her infant son at her breast and her small cask of jewels tucked under an arm, but not before she hid away her husband's portrait, his claymore, bonnet and plaid. Never did she return again to claim them as she made her way to France to reside with other exiles."

"They never do return," Leo said sadly. His eyes blinked heavily with the drug.

"Those spawns of the red devil, Longleigh's sons, found the cache while playing in the old tower. Lady Flora hung the claymore over the fireplace as an ornament, but the duke wouldna have the painting of an ancient enemy hang in the hall. The rest was packed away."

"Sad."

"Aye, vera sad. Now listen, and I'll tell you of the curse. No McLaughlin laird will live long and happy until he takes a bride from the Longleighs and restores the family honor. Then, the clan will regain its pride and the earth will yield its treasures unto us. Tomorrow, ye will break the curse, Leo. Word has come the family is returning midday. I know their ways. Lady Flora will start setting the house in order, making sure all is as it should be. The duke will visit his hounds and thoroughbreds. The lassies will want some exercise after their long journey and walk in the gardens. Their favorite place is the wigwam, and ye will wait just beyond on a sturdy hack I shall provide. Simply scoop up Lady Pandora and fling her over your saddle and be gone to Gretna Green. Do ye understand?"

With closed eyes, Leo answered, "Aye."

"Now, a caution. It's said the duke has armed his daughters and taught them the use of a knife. Keep an eye out for that. 'Tis all. Lie down before the fire and take your rest."

Leo did so, wrapped in the plaid. All night long, Duncan repeated the plot, knowing the lad could hear him in the trance.

Come morning, he left his grand-nephew sleeping and went to the big house to procure his breakfast and borrow a pair of horses to take his visitor to the post house in order catch the northbound coach to Glasgow, he'd say. What could possibly go wrong with so grand and well thought out a scheme?

Four

Leo woke before the cold fire and groped his way in the dimness to pull the pisspot from under his uncle's modest bed. From the duration of his stream, he concluded he'd had quite a bit more to drink than he remembered. His brain, as fuzzy as the old plaid he'd slept upon, seemed empty of all but ancient legends and odd requests. When had he donned the garish trews he'd lowered to gain his relief? Not since his student days had he drunk so much and remembered so little of a morning.

Cotton-tongued, he searched for the water bucket, but found a full pot of cold tea first and gulped it down, cup after cup, hoping to clear his mind. The brew provided no clarity and only appeared to make matters worse. Vaguely recalling he was to go somewhere today, he stumbled to the cottage door, opened it, and reeled back as the sunlight from high in the sky burned into his eyes. Half the day had passed away without his knowledge. What was wrong with him? As a doctor, he should know.

But was he a doctor or a soldier? The two occupations warred in his mind. He took a seat in one of the chairs near the fireplace. A blue Scottish bonnet hung from its knob. Feeling compelled, he pushed his hair behind his ears and put it on. Now what to do? The Highland fog in his mind thickened rather than dispersed. Horses clopped up the lane so slowly he knew they were being led. Yes, he was to meet a coach and go to Gretna Green today. Why?

His uncle Duncan opened the door to the room and greeted him heartily. "I see ye are up and ready to do your duty. Found the tea and drank it. Good lad. Stand and allow me to complete your disguise."

"Disguise?"

"I think perhaps a mask is best under these circumstances." Duncan took a wide band of black silk from the cupboard drawer. "I begged it from a widow lady I sometimes favor with a visit and cut the eyeholes myself. I've a pistol and dirk for your belt as well. No telling when the duke might o'er take ye, and best to be prepared. Here's my own sporran packed with provender for the trip and a wee bit 'o powder and shot. I've put tea in the canteen. Sling it over your shoulder for now. My, but I wish I had a carbine and a sword for ye, too. 'Twould make a grand sight and impress Lady Pandora."

"Lady Pandora?"

"Yes, your bride-to-be. The one ye shall carry away today. Ye ken?"

"Yes, now I remember."

"Good. The family has arrived and taken some refreshment. Soon, the lassies will go for their stroll in the garden. They are sure to come this way. I've brought ye a fine, sturdy mount to carry two of ye into Scotland. Wrap your plaid about ye and come along."

Leo did as he was told and followed his uncle into the blinding sunlight. The mask did shield his eyes somewhat. He mounted a big gray stallion so elderly its dapples had faded and allowed himself to be led down the cottage path and back toward the wigwam.

"Stay ye here in the shelter of the trees until the young ladies come along the path. I will wait further on to make sure ye find your way, nephew. Bear left, always bear left on the trail."

Duncan cloaked his own gray head with a less elegant mask made from a feed bag that covered him to the shoulders and drew on gloves to disguise his aged hands, knotted and callused from his work in the gardens. He rode off to take up his own hiding place.

Blearily, Leonidas thought, "What am I to do again? Oh, yes. Steal a bride."

~ * ~

With a cup of wine by his side and Phemie's copy of *Waverley* in hand, Jason Longleigh settled himself on the terrace overlooking the fountain of Triton. His sisters soon came tripping along, ready for their walk.

"Won't you come with us?" Phemie asked. "Surely you want some exercise after such a long journey?"

"I am content with book and beverage. Enjoy your constitutional."

"Another mind ready to be ruined by romantic fiction," Pandora snorted.

"I will confess I was somewhat disappointed that Fergus Mac-Ivor had no use for the feelings of women and would have married his sister to Waverley without her consent. But oh, how bravely he died." Phemie clasped her hands to the white bosom of her gown. Her ardent emotions set the cheerful red cherries ornamenting the brim of her straw bonnet to shaking.

"There now, you've ruined it for me!" Jason proclaimed.

"Not so! The author admits the first three chapters are rather slow, but necessary. However, read on and you will find lyrical descriptions of the Highlands and much adventure. I do think you and Waverley have a great deal in common."

"Are both their heads filled with poetry?" Pandora said.

"Well, yes, that and not knowing what to do with their lives."

"I can stand no more. I need fresh air and brisk exercise." Moving so quickly her dark dress belled out behind her, Pandora proceeded down the terrace steps.

Phemie took leave of her brother by saying, "We must go to the wigwam and make sure the bearskin and the scalp still remain."

"Enjoy your grisly treasures as only a Longleigh can," Jason replied, waving them off.

She soon caught up with Pandora, despite her sister's martial strides. No lady-like mincing for Panny, never. Having been cooped together in the carriage for so many days, they had no need to converse and walked to their goal in sisterly companionship. The August sun moved along toward high noon. Pandora's deep bonnet, always advocated by their mother to prevent her complexion from darkening any more, shielded her from the sun, but Phemie, feeling her cheeks turn rosy, was grateful when they entered the deep shade of the side path.

At the wigwam, she could catch her breath after attempting to keep up with Panny's longer stride. The quaint hut loomed just ahead and something stirred in the darker shadows beyond it. Other than deer, the more dangerous wild beasts seldom crossed this way so heavily marked by man. Curious, she walked on a bit while Pandora turned in at the Indian habitat.

A masked man astride a large, gray horse burst from the beneath the canopy of trees. She cried out with a loud exclamation, and Panny came running.

Having startled Phemie, the horseman seemed confused as to his purpose and wavered in the lane. Panny threw up her skirt and sought the stiletto she wore in a sheath on her thigh. Encumbered by her petticoats, she shouted, "Drat, drat that Mama would not let me slit a few seams to allow me to get at my weapon. Damnation!"

Both the horse and the rider shied back at the loud words and the flurry of white cloth and undergarments showing. Phemie knew she should be going for her own weapon, but she simply stood there transfixed. The masked man seemed to have stepped from the pages of *Waverley*.

He wore the blue bonnet, the white cockade and the eagle feathers of a Highland chieftain, and truly astounding trousers, the tartan trews Mr. Scott had described. Oh, he was long in the leg and blue of eye. A lion's mane of red-gold hair flowed over his collar and a light stubble of the same shade colored his pale cheeks beneath the swath of the black silk mask.

Having loosened her weapon from female encumbrances, Pandora charged with her stiletto held low and close as Papa had taught. At the very least, she might stab him in the thigh and drive him off if she could not reach his ribs and the heart and lungs they protected. "Panny will scare him away, what a shame," Phemie thought, momentarily beguiled. Her sister had matters well in hand and soon this apparition from the past would vanish, probably wounded or even dying.

~ * ~

Leo stared at the raving woman with the fierce dark eyes who seemed set on killing him. What a face the other lass had, all big brown eyes and a small, pink mouth, so lovely. Without another thought, he moved forward, bent down, and tossed the smaller girl over his saddle. So dainty, she seemed to leap into the air to aid in her kidnapping. Black curls cascaded down her back from under her bonnet and slim, white ankles kicked the air. He turned his mount and spurred the horse just as the charging Amazon slashed downward at his leg. She caught only a corner of his flowing plaid. As he thundered down the path bearing left, he glanced back and saw the frenzied woman draw back her arm and throw her weapon hard as she could. It fell short, and she howled with rage.

Further on, Uncle Duncan waited. "This way to the Scottish border, laddie."

Five

At first, her kidnappers rode two abreast, but the bridle path narrowed when they reached a fork. The man with the muffled Scottish accent led the way onto the lesser trail to the left. Phemie considered trying to throw herself from the horse, but the close proximity of the second animal early on might have resulted in her being trampled. Now, they traveled at such a speed, she'd likely break a bone if she made the attempt.

Rather than panic, she put her considerable intellect to work on the matter. If they remained in Bellevue Park, she had no doubt she could find her way home safely. She and Pandora had done that often enough in the childhood challenges her father devised, his so-called Indian games. Every person on the estate would be searching for her, too, and her sister would have raised the alarm by now. *Show no fear and keep a cool head,* her papa would advocate.

The riders pulled up still deep in the trees, but in view of a high road twining by, brown and dusty. She strained to see or hear if any traffic passed that she could hail for help if she slipped from the horse now, but neither hoofbeat nor the rumble of a coach disturbed the heated air.

"I canna go farther with ye, laddie. Cross the road and stay on this path. "Twill take you into Scotland, then seek a fast track to Gretna Green."

So that was their plot, to abduct and marry the duke's wealthy daughter, not merely to ask for a ransom. Papa had anticipated this. Phemie searched her mind for any of her suitors who might fit the description of this man. None had red hair of any kind, and certainly not as glorious, nor were any so tall and long-limbed. For certain, they were not Scottish. Well, she had only to go along with the scheme until they rode into Gretna Green, and her father's men would rescue her. But what if he forced himself upon her before they arrived? Considering that, she began to wiggle off the large horse to make a break into the forest.

"You must be uncomfortable lying across the saddle." Her captor drew her upright and sat her astride before him, totally unconcerned about the amount of white-stockinged limb she showed as her gown rode up. His strong arms held her firmly in place. "Are you thirsty? Would you care for some tea?" he asked, offering her a canteen as cordially as if they sat in a drawing room.

Her mouth was dry, whether from fear or breathing through her mouth on the rough ride. Besides, if she drank enough, she would have reason to ask for time to relieve herself and possibly escape then. Phemie took several deep swallows and handed the canteen to her captor. "A delightful blend."

"Truly, my uncle's specialty." He partook of the brew as well. She became deeply aware of his warm, orange-scented breath on her neck, and the heat and firmness of the chest pressed against her.

"We have nay time for tea parties now and are in mickle trouble besides. Ye took the wrong lass. This one is the duke's darlin', his Little Dove, he calls her. His lordship will be out for blood and give ye no thanks."

"No matter. I like this one better. Do you know the other tried to kill me? The curse is broken. I have stolen a Longleigh bride!" her captor said blithely.

Ah, that explained the matter. Like so many handsome men, he was less than intelligent and probably addle-pated, too. Phemie sighed. That was ever the case. Would she never find the right man to marry—because she certainly would not have this one? Best to agree to go on to Gretna Green and let the duke's men take care of him. As for the other matter, she certainly could outwit him.

"What's done is done. Go on with ye and wed her. End the curse and restore the clan."

So, they were both lunatics. One must be careful and soothing with the insane. The man with the bag on his head drew back a gloved hand and swatted the gray horse, which sprang out of the woods and onto the deserted highway.

"*Claidheamh Mor!*" her abductor shouted with enthusiasm as they crossed the way and whipped among the trees again, leaving Bellevue Park behind them.

~ * ~

"Aye, *Claidheamh Mor!*" Duncan repeated after Leo with much less joy. "I hope I have not led the last Laird of Laughlin to his death. Come, Brownie," he addressed the nondescript and undistinguished nag he rode. "Back to Bellevue Hall to tell our tale, but first some icing to decorate the cake."

He dismounted, removed his mask, and took aim at a stout oak. Running hard into it headfirst, he sank, stunned, to the earth for a moment. A finger applied to his forehead came away wet with blood. He let the knot from the blow form before he collected his mask, and stowed it in his brown jacket, replacing it with his usual flat cap. Mounting, he took the highway back toward Bellevue. When he reached a portion of the road well-churned with hoofprints and wheel ruts, he picked at the scab forming on his wound and made sure his hat was bloodied before tossing it down in the way. Then, he set his heels to horse and urged it to dash home.

The turmoil at Bellevue Hall did not surprise him. He was about to stir the pot even more. Pelting down the drive, he pulled up sharply before crashing into the roil of hounds and nervous horses. The duke's bellow organizing the hunt for his daughter sounded over the wail of the women.

Lady Pandora, her bonnet gone, her usually tightly knotted black hair streaming down her back, cried repeatedly, "I rescued myself but could not save Phemie. Oh, Mama, I could not save her! Phemie is lost to us. I could not save her."

Although tears wet Lady Flora's pale face, ruining her powder, she consoled her daughter. "You did all you could and were so brave. Thank heaven they did not take both of you."

Duncan felt a twinge of guilt. The duchess had always treated him decently. She loved her flowers and had planned many a garden with him. The duke was a good master, but still a Longleigh. Och well, in Leo they would have a fine and well-educated son-in-law, much more useful than many gentlemen, with his knowledge of medicine and machines.

Armed with sword and pistols, young Lord Jason dashed past the gardener on one of the duke's finest thoroughbreds and made for the road. Lord Bellevue shouted after his son, "Tell my men the blackguard need not be taken alive!"

Calling on the souls of his ancestors to protect his grand-nephew, Duncan slid from the horse and knelt at the duke's feet. Irritated, Bellevue sputtered, "What is it, man? Lady Euphemia has been taken, and we have no time for much else."

"Your horse, Bosworth, has also been stolen, your lordship. As I returned from taking my nephew to the post house, I was set upon by brigands who snatched away the extra mount. I put up a fight, I did, but they bashed me with a pistol butt." He raised his head a bit to show off the bloody wound. "I tore off on Brownie, vowing they would not have both animals, but fell off along the way. As soon as I came back into my head, I made for the Hall to tell ye."

"I care not about the horse, Gardener. My Little Dove is gone."

"Papa," Lady Pandora said. "Now that he mentions it, I believe Phemie's kidnapper did ride Bosworth or a horse very like him, a large gray. Did your thief wear ancient Scottish garb and have red hair?"

"Aye, aye, that he did. Most strange. A small, dark youth rode with him. 'Twas he that hit me."

The housekeeper, who persisted in sticking smell salts under Pandora's nose even though that lady pushed her away saying, "I am not faint. I am angry," interjected. "Duncan's nephew has most extraordinary red hair, more golden like, but he is a fine young man, well-mannered, a physician."

The duke turned a bloody eye on his gardener. *Damn the woman!*

"It wasna my nephew. I put him on the coach to Glasgow myself."

A maid ran down the front steps and handed the duke one of Lady Euphemia's shawls. The duke in turn tossed it to his Master of Hounds, who gave the milling dogs the scent. Bellevue mounted his horse and stared down at Duncan.

"I had best not find Phemie with your nephew. He will be a dead man."

Hounds and horses moved off toward the place where his daughter had been taken. Duncan got off his arthritic and shaking knees. Lady Flora approached the old man.

"Come, Duncan Gardener, we will see to your injury, and perhaps a little brandy would not go amiss."

Guilt stabbed at his Highland heart again. He was to have the lady's care and a wee nip. All he had meant to do was rid them of a troublesome daughter and guarantee Leo a long and happy life as laird of Laughlin. What wheels o' fate had he set in motion?

Six

A gypsy rover came over the hill
Down through the valley so shady
He whistled and he sang 'til the green woods rang
And he won the heart of a lady

Phemie's captor sang the first verse of "Gypsy Rover" in a loud and exuberant, if somewhat tuneless, voice that reminded her of her father. She joined in on the chorus, sweetening the tone. How many times they'd sung the song she did not know. She could have sworn they were intoxicated, but they'd had only the tea in the canteen. It made no sense. She did not care.

At first, it had seemed imperative to gallop as fast as they could to Gretna Green. Then, they had stopped to drink more tea and relieve themselves. She should have run away at that point when she went to the bushes, but instead, she'd spied on her kidnapper as he turned away and lowered his trews enough to relieve himself. Disappointed, she saw only the white moons of his buttocks, fairer than her own. Whatever would her mother think of her curiosity? Phemie giggled and attracted his attention, but he drew up his trews before turning around.

"Laugh at me, would you?"

She should have been afraid, but the blue eyes shone out from the mask bright and merry. Phemie did decide to run then and lead him on a chase, but he soon caught up when she snagged her white gown on a briar and had to tug it free, leaving a patch behind. His long legs caught up with her in an instant, and he spun her round and into his arms.

"I like the length of your limbs, your foolish trousers, and your fine, white arse," she said, feeling remarkably uninhibited. If she had uttered such words in the ballroom at Almack's, she would have been dismissed by the patronesses as Kate had been for daring to take snuff. But during her own season there, she had been the perfect lady.

"And I like your pretty pink lips and raven black curls." He twined his fingers in the hair that spilled out from beneath her bonnet and lowered his mouth to hers. The kiss was warm and firm and not invasive, her first kiss because she hadn't allowed any others. She'd held herself close, and none of her suitors had tempted her enough to do otherwise.

"Your hair is marvelous, too." Standing on tiptoe, she caught up a red-gold lock and twisted it around her finger. He kissed her cheek, her neck, the top of her bosom. Heart racing, she pressed close. Evidently, trews did little to hide a man's desire. Her mother, being outrageously frank, had warned her that a certain hardening in the male nether regions was to be discouraged by pulling away. She did so with reluctance.

"I suppose we should move on to Gretna Green."

"Ah, yes. That was our destination. I remember now."

They'd found the patient gray grazing nearby. Tenderly, he'd lifted her sideways on the saddle this time and mounted behind her. He let the horse set their course meandering through the trees, stopping at a clear running rill for water, walking up the creek bed for a while before clambering out to graze on some tempting greenery. They finished the tea and filled the canteen with water.

At some point, singing to pass the time had seemed a good idea. Phemie sang the second verse:

She left her father's castle gate.
She left her own fine lover.
She left her servants and her state
To follow her gypsy rover.

Her captor took the next after the chorus:

She left behind her velvet gown
And shoes of Spanish leather
They whistled and they sang 'till the green woods rang
As they rode off together.

Phemie astounded him by whistling the chorus. "My brother, Jason, taught me. It's my most unlady-like accomplishment."

"All ladies should learn to whistle if they can do it as charmingly as you." Leo belted out the next stanza. They did make the green woods ring with their enchanting duet.

Last night, she slept on a goose feather bed
With silken sheets for cover.
Tonight she'll sleep on the cold, cold ground
Beside her gypsy lover.

He took a turn at whistling the chorus and did it so much better than he sang. She took up the next verse:

Her father saddled up his fastest steed
And roamed the valley over.
Sought his daughter at great speed
And the whistlin' gypsy rover.

"He will, you know. My father will never stop searching for me," she added before he could burst into the chorus again.

"No matter. We shall be wedded by then. Give me the lady's reply to her papa."

"He is no gypsy, my Father," she cried
But Lord of these lands all over.
And I shall stay 'til my dying day
With my whistlin' gypsy rover."

"Och, we've skipped a verse and must begin over." Leo grinned at her. The girl was such congenial company and sang with a pleasing lilt. He had chosen the right lady, no matter what his uncle thought.

"Haven't we passed this rock before?" she asked.

"It is a vera fine rock, as my uncle would say, an outstanding rock. Look at the wee cave at its base, perfect to spend the night as the sun appears to be going down. I shall cut some bracken for our bed. Do I have a knife? Aye, I do."

The cave was more of a deep overhang that had shaded out the surrounding vegetation. Phemie stood watching before the shelter as her captor hacked down the large ferns some distance away and sometimes pulled the plants up by the roots. When he had amassed a large heap, he carried it all back to the shelter and bending nearly double, spread it under the rim. Unwrapping from his plaid, he covered the bracken with this blanket and gestured for her to sit.

"Your bower, milady. You need not sleep on the cold, cold ground. Now, what have we to eat?" He rummaged in the sporran and took out a piece of hard cheese, a brown loaf, and a small flask. "All we need to be content, but each would be better taken before a fire. Allow me a moment."

He went off again, this time foraging for dead bracken, twigs, and fallen branches. Phemie settled herself demurely on the plaid with her legs turned to one side and completely covered by her skirts. She enjoyed watching him work, especially bent over in the in the tightly fitting trews. She hummed "Gypsy Rover" as she waited, not at all worried about what might come when the sun vanished entirely.

Crouched down, her kidnapper assembled the makings of the fire on the barren floor of the cave, then sat and stared at his creation.

Phemie prompted, "Have you any means of starting it—other than the power of your mind." Yes, he did seem to be a simpleton, although a lovely one. His intellect would not light so much as a small candle.

"I do! I have this relic of a pistol." Immediately, he dumped the gunpowder from the pan onto the bracken and holding the weapon close to the heap of wood, pulled the trigger. The spark of the flint meant to send a bullet flying ignited the fire with a huge whoosh. The flames shot up to the low roof of the overhang and left a sooty mark before dying down again.

"How wonderful is chemistry," he remarked brightly, so proud of his achievement.

Phemie drew her skirts tight to keep them from catching fire and thought, "Not an idiot, a madman."

Her abductor immediately broke off a piece of cheese and skewered it on the tip of his dirk. Holding the morsel over the fire until it began to bubble, he smeared it on a hunk of bread and presented it to her with a grand gesture.

"Your dinner is served, milady. What would you have to drink? Water?" He held up the canteen, then the flask. "Or something better?" Opening the flask, he sniffed the contents. "As I thought, good Scotch whisky. But I don't suppose young ladies like you imbibe."

Phemie flared up exactly like the fire a moment ago. "My sister, Pandora, says women should be allowed to take hard liquor if they wish." She seized the flask and downed a large swallow. The liquid burned all the way to her belly and lay there like a smoking coal. She gasped and coughed. He laughed with head thrown back and very nice, strong white teeth showing.

Defiant, she took another slug. With her throat already numb, it did not hurt as much as the first. She nibbled her bread, hoping to keep it down.

Her captor retrieved the flask and sipped more prudently. He toasted cheese for both of them and shared the bread.

"I can toast my own cheese," she said defiantly. "Because I have my own knife." Tossing up her white skirts without another thought, Phemie drew her stiletto from its sheath on her rounded thigh.

"So you do," he said. "I'm grateful you only want to toast cheese with it." But his eyes skipped over the tip of the blade and followed her white stockings clear from her slippers to the red garters that matched the ribbon under her breasts and on to the slit in her undergarments. With difficulty, he raised his eyes to hers and asked, "Still hungry?"

"For your kisses," she answered and threw herself upon him in a flurry of white like a turtledove flushed from its nest. Obviously, she had been reading too many romantic novels, but knowing that did not impede her.

~ * ~

Startled, he drew back, but only for a moment. "What is a man to do with such a bonny offer? What would my fierce Highlander ancestor, Ian McLaughlin, have done? Accept it!" he declared.

His kisses were hot, wet, and open-mouthed now. She answered him with the same. He yanked down her bodice and exposed two small perfect breasts tipped with pale brown nipples peaked in excitement. He took his kisses there, sucking and laving. Phemie tore off his Scotch bonnet and cast it aside so she could have her way with his hair. He paused long enough to do the same with her hat, then back to business.

Something lurking in the misty mountains of his mind prompted him to say before going further, "Tomorrow, we shall marry in Gretna Green. Never fear!"

"Yes, yes!" she cried. "I am not afraid."

He was not sure if she believed his promise or responded to the opening of her undergarments and the stroking of his fingers in the place most likely to elicit such a response. How wet and ready she was. He pushed down the trews and positioned himself between her lovely, open limbs. Out of consideration for her virginity, he would go carefully, slowly. He'd give her an inch, then let her adjust, then another inch. So tight and steaming inside, he had difficulty keeping to his plan. When her small hands reached down, clasped his naked backside, and gave him a great push, the plan changed.

He took her hard and deep and all at once. She gasped from pain or ecstasy, which he could not tell. Leo paused. She rose up beneath him, craving more. Not pain then. He'd done well by her. He picked up his rhythm and kept on until a long, shuddering spasm overtook his intended bride. Now, he could freely forget himself and ride on to his own oblivion. She came along with him.

He cradled her in the aftermath. She wanted to talk. He wanted to sleep.

"I think you should remove your mask now and tell me your name," she persisted.

"Am I wearing a mask?"

"Of course you are. All highwaymen and kidnappers do."

"Then take it off, by all means."

She moved her fingers delicately over his face and under the mask until she pulled it off. Her small thumbs smoothed his ruffled brows sitting like two small flames above the blue of his eyes. "I am so glad the lighting of the fire did not singe these away."

"No more than I."

"Tell me your name."

"Ian, Laird o' Laughlin," he answered, only a small jest to silence her. With one hand tangled in her black curls, he closed his eyes.

"Truly?"

Her captor did not answer. Phemie recognized the light snore of a man dead to the world. Her brothers slept like this. Why, a prankster could enter their bedchamber and pour treacle in their hair, and they never noticed until morning. As small children, she and Panny had done that once very successfully.

Sleep did not come as easily to her. As she'd always suspected, she could be as wanton as her mother with her father. Oh, no matter. Tomorrow, she and Ian of Laughlin would be married. Phemie arranged her clothes more modestly and tucked in against her lover's side. His heat and the length of his body kept her from the dew and damp all night long.

Seven

Phemie woke first. An early ray of dawn had found its way into the shallow cave and slanted across the cheek of her captor. The light turned his beard a sparkling reddish-gold, as if he had been touched by Midas. Simply enchanted as she had been the first time she had seen him wrapped in his plaid and wearing the blue bonnet with the white cockade, she drew a finger down the curve of his cheek. He startled awake, blue eyes flashing open. Sitting up abruptly, he immediately conked his head against the low overhang.

"Where am I?"

She'd fallen off the plaid blanket when he moved so suddenly. Her hand came to rest on a metal object deep in the pile of bracken. Recognizing her stiletto, however had it gotten there, Phemie grasped the handle and held the knife out in front of her. The tip was besmirched with some kind of crusty substance, but it would do well enough if he proved violent.

She addressed him. "Not a comforting question coming from my kidnapper. If you do not know, how should I?"

He held up his hands and kept his eyes on the knife. "Kidnapper? No, I am a reputable physician, Leonidas McLaughlin at your service.

I mean you no harm." As if the duchess had just introduced them at Almack's, he bobbed his head, then rubbed the top where a lump was rising.

"I remember very clearly being swept off my feet and thrown over your saddle while I walked in the gardens of Bellevue Hall yesterday. After we left the park, my recollection is not as sharp. I believe you told me another name, certainly not Leonidas, which I would recall. You seem to be a horse thief as well. That is Bosworth, one of my father's old mounts, grazing over there."

At the mention of his name, the large gray raised his head and nickered in recognition. Leo turned and regarded the horse with horror. By the look on his face, the animal might well have been a dragon or a troll.

"No, no. I know my unc...a deranged friend tried to convince me to take Lady Pandora Longleigh as a stolen bride, but I would never do so. Still, as a man of science, I believe in tangible proof. The evidence is right before me holding a knife, and the horse is surely stolen—unless I borrowed it. You must be Lady Pandora. I do beg your pardon. My mind was poisoned by that wretched tea. You can put down the knife. I am in my right mind now and will not hurt you."

Phemie lowered the stiletto to her lap. "No, I am Lady Euphemia Longleigh, her sister." Her heart gave a small twinge that he did not even recognize her name and mistook her for Panny. They were close in age but looked nothing alike. The ache in her chest slightly mitigated the one in her head.

He gave her the slightest of smiles. "A very long name for a so tiny a lady."

"As if I have not heard that before from many men. Do you think Leonidas is any better?"

"He was a Spartan general, and it can always be shortened to Leo."

"Well, Euphemia was a saint. My mother distressed the vicar with her choice of so many pagan names, and he convinced her to use this one."

"In Scotland, we would call you Effie."

"We might be in Scotland, for all I know, but my family calls me Phemie. The Longleighs never do anything as others do. They make a point of it."

A sudden flush colored Leo's cheeks. "Last night, I did nothing untoward, offered no insult to your person. Did I, Lady Euphemia?"

Oddly, she could not recall. Phemie took stock of her aches and pains, a pounding head, sore across the stomach and between the legs. "I seem to have a headache, a bruised middle and some discomfort in my nether regions," she told him.

"I suppose I did throw you across my saddle, and we seem to have ridden a long way. That, a bit of whisky, and the strange tea would account for your discomforts. However, as I am a physician, I could exam—"

"Certainly not! Make way."

As he drew his long legs up, she ducked from under the overhang and made for the nearest stout tree. On its far side, she lost whatever meal she'd eaten, cheese and bread most likely, then answered the call of nature. Her undergarments were tinged with a distinct brownish stain. She had started her monthlies right here in the woods, and while wearing a white dress, what a calamity! Or she had slept with a man for the very first time and could not remember a moment of it, even more distressing.

In case she had to deal with the first problem, she removed the broad red ribbon that tied her dress, lapped it over, and stuffed it between her legs. If the second were true, she was ruined. Rumors would fly once word got out that Lady Euphemia Longleigh had spent the night in the woods with a man. She would be obliged to accept any who offered to restore the family honor. By doing that, she would lose what her unorthodox mother considered to be the most important element in a marriage—love.

Despair threatened until she remembered the Longleighs never did as expected. They would have some other plan, and her dear papa would never force her to marry without love. Relieved in many ways, she cleaned her stiletto on her hem, returned it to its sheath and went back to the cave to find Leonidas McLaughlin, M.D. examining a dark stain on his plaid. He wet a finger, rubbed it against the spot, and regarded the color.

Glancing up at her, he said, "I believe we were on our way to Gretna Green and should go there at once."

"Since you are a physician, I feel I can say it might be my time of the month," she answered. "Besides, Gretna Green is the last place we should go. My father has posted men who will shoot you on sight."

"The duke keeps a personal army in Gretna Green?"

"Until yesterday, I had a great many eager suitors he thought might prove impetuous."

He appeared to note the slight trembling of her lower lip, which she quickly bit to still. She put her small shoulders back and raised her chin.

"Do your courses come regularly? When was the last time you bled? If you would allow me to examine you…"

Her courage broke beneath the weight of these questions. She brushed aside a few errant tears and straightened her shoulders again.

"Where would you have me take you, then? Back to Bellevue Hall if we can find the way?"

"My father would personally run you through and take your scalp. He has done it before when he thought another man offered bodily insult to my mother. That turned out not to be the case, but he did not wait to find out. You have a very nice scalp. I would hate to see it hung in our wigwam." What wonderful hair he possessed. She could almost feel its thickness running between her fingers. Had she done that last evening?

"I know a place we could go until your father's temper cools, if only we knew where we are now. You are so lovely, who would not want you for a bride in any condition?

The tears escaped again. She swallowed them and concentrated on the immediate problem. "I hear a brook nearby. Papa always says if you follow a stream downhill you will eventually find a town and have drinking water as you go."

"A sensible idea. We will follow the stream back to civilization."

"I believe we should go upstream instead, riding in the water, if possible, to throw off the hounds."

"Hounds?"

"Oh, yes. Papa will have put his pack on our trail."

"You seem very knowledgeable about such matters for a young lady."

"The duke taught all his children how to survive in the wilderness. He does not consider women to be a weaker sex or less intelligent than men. Quite the contrary."

"From my own observations, I believe this to be true. If women were not burdened by childbirth, their achievements would equal ours."

"Ours?" Incredible, this wondrous man shared the Longleighs' belief in women's equality.

"I dabble in inventions, but the sun is rising and the hounds are on our trail. Here, have a sip or two of water. When you feel better, you may have this heel of bread. We must be going." He ate the remaining lump of cheese and finished off the last drops in the flask. "For fortitude," he added.

~ * ~

Leo sat his stolen bride sideways on the saddle and mounted the purloined horse. They took to the stream and followed it northward. At least, that is the direction Euphemia told him they went, judging by the thickness of the moss on that side of the trees. When they came to a fast running, rocky part of the rill, he steered the placid animal to shore. They continued to follow the water until the forest thinned and a narrow road appeared. A croft lay nearby the stream and its owner grubbed in a potato patch with a hoe.

Leo stopped to ask their way. "My good man, are we in Scotland?"

"Aye," the farmer answered. He eyed the pretty lass in the soiled white gown and the gentleman in antique dress. Pointing, he said, "Gretna Green is that away."

"And Glasgow?"

"Bear right at the next fork. Bring ye out on the new paved road."

Leo searched in the bottom of the sporran for the small coins he'd found there along with the flask. "Could you spare us some food and drink?"

The place did not look any too prosperous. He offered only a pittance.

"Ale and sheep's cheese. Might be some oat cakes."

"No cheese for me. Would you have a boiled egg?" Phemie asked.

"Perhaps."

Leo weighed the time it would take to boil an egg against the chance of being torn apart by the Duke of Bellevue's hounds. Phemie, pale from the loss of her dinner and the long morning's ride, gazed pathetically at him with those huge brown eyes. "Eggs, ale and oat cakes then, as quickly as you can."

They ate and pounded on, not for Gretna Green but for Glasgow.

Eight

When Pearce Longleigh burst from the woods on his huge, black charger, the crofter dropped his hoe and crossed himself as if the Wild Hunt had appeared on his property. The duke supposed with his fierce bronze face, his hounds running before and his minions riding behind, he might resemble some damned soul condemned to course the forest forever. But only one person would be sent to perdition today—Phemie's captor.

Reining in his horse near the man, he searched the pocket of his outdated greatcoat and offered the miniature painting of his daughter made just before her spring debut. "I am the Duke of Bellevue. This is my daughter. She was taken by a man wearing Highland dress and mounted on a big gray. Have you seen them?"

The farmer furtively made the sign of the cross again as if having an English lord on his land was as bad as hosting the devil. "Aye, they passed by here."

"Which direction did they go?"

"Why, west to Gretna Green. They had the look of runaway lovers. Tried to fool me by asking the way to Glasgow, but I kent what they were about."

"My daughter was kidnapped, and the man has seen his last day on earth!"

"Aye, aye. I'm sure o' that, your lordship," the crofter replied, as if disagreeing might prove fatal.

"Men, to Gretna Green. The Armstrong boys must have him by now."

The Master of Hounds rode up on the duke's left. "If you will pardon me, Your Grace, the men and animals are in need of food and drink. We had only stream water for supper and breakfast and a bit of the dried meat I brought for the hounds."

The duke quelled his disgust at their weakness. Thanks to his good management, his servants never went without a meal and did not know the meaning of fasting when on the warpath. He'd wrapped in a blanket and slept in the bracken, dined on water, and heated himself with the fire of his hatred for Phemie's captor. However, he was certain Jason and the Armstrongs would have stopped any forced marriage by now. He relented.

"Food and drink for all. I will pay you well."

The crofter led the way to his humble home. The men and animals settled in the yard while the duke went inside to occupy the largest chair and the table. The good wife, as browned as her husband and bearing a bruise high on her right cheek, set a bowl of boiled eggs and fresh oatcakes before him. She drew off a pewter tankard full of foaming, home-brewed ale from cask before her husband carried the small barrel outside to set up on a trestle. Adding a bowl to the array, she filled it with the mutton stew intended for their own dinner and passed the duke her best spoon. The rest of the pot she carried outside to feed the others. He didn't touch his food until she returned.

"Sit, goodwife, and eat. I know we take your dinner."

Timorously, the woman took a rush-seated chair and selected a boiled egg to peel. Bug-eyed, she watched the great man devour his stew as if he were a talking bear in a children's tale.

The duke rambled on, speaking more to himself than to the woman. "Canny bastard knew his way around the woods. He led us in circles, in and out of the water, but my daughter left a sign, a small scrap of her dress on a bush. Oh, but we wasted time when we came to the edge of the park and found blood on a tree. I sent half the hounds one way on the road and the rest the other. They found only my gardener's cap in the path. Of course, her kidnapper went directly into Edgemont's forest and stayed off the highway."

Bellevue quaffed half his ale and slammed the tankard down, making the woman jump. "No need to ask the Earl of Edgemont's permission to search his land. That soft and silly boy has gone off to fight Napoleon and left his ailing mother. He'll be the death of her. Edgemont was supposed to offer for my other daughter, Pandora. How will he face Nappy if he is afraid of a girl?"

"Don't know, milord. More ale?" She winced at the sound of her chickens being thrown to the hounds.

The duke held out his tankard. He plucked an egg from the bowl and cracked the shell against the rough table. The farmer's wife returned with the filled cup.

"I should have gone immediately into the woods. We have lost both time and daylight. Had to camp in the forest as I would not go back. Near noon, we found the place where they spent the night, a small cave lined with bracken big enough for only two. Two pressed tight together."

His fist crushed the egg until it oozed between his thick fingers. He brushed his hands off over the bowl of stew and continued eating.

The farm wife hovered at his elbow, then said, "I fed eggs and ale and oatcakes to them, milord. Your daughter has not gone hungry, and the young man worried over her. He seemed not a rough sort, not like some." Her faded blue eyes shifted toward her husband throwing down hay for the horses in the yard. "He spoke like a gentleman and won't harm her, I'm thinking."

"He'd best worry about the harm I will do to him once we catch him, but I thank you for your words." The duke tossed down enough guineas to pay for the cask his men had drained, the fodder for their mounts, the chickens that would never lay eggs again, and her husband's supper. He added a few more to the pile. "For any daughter you might have to dower," he said as he strode for the door. "Mount up. Gretna Green by nightfall, men."

The crofter's wife slid the extra coins into her apron pocket and went outside to see her second set of strange visitors ride off. Bloodied feathers stirred in their wake. What came as a misfortune to one person sometimes made the fortune of another.

~ * ~

Phemie lay against the haystack and watched a red August sun descend behind the western hills. A couple of hares came out to nibble herbs and play in the twilight. Leo carefully drew a bead on the largest and pulled the trigger of the ancient pistol. The loud click sent the rabbits scattering.

"Curse it! No powder."

"You should always reload immediately, if possible, Papa says."

"But I haven't fired the thing before, have I?"

"No matter, we have the extra eggs and oatcakes from our earlier meal."

Phemie shivered a little, recalling the clout the crofter had given his wife for handing over extra provisions. Leo had stepped between the couple and offered another small coin to take care of the matter. Her father or brothers would simply have flattened the man with a blow of their fist. She found her companion, no longer thought of as a captor, to be both reasonable and gentle when in his right mind. Surely, he would try to explain the situation logically if they were overtaken, and one of the Longleighs would shoot him dead as he spoke. She must take care of Leo, or he hadn't a chance to survive.

Such a lovely man; losing him would be a shame. The setting sun brought out a blaze of red in his hair, overpowering the gold. He carefully peeled a brown egg with his slim, white fingers and, checking to be sure no specks of shell remained, offered it to her on an open palm. Beautiful hands, healing hands, pallid and uncalloused, they confirmed he was no sportsman. Those hands would never strike a woman.

She accepted the egg, their fingers touching in the transfer. A current of electricity akin to the one Mr. Benjamin Franklin had coaxed from the sky passed through her, or so it seemed. Leonidas must have felt it, too, because he took his hand away as if shocked by a spark and put those fingers immediately to work peeling the second egg.

Earlier today, held close as they rode along on Bosworth, she'd observed a few faded freckles visible only in very good light scattered across the bridge of his long, straight nose. His lips, so close to her cheek, were narrow but sensitive, often quirking into a white smile surrounded by the start of a reddish beard when he considered his ridiculous costume and equally ludicrous predicament. What a pale and noble brow he had—and how Pandora would laugh at that description.

Her sister often warned her not to be taken in by handsome men as those were the most likely to be arrogant and full of themselves. In fact, Panny had tried to convince her to consider spinsterhood and remain forever at Bellevue Hall, her own mistress and subject to no husband who might abuse her like the abused wives she espoused as another of her good deeds. What causes they could embrace together instead of a man! Phemie found that a cold future. So, she had enjoyed her season and listened to the entreaties of her suitors, finding them all about the same. None stood out—except Leonidas McLaughlin.

He laid the ragged napkin containing the crumbles of the brittle oatcakes between them and wiped off the lip of the canteen with a spotless handkerchief he took from his jacket before offering it to her. "Lukewarm water and the humblest of breads for the duke's daughter. I am sorry I could do no better," he said in that self-mocking way of his.

"Did I ask for more?" Phemie nibbled on a broken piece of oat cake.

"No. I find you to be a most extraordinary young woman, Lady Euphemia. Others would be hysterical, given the circumstances."

"I am a Longleigh, and they are not. We relish adventure. My mother was once abducted by red Indians and managed quite well. I believe I am more fortunate in the gentleness of my captor, and given the circumstances, I want you to call me Phemie."

"Not Effie, even though we are most certainly deep into Scotland now? Please call me Leo and never your captor again."

The light of the rising moon turned his mane of hair tawny. She would have loved to let him lay his head in her lap and stroke back the strands, but she was too much of a lady to suggest it, and he too much of a gentleman to do so. They remained seated side by side with the ragged napkin between them, proper as picnickers in a park.

"I've always hated my name, but it does come with a good story. Do you know it?"

"Presbyterians aren't much for saints and martyrs."

A working physician and a Scottish Presbyterian! How people would talk if she settled on this man. Undiscouraged, she told her tale as the moon rose higher in the sky.

"Then you have missed some good gory tales. St. Euphemia, the All-Praised, was the virgin daughter of a Roman senator. Having converted to the worship of the One True God, she refused to make a sacrifice to the idol of Ares, god of war. The local governor demanded she recant, even offering her bribes, but she refused. He had her tied to a wheel of knives, but when she cried out to God, the wheel jammed. Next, she was taken to a red-hot oven. Angels appeared in the flames and her guards would not cast her inside, but others did. She remained unharmed. After that, her tormentors prepared a pit full of knives for her doom and covered it with grass and earth to deceive her. She walked right over it."

"Quite the girl, our Euphemia," Leo said, his eyes never leaving her face.

"Yes. At last, the governor condemned her to the arena to be torn apart by wild beasts. The lions came to lie at her feet. None of the other animals would touch her until at last a bear bit her in the neck. Angels swooped down to collect her soul, and the Lord shook the theater with an earthquake. She is usually pictured as a blond young woman with two lions at her feet, not even slightly resembling me."

Leo's smile came again. "Oh, I believe you could tame lions and have them do whatever you commanded. Coincidentally, my coat of arms has two golden lions upon it, rampant on either side of a tower shown on a field of green, ah, vert. Compared to the mighty Bellevue crest, it's quite shabby and of no consequence. Only my uncle and some kin put store in it. Why, once when seventeen, I tried to impress a lady with it. She replied she didn't care if I were the King of England, I'd have to pay for her time. Excuse me, that was a crude story, not for young ladies."

Instead, she laughed and clapped her hands together, thoroughly delighted. "You have a coat of arms? I knew you were a gentleman!" One impediment out of the way.

"Do not confuse me with the Gypsy Rover, Phemie. I have no riches and the castle belongs to someone else. What part of my commoner mother's fortune my father did not spend, she used to make a gentleman of me. It did not take. I preferred my studies to swords and pistols and lying about wasting a woman's money. After settling my father's estate upon his demise and paying off his debts, she did see the sense of using what was left to teach me a profession. I chose medicine, though perhaps it should have been engineering. I like to dabble with machines."

"As do I! I can disassemble a watch and put it together again in perfect working order."

There, she'd done it once more, tried to make his life dovetail with hers into a tight bond.

"A most unusual accomplishment for a young lady, a most unusual young lady."

"You find me eccentric." She'd been warned not to flaunt her mechanical abilities lest she scare off any suitors. Now, she'd put off the only man of interest.

"Charmingly so. I suggest you take your choice of necessaries before we settle for the night." He made a wide gesture toward the field of haystacks.

Phemie rose and shook the dried grass from her skirts. Before following the path of moonlight across the stubble to the nearest pile of hay, she asked, "We were speaking of lions when suddenly you mentioned the Gypsy Rover. Why?"

"No idea. It popped into my head. I have always considered it a dangerously sentimental song and the chorus ridiculous with all those ah-dee-doos in it."

"Oh, I'm rather fond of it. Lately, it won't leave my mind."

"You should try to forget it." He gestured again to the haystacks, and she moved away.

Leo pulled down enough hay to make her a comfortable bed and arranged the plaid over it. When Phemie returned, he tucked her in, then lay down outside the covers, his back to hers, too much a gentleman, no matter what he said.

"Sleep well, Little Dove."

"That is what my father calls me."

"I must have heard somewhere." He sunk into sleep like a drowning man, deep and heavy.

Phemie stayed awake considering. Mama had pursued her father all the way to America once she had made up her mind to have him as a husband. He had resisted. Sometimes logic stood in the way of romance and had to be set aside until after the wedding. She hummed "Gypsy Rover" and whispered the very last lines.

And I shall stay 'til my dying day
With my whistlin' gypsy rover.

Nine

"What do you mean, they have not come here?" the duke roared at his third son.

Jason Longleigh knew better than to step back as most men did when his father bellowed. The family motto should be, "Never show fear," though that phrase came from his Shawnee heritage, not the English. He might be a poet who preferred words to weapons, but he had learned all the Longleigh virtues well enough.

"No one in Gretna Green has seen anyone resembling Phemie or her kidnapper. One of the Armstrong boys loiters near the blacksmith shop where the weddings are performed before the anvil. He would recognize Phemie at once. The man who unites elopers swears he has not seen them either...no small girl with dark curls together with a tall man having reddish hair. All in town providing the service say the same."

The duke ground his teeth. "I wonder what he would say if we laid him across his anvil and applied a hot coal to his privates."

Jason suppressed a shudder and remained perfectly still. How to calm his father? Though Pearce Longleigh would never admit it, he favored his youngest daughter, perhaps because she so resembled their mother, except for her dark hair, eyes, and complexion. The duchess could control her massive husband with a crook of her finger despite her small size. Jason felt the need to invoke her name.

"Mama would not approve. We live in more civilized times now, she would say. Besides, I rode here on your fastest horse by the best roads. There is no way two astride old Bosworth taking the back ways could reach this place before me. Boz has strength and stamina and bore you for many a year, but he is no racer."

His father's great chest heaved with an indrawn breath and exhale. "Yes, of course. He has taken her into the Highlands then. Let us hope he holds your sister for a ransom and nothing more. We must check one other possibility as well. Duncan Gardener's nephew does fit the description of the kidnapper, no matter what the man claims about putting him on the northbound coach. I secured this doctor's direction before we left and have an address in Glasgow. We will go there and find the man, and perhaps, Phemie. If that fails, and a ransom letter does not come in a timely manner, we shall scour the Highlands for her."

Astounding how his father could be the ferocious savage one moment and the cool Englishman the next. How difficult it must be to contain two such opposing forces in one bronze skin. Though all his many offspring had some semblance of the man, only James, the heir, resembled their father in nature. Jason wondered if the duke felt a disappointment in his other sons: Joshua, the dandy and barrister; himself, the poet and lover of older women; Justinian, the baby of the family and destined to be a scholar. Raised to be warriors, none had taken up the sword as a career, though Josh had considered the military at one time and been denied.

As for the six Longleigh daughters, they had been nothing but trouble. All were settled now except for strident Pandora and Phemie, so gentle and sweet, if a trifle mischievous. Would the duke scour the Highlands for any of the rest? Jason knew the answer to that. Yes, Bellevue would go for any of his children who needed aid. You did not take what belonged to him.

"The dogs be damned. We will send them home. You and I go on to Glasgow, son."

~ * ~

Tonight, the couple sheltered in an orchard surrounded by the soft, ripening fruits of August: fuzzy peaches and smooth-skinned plums. Leo kicked aside early fallen peaches and released their aroma into the cool night air as he made up their bed. Earlier, they had eaten their fill, along with bread and a soft, buttery Dunlop cheese obtained at a prosperous farm along the way. They'd traded her straw bonnet with its merry red ribbons and jolly cherry trim for the food. Leo scolded her like a child when she reached for a third peach.

"Do not make yourself sick, Phemie. We have a way to go still, but once we get to Glasgow, I promise to feed you better."

"As I said, I am not complaining. Is that our destination then? Glasgow?"

"No, but I have a friend there who keeps a change of clothes and a small purse for me when I come to the city."

"How fortunate. Who is this friend?"

"The Widow Cunningham, my former landlady."

"I suppose many poor elderly widows must turn their homes into lodging houses to earn a living."

"Oh, Agnes, I mean, Mrs. Cunningham, would take exception to that description. She fancies herself in the prime of life, and there is some doubt as to her widowhood. She married a sea captain who never returned home, fate unknown."

"How terrible," she answered, not meaning a word of it. Jason's antics with women like Lady Tartte had made her only too aware of the taste widows had for handsome young men. She felt a tightening around her heart and knew it for jealousy.

"She seems to enjoy her life, so I would not fret about her. Here, settle into the plaid and let me wrap it round you."

"I am not ready for sleep. I would like a story first." Oh, how childish that and a yen for more peaches made her seem. "I mean, I should like to know the meaning of your name. I told you about mine last night."

"Leonidas? It means lion's son. He was the Spartan general who held the pass against the Persians at the Battle of Thermopylae and eventually died a great hero in the effort. I believe my father intended me for a military life, but expired before he could put that desire into effect. Regardless, I have little in common with the King of Sparta or my war-like Scottish ancestors. If I had joined the army, I would be working in the surgeons' tent saving men or helping the engineers to put up a bridge rather than counting the number I'd slain."

"Herodotus said the King of Sparta and his three-hundred troops killed twenty-thousand of the enemy," Phemie said, filling in the numbers for him.

"You've read Herodotus?"

"Only in Latin translation," she replied modestly.

"A great but odd accomplishment for a woman. Your father allowed this?"

"He did indulge me, but drew the line at my learning Greek. He said the language was a plague to young scholars, and he would not have me worry myself with it." Oh my, now he thought her odd...odd *and* childish. She rushed to change the subject. "Since we both know the story of Thermopylae, tell me of your war-like Scottish ancestors."

Leo stared out through the low-hanging branches of the heavily laden fruit tree and gazed at the moon growing in fullness each night. "We should sleep. The road will be well-lit tomorrow evening, and we can ride much further."

"Please." She coached herself to say that word softly in the way a woman would plead and touched his arm, gazing up at him through a veil of long, dark lashes. She'd mastered the technique by watching other girls at Almack's, certainly not from Pandora, who despised such manipulations, always looking men in the eyes and scaring them off. Though she would not want this man, how envious Panny would be of their adventure.

With the small hand resting warm on his sleeve, and her wide, beseeching eyes, she forestalled the idea of going to bed. Last night, he'd tried to point out the difference in their status to no avail, slept atop the plaid and fully clothed to place a barrier between them. He regarded her as very young and impressionable, hardly more than a child—but she knew her womanly wiles and worked them on him.

Swallowing hard, he said, "Very well, Lady Euphemia, as you wish it." She smiled at his courtly language.

"It is said the McLaughlins are descended from Vikings who raided the west coast of Scotland and sailed up one of the firths to found a settlement there. From them, we get our height and our hair color from mingling with the red-haired Pict women. But they were overcome by another of their kind, Somerled, the Lord of the Isles, who sailed out of Ireland and defeated their longboats with an invention of his own. He used a small ship with a fixed hinged rudder, very maneuverable. His fleet drove away the bigger, slower ships."

Leo sketched a *naibheagan* with a peach tree twig in the dust. In the moonlight, Phemie gazed at it avidly as if Somerled himself might jump from the deck and into her arms.

"The Lord of the Isles conquered the western coast and all the islands, but he suffered from *hubris*. Do you know the word?'

"Excessive pride."

"Exactly. He challenged Malcolm, the king of all Scotland, for the throne, and might have won if a treacherous relative had not stabbed him to death the night before the battle. However, he left three sons who prospered in their island strongholds and eventually formed the Clan MacDonald. The McLaughlins have blood ties to them. I'd like to think my knack for innovations comes directly from Somerled, a silly notion of course. However, a new invention often overcomes brute force."

"Your clan is far more ancient than the Longleighs. They came to Britain with William the Conqueror."

"Ah, Phemie, the stars shine in your eyes. My family is in no way equal to that of Lord Bellevue. The Normans were also descended from Vikings—who were ruthless marauders as was Somerled—not figures of romance. No more of this nonsense. We must rest."

He again arranged the plaid with a large fold between them and turned his back toward her. She went to sleep as easily as a kitten cuddled by its mother.

~ * ~

He laid awake disturbed by her nearness. Once before, she'd looked at him with adoration, but he couldn't quite place the moment, *damn that tea.* She shifted, and her small hand crept out of the blanket and settled on his waist. He tried to return it to its proper place, but her fingers felt cold, and so he covered them with his own and dozed off holding her hand.

Long after the moon had set and left them in darkness, that captured hand jerked free and pounded on his back. "No, no, no," she cried.

"Your pardon. I meant no harm. Your hand was cold and seemed to seek me out."

"What? Leo, I had the most terrible dream."

She trembled so, he had no other choice than to gather her into his arms and hold her close. Her heart beat as rapidly as a captive dove against his chest. He rubbed her shaking back in soothing circles. "There, there, only a nightmare."

"I dreamt I truly was St. Euphemia in the arena. A tame lion lay at my feet. Then, the bear came lumbering up to kill me, but instead, it savaged the lion, tearing it all to pieces."

"Well, I am glad the beast spared Euphemia in this version. The lion was probably most pleased to give its life for her. Think no more about it."

"You do not understand. The Shawnee call my father Great Bear. You were the lion. Leo, you must promise me not to be brave like King Leonidas of Sparta. If Papa should discover us, I want you to run."

"I said I am no warrior, but neither am I a coward, Phemie. I have a plan to return you safely to your family without confronting Lord Bellevue. If that should fail, I will face him and apologize for this foolish escapade. All will be well. Now settle yourself." He smoothed back her dark, tangled curls and brushed a chaste kiss on her forehead.

Phemie surged up and cupped his face with her hands, stroking his growth of red-gold beard with her thumbs. Deliberately, she placed her lips on his and put all her heart into the kiss. The bristle of a man's unshaven face so close to hers did not deter her. Her lips still held the sweetness of peaches. Running the tip of her tongue along his sealed lips, she broke his reserve. He answered her kiss, going deep and far beyond a mere brush of her forehead, and she answered him lick for lick. He broke it off.

"Jesus," he said, "It's now I should run while St. Euphemia is still a virgin."

"Too late for that, I think. My monthly never came. I believe we left my virginity back in the cavern, and I am most confounded that I have no memory of losing it."

"We cannot be sure until I examine you—which I hardly can do in a peach orchard in the dead of night. We must not make this worse, Phemie. Turn around, go to sleep."

"Very well. I think you *are* a coward." She wrapped in the plaid, leaving him not an inch of blanket and turned her back.

He had the rest of an uncomfortable night to consider her statement. Truthfully, he feared his desire for Euphemia Longleigh far more than her father.

Ten

Leo insisted they ride far into the night and drop exhausted beneath any shelter that came their way. The Glasgow road was fine and fast, but also more crowded with drays hauling goods from the port, swift coaches, and single riders. The traffic often forced them to skirt the road. As he pointed out when they dashed into the bushes the first time, a man in tartan trews riding with a beautiful young lady on a single horse would be a memorable sight. To which Phemie replied, "Do you think me beautiful?"

"Och, aye," he said, affecting a Scottish accent. "Vera, vera beautiful."

"I love when you speak that way," she answered, tracing the line of his lips with a finger and making them quirk up into a smile.

He'd succumbed to another kiss and blamed himself the rest of the day. Yes, they rode hard and late. With Phemie no longer angry, anything could happen when they ceased riding. He allowed only brief stops to refresh themselves and gobble down the rest of the Dunlop cheese and stolen peaches.

Peaches…he would never eat another without thinking of Phemie. Perhaps it was best the unbroken curse promised him a life cut short if he had to live it without her. He'd stolen the bride, but could not marry her for her own sake. She had greater prospects than he could ever provide if he left her undamaged.

Just short of Glasgow, they took shelter in the shadow of a large oak, not a moment too soon. Two riders thundered round a bend. The moonlight glinted off their weaponry. Bosworth drew back his pink lips to neigh, but Leo swiftly covered the horse's nostrils to prevent him.

"Would you look at those two," he whispered to Phemie. "The big one could be a highwayman of old, sword and pistol by his side, and the younger, what a sleek, deadly-looking hound he is."

"Papa and Jason, my brother."

"I see what you mean about them. But, Phemie, tell me now if you want me to put you up on Bosworth to ride after them. You can say you have escaped."

"No. I want to stay with you. Are we going into the Highlands?"

"That was my plan, but we have no need of it now. Quickly, let me lift you up. This tired old steed will not be able to catch them if you wait any longer."

"No, I won't go!"

"You must, for your own good." He reached for her waist to hike her into the saddle, but Phemie took advantage of her small stature to duck under Bosworth's belly and dash behind the huge bole of the oak.

"Phemie, Phemie! Don't run into the forest. You will be lost."

Leo tried the same maneuver, but Boz took offense this time and shifted to block with his haunches, nearly knocking him to the ground. He found his feet and pelted after the girl. Tripping over roots and shoving greenery aside, he would have been lost himself if the woods had not turned out to be merely a green verge rimming a small field of ripe oats rattling their hulls in a stiff evening breeze. He paused at its edge and looked for signs of trampled grain or an indentation where his quarry might have lain down to hide. He found no sign of her.

Well then, she must have run parallel to the road. He made his way back to the oak, following his own trail of crushed vegetation. Now, he noticed the rear of the tree had a deep cavity. Aha! He peered inside. No Phemie. The wind grew stronger and veiled the shining moon in clouds dark as widow's weeds. A single fat drop of rain found its way through the canopy of leaves, hit him on the bridge of his nose and slid down its length to drip off the end. Wonderful...in her thin summer gown, the duke's daughter would catch a chill and die of it. The guilt would be his for all of his life.

He heard the giggle two branches above him. She sat swinging her feet on a stout limb. Phemie called down to him, "Papa says people rarely look up when searching. He used this ruse when fighting Indian enemies."

"I see you have yet another strange and wonderful accomplishment for a young lady—tree-climbing."

"I am a bit rusty or I could have gone higher. Mama put an end to our climbing several years ago. Catch me, Leo!"

She spread her white-clad arms and fell into his embrace as lightly as a piece of thistledown. He might have held her far longer if the rain had not begun to pelt down harder. "Get the plaid," she ordered, slipping away from him and ducking into the cavity of the tree. He tied the horse and fetched the blanket to make a nest for them inside the oak. Giving no thought to putting a space between them, he arranged the plaid under and over them and cradled her in his arms.

"Pandora and I once spent the night in a hollow oak when our brothers failed to find us after a game of pursuit."

"Hide-and-seek, do you mean?"

"No, far more serious than that. Papa wanted all his children to be able to survive in the outdoors. He trained the boys in the Shawnee way, but Panny and I did not want to be left out, so we were to make a trail and they would find us. We did our task too well. Papa's best hound found us the next morning and awakened us by licking our faces. We were very proud of how well we had hidden, but Mama did not share in our joy. Another good sport forbidden."

"And people think the Scots were wild."

"I have a drop or two of Scottish blood, you know."

"I do know—from Rose of Laughlin."

"Why, yes! Laughlin, McLaughlin. You belong to the same clan. Our family legend claims she was a bride stolen from the Highlands by Hugh of Bellevue. Her portrait hangs next to his in our gallery. She wears a plaid much like this one attached to her gown at the shoulder with a thistle pin. Her hair is redder than yours. Mama says judging by her self-satisfied smirk, Rose most likely had a hand in her kidnapping and got the man she wanted."

"And she so cursed her brother and all future Laughlin lairds to untimely deaths and near-poverty until avenging the slight by stealing and marrying a Bellevue bride. It makes no sense if she helped with her own abduction, but then legends seldom do." Why had he said that? She had no need to know the old rubbish.

Phemie shifted in his arms to face him even though the darkness hid all expression. "I never heard that part of the story. Perhaps she found herself supremely happy later and regretted her words. Leo, is that what you were doing, stealing a Bellevue bride?"

"Perhaps. I was under the influence, you know, drugs and Scotch whisky. My unc—friend spoke of the curse while we shared a dram or two. Then, I awakened in a cave with the Duke of Bellevue's daughter."

"You thought I was Pandora. You intended to take her. But I heard you tell your confederate you liked me better before we went into the woods."

Did he detect jealousy in her words? He tightened his arms around her. "I do like you better than anyone, Phemie. We should attempt sleep now."

"First, tell me, are the lairds of Laughlin truly condemned to early deaths and poverty because of the Longleighs?"

"They never were rich. The McLaughlins held a keep on the coast for the greater McDonalds. The sea, sheep, cattle, and game fed them. When Ian McLaughlin fell at Culloden, certainly an untimely death, my great-grandmother fled to France with her son and what few jewels she had."

"Ian McLaughlin...I've heard that name."

"Um, possibly I borrowed it for a while. I am unclear about that. My friend and I did discuss him before my mind went blank."

"To think, he died in glory at Culloden."

Leo heard her little sigh, felt the flutter of her heart pressed so near his. "Phemie, have you been reading *Waverley*?"

"Yes, just recently."

"I thought as much. Listen to me. There is no curse, only consequences. Ian McLaughlin chose to fight at Culloden. His widow was reduced to teaching harp to the ladies of the French court."

"Like Flora Mac-Ivor."

"I doubt if she thought it such a fine thing. Her son married a French woman with the best dowry he could obtain, but he left her soon after my father's birth to be a noblewoman's lover. I understand he was still quite vigorous when he went to the guillotine with his mistress in the year of my birth. As for my own father, he chose an English merchant's daughter and neglected her in much the same way. That he walked in front of a carriage and got trampled to death, merely an act of inattention, not a curse. If I die with a bullet in my breast delivered by the weapon of the Duke of Bellevue, that will be the consequence of my foolish act."

Phemie struggled from his arms and her hands went flying. She barked her knuckles on the rough interior of the oak which only made her angrier.

"So, you regard this adventure as idiocy and taking me as a mistake!"

"Of course, taking you was a mistake, but my concern is only for you. I am merely a Scottish physician who dabbles in experiments, not Angus Mac-Ivor, not Ian McLaughlin, no great romantic figure from the pages of a book. Do you understand, Phemie?"

Her arms flailed again, one hand catching him across the cheek. He sat up to contain her and immediately hit his head in precisely the same spot wounded in the cave. Putting his own pain aside, he pinned her arms. "There, you will hurt yourself."

"I already have." As he loosened his grip, she raised a skinned knuckle to her lips and sucked on it for a moment.

"Let me collect some rainwater and clean your wounds."

Drawing away again, she answered, "No, I do not need your help. You sound exactly like Pandora. You should have taken her. Only she would have killed you by now."

Exasperated, Leo fumbled with his jacket buttons, and then his waistcoat. He pulled up his shirt and exposed his pale chest in the darkness. "You have a weapon. If you want me dead, go ahead. Send me to my untimely death. Fulfill the curse."

Her small hands touched him, flesh against flesh. "You are so warm and your heart beats mightily. I could never slay you, Leo."

Just like that, she folded against him, laid her head over his heart, and ran her fingers over the light covering of hair on his chest, rousing that frisson of small sparks wherever she touched. "You did not tell me, but I know who you truly are—the Last Laird of Laughlin."

He nearly wished she had killed him and put him out of his misery.

Eleven

The Duke of Bellevue rode on through the rain as if he were a large frigate cutting through the sea. Jason, a lesser craft, bobbed at his side. They dropped anchor at a tavern only to take on mulled wine, a bowl of hot beef stew, and ask directions to the street where Leonidas McLaughlin had his lodgings. Then, out into the slop again with some compliments to good Glasgow paving.

Near midnight, the duke clapped the knocker on the green door of a narrow three-story brick dwelling near the university. He followed that with a pounding of his fist on the wood. Footsteps approached and the door opened on a woman wearing a large nightcap to cover her rag-wrapped hair and a floral dressing gown inadequate for the size of her bosom. Only a fringe of bright red hair across the brow escaped her cap, but a great deal of breast made more prominent by an arm bent behind her back eluded her nightdress.

"I've told ye and told ye, if ye canna come in at a decent hour, then sleep in the gutter. I only answered tonight because of the rain you might drown. Oh, not one of my tardy lodgers, then." She peered at him more closely and stepped back a bit.

"Your pardon, madam. We seek a man who stays here, one Leonidas McLaughlin. It is most urgent we see him."

66

Shrewd blue eyes crinkled at the edges as she gauged the visitors from the tips of their muddied, fine leather boots to the rain-wilted lace at their sleeves and necks to the ruined hats atop their heads. They stood tall and let her peruse them. Their stance told her they had no regard for the ruination of good clothing. Those blue eyes lit as they examined Jason's lean, swarthy face and scanned his lithe and youthful form.

"Who might ye be seeking young Leo?"

"Pearce Longleigh, Duke of Bellevue. My son, Lord Jason Longleigh." The duke bowed slightly and rainwater poured from the tip of his expensive but unfashionable gold-laced tricorne.

"I do believe it. Agnes Cunningham, widow and owner of this establishment, Your Grace. Come out of the weather," the landlady beckoned as she drew her hidden arm forward and stuck a pistol into the already strained sash of the dressing gown. "I willna be in need of this, I see, but a poor lady all alone must take care."

"Of course," the duke conceded. "Is Dr. McLaughlin in residence?"

"Nay. He went into the Highlands several years ago to start a medical practice. I suspect he wanted more time and space to work on his contraptions than a city practice might allow. Someone gave you the wrong direction for the lad."

"His Uncle Duncan."

"Ah, the old man, always pestering Leo for a visit in his letters. No wonder he didna share his new address. Now me, he visits when he gets to Glasgow as I was like a mother to him. He came to me all gangling limbs and clumsy feet and grew to be a man in my keeping."

"Indeed. So, he has not come here lately bringing a young woman with him?"

"Leo? Not much for the ladies, always head in the books, always tinkering. He had no idea what a handsome young man he became under my care. He wouldna notice a willing woman if she sat upon his lap."

"Then, he might not be the man we seek. Could you suggest a nearby inn for the night?"

Eyeing Jason again, Mrs. Cunningham made a suggestion. "One of my students—I let rooms to the medical variety mainly—is away, his mother taken ill. If ye have no problem with a study skull and monstrous things pickled in jars, you may have his cot and a private chamber. I will give my own bed to your poor son and sleep in the rocker. All soaked through he is."

"Yes, he is. Would you have a place for our horses and a boy to see to them?"

"I have a shed in back where I keep my milch cow. Clover willna mind the company of such distinguished animals, but the boy does not come around till morning to feed and milk her and take her leavings to his mother's garden."

"Jason will see to the horses, and I will gladly pay for the hay. Come, son, I will help you settle the beasts. Your offer is greatly appreciated, madam."

"I will open the door round the back, Your Grace." The landlady performed a deep and greatly revealing curtsy as they stepped into the rain once more.

As they led their mounts down a narrow aperture to the rear of the establishment, Jason whined, "I had more luxurious accommodations in mind after such a foul ride."

"If I can endure a death's head staring at me all night, you can milk the widow of any information she might be withholding on this Leo McLaughlin. She fancies you, and your specialty *is* randy widows of a certain age."

"Acknowledged, but usually I do the choosing."

"We must all do our utmost to find Phemie."

The duke, being of the belief that a man should be able to care for his own horse, pushed aside the mild and dozing cow in its byre and soon had both mounts stripped of their tack, the saddles resting on either end of the manger. He picked up handfuls of clean straw, began rubbing down his great, black stallion, and beckoned Jason to do the same with his sleek bay racer. The animals dined on hay pulled from a small ledge above the cow's reach, and Clover benefited from some extra supper because of them.

"I shall return to the house first. Come after me, seem in need of her comfort, and learn what you can, boy."

The duke strode out into the rain and followed the slate flags to the rear of the house. His hostess greeted him with a candle in hand and took his sodden coat and hat to dry in the laundry. Soon ensconced in a front room on the second floor decorated with enough gory objects to give nightmares to the less stout-hearted—a jawless skull on the bedpost, a pickled hand bent as if trying to claw its way out of the jar on the dresser, a fetal pig dried and half-dissected on a table—he shed the remainder of his clothes to hang on a chair back and rolled into the extra blankets provided by the landlady. The rest he left to his son.

~ * ~

Determined to do his duty, Jason made his way to the house. Mrs. Cunningham lay in wait, ready to strip him of his wet garments. He managed to retain his shirt and snug trousers until he reached her bedchamber, still warm and cozy on a wet night from a small fire recently banked. Though he shed the remainder of his damp clothes behind a screen, he had the feeling Mrs. Cunningham watched him disrobe in the mirror above the bowl and pitcher set well-illuminated by candles set on either side. She was a tall enough woman and had the inclination to do so. Wrapped in a sheet, he made his way to a commodious bed with a feather tick and sank into its depths.

The landlady hurried to raise the covers over him and made no move to take her place in the nicely-padded rocker across the room. "There now, my handsome lad, I've left my own heat in the sheets for ye." She brushed his dark hair from his forehead. "Och, so chilled ye are. What can we do keep ye from taking a cold?" Her ample breasts looming above him blotted out the light from the candles.

He wanted to suggest she bring him a hot brick for his feet or a toddy to thaw his insides, but instead, he drew in his breath and said, "I see no reason why two people should not warm each other on such a miserable night. I would not have you sleep in a chair."

"I thought the same!"

The widow hastened to blow out the candles and throw her dressing gown over the screen. The billowing white mass of her nightdress followed. Quite naked, she came to him. Jason moved to the far side of the bed to accommodate her. The mattress sank down. Neither of them moved to turn their back to the other. A plump but strong and knowing hand made its way under his sheet and cupped his cock and balls. Already shriveled with the cold, they drew up a little further. Then, she began to stroke him vigorously.

"This will bring the heat back into your blood, my young lord. I canna have ye die of a lung inflammation."

She did know how to inflame other parts of the body, however. Jason closed his eyes and imaged Lady Tartte doing the same, but that high-born and well-preserved widow was not a particularly generous lover and usually, he did most of the work. Still, he managed to lose himself in the vision and came close to meeting his goal when the stroking ceased and the Widow Cunningham straddled his hips.

"Lie there and do not strain yourself. I will revive ye from your ordeal, Lord Jason."

He had to admit the landlady possessed strong thighs and a pretty rhythm that teased by stopping and starting, going fast and slow. She drew it out but finally finished both him and herself. He wanted nothing more than to go to sleep after she rolled off and cuddled him on her great bosom. Agnes gave off the heat of a burning coal fire, very comforting. But no, he must question her about Leonidas McLaughlin.

"My dear Mrs. Cunningham, did Dr. McLaughlin ever avail himself of your bounteous charms?"

"Leo? I offered many a time to show him the ways of a man with a woman, but he accepted only the once. When he got word of his mother's death, he cried in my arms. I comforted him as best I knew how, but there was nay passion in it. Blamed himself for being so far from her sickbed and unable to save her, for all his learning. His father gone some years, other family lost in that French upheaval, he really had little kin left but his great-uncle and some other elders up Ben Lomond way."

"Ben Lomond, you say."

"Aye, but I canna say where exactly. He keeps a change of clothes here and a few coins for when he visits in town. If a letter or a package comes, I keep it for him."

"What a good and kind woman you are, Mrs. Cunningham."

"Agnes, do call me Agnes." She squeezed his shoulders a bit too tightly and tucked his head more firmly under her chin.

"When do you think he might come here again?"

"No way to tell. When he needs parts for his contraptions."

"Is he some mad inventor, then?"

"Nay, nay, I've never known a gentler or more sensible young man. He hopes to make money on his devices and raise up the name of McLaughlin in his mother's memory. Poor lad, poor lad. He is the last of his kind, the Last Laird o' Laughlin."

He rolled free of her embrace and sat up. "This man is a Scottish laird?"

"With nothing to show for it, his lands all lost in the Rising back in forty-six." Agnes sat up, too, and exposed her large breasts. "I do like a young man who doesna go to sleep on me. I see by all this talk you are warmed up and ready to go again."

She forced her bulk beneath Jason and heaved him into position between her mighty thighs. "Now, laddie, your turn to keep us warm beneath the covers."

~ * ~

Jason rose weak-kneed from all his exertions, washed and dressed behind the screen. The widow had risen early and left him to get in another hour of sleep. He followed his nose to a private parlor across the hall where his father sat at a round table covered by a pretty cloth and brimming with breakfast: fried sausages and eggs, brown toast, crumbly scones, tea and coffee, sugar, cream, and jam. Obviously, the duke had finished a large platter of the offerings as he blotted his lips on a napkin.

"Did you sleep well, Papa?"

"Yes, I did despite all the horrors in my chamber."

"The horrors in *your* chamber—do you know what I had to do last evening?"

"No matter about that. We must each do our part to recover your sister. What did you learn?"

"I'd say we are searching for the wrong man as she described McLaughlin as scholarly and immersed in his inventions, not one to chase women, not an ounce of mayhem in him—except for one thing."

Bearing a fresh pot of tea, Mrs. Cunningham bounced cheerfully into the room. Some of her red curls released from their rags were drawn up into a topknot above her broad face, and others jiggled down beside her ears. A small wedge of lace pinned to her hair served as a cap, and she wore her Sunday best, a dress of dark blue silk with many flounces under her white apron. She'd taken the time to powder and rouge and douse herself with the scent of lilacs. Agnes beamed at Jason. "Here ye are, just in time for a nice hot cuppa."

Jason accepted her offering gladly and applied liberal doses of sugar and cream, hoping to restore his energy. Any moment now, his father would suggest they ride on. He took toast, eggs, and a sausage.

The landlady nodded with approval. "Ye still seem peaked this morning, young Lord Jason. Eat hearty and perhaps consider spending another night."

That would be the death of him. "We must ride on shortly, my dear Mrs. Cunningham, but I shall never forget the night spent under your roof." He was far too much of a gentleman ever to imply the evening to be less than wonderful. Certainly, her crude skills had been extraordinarily robust and, yes, memorable.

His vague compliment pleased her, and she insisted on wrapping the remainder of the sausages and scones to take on their travels. The duke pressed enough payment into her pudgy hands to cover both the food and the fodder for their horses. As they passed through the house to the reclaim their mounts, the other denizens of the house began to stir.

"Medical students, they keep the Sabbath by sleeping in, and those who did not make curfew stayed at their usual haunts," Agnes remarked. "If I do see Leo McLaughlin, I will tell him the Duke of Bellevue seeks him."

"I imagine he might already know. Good day, madam, and our thanks for your hospitality." The duke bowed over her proffered hand as Agnes sank into her deep curtsy.

"My pleasure, Your Grace."

In the privacy of the byre, with only the cow to overhear, he asked his son, "What was that one thing you were about to reveal when our hostess interrupted."

"Only this, she called Leonidas the Last Laird of Laughlin."

"Laughlin, our holdings in the north? Your brother is Viscount Laughlin. The lairds died off long ago."

"Evidently not."

The duke's broad fist slammed against the side of the byre, causing the cow to moo in distress, but the hay shaken down soon calmed the beast. "I see it now. This McLaughlin took Phemie hoping to regain his lands. There is not room in the world for two lairds of Laughlin. Your brother must retain the title."

"He hardly takes an interest in it. Now, if I had a Scottish castle and the lands surrounding it…"

"You would write a lay to its beauty. Mount up. We ride for Castle Laughlin."

After leaving Glasgow, they turned north at a white-planked Presbyterian chapel, its bells calling the congregation milling before the door to worship. They took no notice of a small woman, her head and shoulders wrapped in a plaid, entering with the crowd, nor of the tall man on a great dappled horse who waited in hiding to see her go safely inside.

Twelve

Phemie drew the plaid tighter around her face, hiding her chin and lips as the great, black horse galloped past the chapel. Jason's mount trailed behind, and she thought her brother looked exhausted from the chase. Fortunately, Leo had retained his Scotch bonnet, and the brightness of his hair would not give away his hiding place as he watched her to safety. She inserted herself into a group of sizeable women entering the sanctuary and took a place on the last row of benches.

Leo thought it best they not enter Glasgow together, even on a quiet Sunday morning. He would go to Mrs. Cunningham's house, change his clothes and retrieve his purse, make some arrangements for further travel, and return to the church.

"The sermon will be long, and the ranting will keep you awake. Since many will have come far to hear the preaching, they will have food afterward, and someone will offer you a bite. I haven't provided for you very well and see it in your cheeks." He'd drawn a long, white finger down the side of her face.

"I do not care. You will come back for me?"

"Lord help me, I will, but I should leave you with these godly people instead of taking you with me."

Then, he'd raised her chin with that finger and kissed her good-bye. But moments later, her father passed turning north, not back to Bellevue, and still in pursuit. The sermon did go on and on, raining damnation on those who shirked the laws of God. Her mind returned to the hollow oak and her awakening on Leo's bare chest, his embarrassment as he pulled down his shirt and buttoned up tight again. Bosworth had wandered off in search of better grazing than bitter oak leaves, but an animal that big was easy to track with his large hoof prints impressed in the wet ground. They found him dining in the oat field and had a time leading him away. At least one of them had gotten breakfast. She looked down at her mud-caked slippers and smiled at the memory.

During prayer, while the minister called on God's succor for the sick, and salvation for the sinners who had left their appointed path, Phemie asked only that Leo return. She knew his mind already. He would want to do what was best for her—such as leaving her with this godly congregation, knowing some Christian family would care for her until word could be sent to Bellevue of her rescue. However, she knew her own mind even better. Like her mother before her, she had decided to have this man and would—if he only came back for her.

As the service lengthened, she dwelt on Leo's long limbs, his gentle white hands, his red-gold hair, so different from her dark-visaged, superior brothers. All of them stood six feet and over, except for Justinian who hadn't his full growth yet, but she was certain Leo had several inches more than that. The thought of a man's inches made her want to giggle. Leo's shoulders were not quite as broad as those of her brothers, but he might make up for that elsewhere. Maids did gossip, and she and Panny had kept their ears open to learn what they could. Color flooded her cheeks as she recalled the kisses she had teased out of him and taught him to return by raising her eyes and lips just so. What might come next?

Abruptly, the congregation stood for a final hymn and let the blood flow back into their buttocks after such a long stint on the hard benches. A little wobbly, she rose, too, and joined in the song. The minister gave a final blessing and moved to the front of the chapel to greet his congregants. His stern wife stood beside him. Presbyterian she might have been, but her dark bonnet had a lining of black lace and velvet cords tied beneath her sharp chin. Even in the warmth of summer, she wore long sleeves and a high neckline punctuated with a mourning broach from some recent bereavement. The preacher, her match in dour looks, inquired if Phemie were new to their group.

"No, my—my husband and I were passing when the bells tolled and I asked that he put me down to worship while he went about his business in Glasgow."

"Business on the Sabbath?" The man's dark eyes still burned with hellfire and brimstone.

"Of a personal nature only."

Whether it was the strong look that said he knew she'd had impure thoughts during his sermon, or the lack of a morning meal, Phemie felt her legs tremble and fold. The wife caught her, not the man, and took her to a bench. Her dark bonnet so close it shielded Phemie's face, the woman asked, "Are you with child?"

"No. I am without breakfast but thank you for your concern."

The preacher's wife seemed to regard that as a flippant answer. "I can remedy that, but not your sins. Your name, girl."

"Um, Effie. My name is Effie McLaughlin, Mrs. Leo McLaughlin."

Her interrogator's eyebrows rose in doubt. With a sturdy hand on Phemie's elbow, the woman led her to a wagon where a family laid out a meal to sustain them through the afternoon service. "As you can see, this poor young woman is in need of your charity. Might you spare her something to eat?"

"Be happy to share, Mrs. Reverend MacLean," the kindly farm wife replied, though her husband frowned into his beard. She poured cider into a tin cup and offered Phemie half her sandwich of roast beef made tangy with horseradish. Three young children sitting in the wagon bed watched the sandwich go and applied themselves to smaller versions.

"Thank you, Mrs. Lamont. I must see to my husband's dinner. He needs his nourishment to serve the Lord." The minister's wife walked off to a substantial stone house a short way from the chapel.

"Humpf. She willna dirty her own floors with the feet of the poor," the farmer remarked. "Pastor MacLean took her off her parents' hands and got himself land for a church, and now with the old man dead, he has the house and acreage, too. Canny, vera canny for a man of God, but I wouldna have her for all the land in Scotland."

"Archie, for shame. A peach, my dear." Mrs. Lamont, a smile on her pockmarked, homely face, held out the offering.

Peaches. Would Leo return for her? Phemie accepted the fruit, but felt she had to explain. "I am not poor, only without money at the moment."

The farmer laughed, considerably softening his deep-lined face. "That is one way to look at it, lassie."

With her father long gone, she'd let the plaid slide down to her shoulders in the warmth of the afternoon. No need for disguises now, but it seemed she had one, anyway. Their travels and rough nights had taken a toll on a perfectly simple but lovely dress made from layers of fragile white lawn and tied with a red ribbon, a light airy gown she'd changed into after the long carriage ride home. The soiled ribbon was long gone, and her skirts were tattered and besmirched. Add her muddy slippers and dirty stockings, thanks to Bosworth, and she looked like a woman who had slept in a haystack—which she had. At least, she'd washed her hands and face in a rain puddle this morning.

Mrs. Lamont unpacked a crock of pickles, boiled eggs and cheese from a basket and laid out slices of a dry but currant-filled cake on a cloth. "Eat all ye wish, Miss...?"

"Mrs. Leo McLaughlin...Effie. So pleased to meet you." The lie came easily to her now. The name seemed to fit her perfectly, like her best kid gloves. "My husband has gone into Glasgow and will repay your kindness upon his return." She hoped so.

"No need. We have enough, thanks to the Lord's blessing." Mrs. Lamont pressed a piece of the currant cake into her hands and slapped away the grab made by her eldest son. "Guests first, Donal."

Suspecting Mrs. Lamont had made them all, Phemie nibbled the cake, sampled the cheese and pickles, and exclaimed over their excellence in her best manners. As the country wife repacked the remainders of their picnic, no cake remaining after Donal and his brothers were given their turn, Phemie thanked them again. She startled when a hand grasped her shoulder.

Mrs. Reverend MacLean said, "You have very pretty manners and refined speech for a poor waif. Confess that some unsavory man has seduced and abandoned you. Receive the Lord, and I shall take you in and train you to be my parlor maid. You have no better future than that."

"No, no! My husband will return for me. See, there he is."

Phemie shook free and ran toward the big gray horse bearing Leonidas to the church. He looked so different, all dressed in somber black with a plain white neckcloth and no hat upon his head. How his hair blazed in the sunlight. Clean and fresh-shaven, so very much the handsome gentleman, she could not race to him fast enough.

"Stop," Mrs. MacLean shouted. "You will ride to perdition with a man such as that. Save yourself from damnation and stay with us!"

Phemie leapt up, and he caught her round the waist and set her in the saddle.

"Ride," she said. "Even if we do go to hell, I will not stay here."

~ * ~

To think, he'd nearly left her, considering her to be in good Christian hands, and sought his own safety in his private haven. Mrs. Cunningham had pinched his cheek and declared she knew he'd gotten into some mischief and about time, too. A duke and a young lord had come looking for him, and she might have talked too much after a night of carnal persuasion, not mentioning whether it was the lord or the duke she'd entertained. He suspected the younger. He had an impulse to flee, but thinking of leaving Phemie among strangers, even godly ones, stopped him. Simply the prospect of a few more days in her company, another kiss or two stolen like the thief he was, brought him back to the chapel.

The excitement in her eyes when she saw him approach he'd seen before, but could not remember exactly when. No matter. He turned back to Glasgow and its port beyond with Phemie in his arms. A day's sail up the coast, and they would arrive at the safest haven he could provide, where the duke's own retainers would take care of her and restore her to her family—Castle Laughlin. He felt her loss already.

Thirteen

They quarreled. Phemie would not leave Bosworth with Mrs. Cunningham, though she trusted the landlady enough to store the trews and Scotch bonnet with its white Jacobite rosette. Leo supposed they would need Boz once they reached Strachur and went inland. Fortunately, the coastal craft was a shallow draft and could be boarded by plank. Blindfolded, Bosworth accepted his fate and soon stood cross-tied midship. An offering of hay calmed the animal further.

As for Phemie, she delighted in the spanking breeze that pushed the ship along and the sights on shore, especially the castle that perched on a cliff, and, eventually, the great bulk of the mountain, Ben Lomond. Leo made no mention of the castle being their ultimate destination.

"Have you never been to the Highlands, then?" He watched the wind tangle her wild gypsy curls. The seamen probably thought her a light lady he'd brought along for amusement in her soiled gown and without a bonnet, but oh, so lovely.

"Only once. I was but seven when I traveled here with my mother. You see, my elder brothers had come with my father to hunt, and all took a severe chill. Thanks to strong constitutions, they survived, but my mother descended on their hunting lodge, really a ruined castle, calling it a dreary, damp death trap. Wagons carrying carpets and antique tapestries, feather ticks and furnishings stretched out three miles behind our carriage. When we arrived, she had the garderobes mucked, the grand fireplace in the great hall cleaned, the floors covered in the best a Persian could weave. The servants hiked the pieces of bed frames up the winding staircase to my father's chamber and even higher to the room where the ladies-in-waiting once stayed and where my brothers were to sleep. The solar of the tower, she outfitted as finely as any sitting room in London."

"The duchess sounds like a lady to be reckoned with." Like her daughter, Leo thought.

"Same as a general on the march. The boys said she ruined the place. They used to sleep before the fire in the great hall and rampage up and down those twisting stairs. During our stay, Jason and Joshua lured Panny and me into the dungeon. They put us in manacles and locked us in a cell, all in good fun, as the manacles were much too big and would have fallen off our wrists if we hadn't held them on. The boys threatened us with the rack and thumbscrews if we did not reveal where the castle's treasure lay hidden. We wailed and cried for mercy, a marvelous game, but Mama, who has ears sharp as a fox, overheard and had every last chain and remnant torture device thrown into the sea. She always says she does not know how she raised us all to adulthood. Regardless, we girls were never allowed to go back. Men must have a place to be men, Mama said."

Leo watched the animation of her face, the merriment of her dark eyes as she told her tale. "You would like to live in a Highland castle then?"

"My, yes! Ever since I read *Waverley*, I've been thinking of asking Papa if we could visit Castle Laughlin again."

"That book! You should put it out of your mind, Phemie. Castles and curses have no place in the nineteenth century. We are entering the age of steam. Why, did you know the famous Robert Fulton has a steam-powered warship in the works to use against our forces in

New York, and the *London Times* will soon be produced on a steam-powered press?"

"I do know that. Papa subscribes to several scholarly journals but never reads them. I suspect he leaves them lying about for me to pick up and peruse. But Leo, I do not see why we cannot have steam warships and presses, castles, *and* curses."

"A duke's daughter might have them all, but not the rest of us. Curses have no basis in science, and castles have no use at all, except to serve as some fine lord's hunting lodge." Bitterness edged his statement, and its taste caught him by surprise. He'd never minded making his own way, working to gain his fortune as his merchant grandfather did—until he'd kidnapped Phemie. By the time he amassed enough money to support a lady like her, she would be long married to someone born with a fortune. As *he* had been before his father spent it in gambling dens and the beds of high-classed whores.

Phemie raised her big brown eyes to his. Her rosy lower lip trembled. She wanted to be held and kissed right here in front of the sailors. He would not do it. Leo crossed his arms across his chest.

"I do come with twenty-thousand pounds," she said, as if he would have to be paid to take her. "That would build any number of steam machines."

"I despise men who marry for money."

"Who is the romantic now, Leo?"

"I mean to make my own fortune."

"Admirable. You could pay me back."

"Phemie, much as I hate the idea of parting from you, I must return you to your family. It is the right thing to do."

"And I have no say in the matter?"

"Correct."

Her round eyes narrowed. She crossed her arms, mirroring his stance and turned away. They passed the rest of the trip in silence until at last, the ferry docked. Leo led Bosworth ashore and saddled the horse again. The sun was descending, shooting its rays out across the water. Its blaze reflected in Phemie's eyes.

"So, here we are in Strachur, the Glen of the Herons. Pretty name, no?" Leo said as he mounted.

"I have not come here as a tourist," she proclaimed.

"Very well then. We have a way to go before dark. Come along."

She did not leap into his arms this time, but stood there, arms still crossed under her bosom. He got down and lifted her into place. She refused to relax against him but sat stiffly erect.

"You will be uncomfortable, but suit yourself, Lady Euphemia."

"I shall."

Several miles on their silent way, Leo pulled up. "Now, I must ask you to trust me. I would not implicate any of the good people who have taken me in, and so I must blindfold you for the remainder of our travels."

He took the black silk mask from his jacket, doubled it over to cover the eyeholes and bound it around Phemie's eyes. "You do not think a man riding along with a blindfolded girl will draw attention?" she said.

"This road is not much traveled, and day draws to an end. We will be fine. Not much longer now."

The words were barely spoken when a rider approached and hailed them. "Dr. McLaughlin, is it you?"

"Yes, good day to you, Mr. MacEwan."

"Who might this young woman be?"

"A patient—with an eye disease. I am taking her for treatment. I would not come too close as it might be catching."

The man veered off and waved his goodbye.

"Why, you are very inventive, Leo." Phemie's bowed lips quirked up at the corners. He did not reply but set his heels to Bosworth's sides and urged the animal on the last few miles.

They did not beat darkness to their destination, but someone had left lanterns burning on either side of the entrance to the old bailey of the castle. The stout doors and portcullis were long gone as were most of the once mighty walls. Cotters had taken the stones to build homes and erect barns. Now only the crumbled base remained, poking up like broken teeth in a skull through a covering of yellow rambling roses.

The buildings that would have cluttered the area in medieval times had vanished, leaving only a wide-open court, but the castle keep still stood four-square with the great hall jutting from its side and a small chapel tucked in under the exterior stairway leading into the tower. Castle Laughlin—he called it home.

Leo approached quietly to where another stone staircase led not up but down under the great hall. Someone expecting his return had left a lantern glowing there, too. He dismounted and took Phemie from the horse.

"I must carry you. I don't want you to stumble."

"Where are you taking me?"

"You will see soon enough. Sit on this step for a moment."

He found the fisherman's boots and drew them on over his own. Then, he picked up Phemie and waded into the water flooding the tunnel. A few paces took him to the small dike creating the pool. He bent low and stepped over the partition into the dry portion of his hideaway.

"Leo, are we in a watery cave like the one belonging to the cattle thief in *Waverley*?"

"*Waverley* again! No, we are in my living quarters."

He sat her beside him on the last step, took off the boots, and next, her blindfold. Not that it made any difference as the chamber was pitch black. A ghostly voice echoed in the void.

"Leonidas McLaughlin, are ye down there? We been awaiting ye these many days. When ye did not arrive on the coach, and Ben returned in the pony cart without ye, we feared the worst, the Last Laird of Laughlin dead and gone."

"No, I am quite well. Could you send down a lantern?'

"I left one by the stairs."

"Yes, well, my hands were full."

"Full o' what?" The spirit, speaking in the high cracked voice of an elderly woman, seemed inclined to converse at length.

"I will explain later. Please send down a light and any food that might be at hand, but I do have a mighty hunger. Oh, and I've come by horseback. Would you have Ben see to my mount?"

"Surely. Give an old woman a few moments."

"Who was that?" Phemie asked.

"The steward's wife, as it happens, my great-auntie."

"Are we simply to sit here and wait?"

"That would be wise, considering the place is quite cluttered, and I would not want to damage anything."

They sat until a squeaking sound filled the chamber, followed by a dim light and the distinctive sheepy aroma of mutton stew. Leo made his way to an opening where the lantern and steaming bowl had magically appeared. Taking the candle from the lamp, he made his way around the chamber, lighting a festoon of lanterns that hung from hooks in the low, vaulted ceiling. As each flame caught, another portion of the room revealed itself. Dark doorways gapped open off the main chamber. Strange metal objects and rolls of paper appeared on a long central table resting on a threadbare crimson Turkey carpet woven with a pattern of fantastical beasts. Leo carried the bowl to a smaller table with two rush-bottomed chairs on either side and went back for bread, a cheese, and a pitcher of ale.

Still taking in the revelation, Phemie sat on the step and pondered. "You live in a dungeon. That explains your pallor. But why?"

"A private space in which to conduct my experiments rent-free. The current proprietor would not approve of my presence, even though I do give medical treatment to his tenants at no charge, if only he knew."

"His people hide you?"

"While they think he is a good enough fellow for an Englishman, their loyalty is still to the clan, to the Last Laird of Laughlin. He comes only twice a year to hunt, fish, and look over the books for the grazing, quarry, and fisheries income. It's easy enough to stay below while he visits as he is out most of the time. I contrived the dike to make the dungeon appear flooded. Though he ordered it pumped out by his next visit, the staff has neglected to do so."

"Very clever of you." It took Phemie only a moment to add the facts in her head. "I believe we are at Castle Laughlin, my father's

Scottish holding, the one he gifted to my eldest brother who is always abroad. This is the dungeon where I once played."

"I see all my secrecy was for naught. But you cannot be safer than here on your father's own land."

"Which should be your land, and that is why you took me."

"No, no. I took you because I was out of my head at the time. Come eat before the stew grows cold." He held a chair for her like the best of footmen.

Though she was hungry, Phemie did not go to him immediately. She paused by the opening braced with iron in a round bulge in the wall and peered upwards to see how the food had been delivered. Ropes disappeared into the darkness of the hole.

"The castle oubliette. It opens into the great hall. My savage ancestors could drop an enemy into the hole from above and torment him while feasting and drinking. He starved unless someone threw him a tidbit. Not enough space to lie down, only to stand or sit with his knees drawn up...quite barbaric. The oubliette has been covered by a wooden plug since one of your brothers fell through the rusty grate."

"Josh pushed him. Jason broke a leg in that escapade. I've heard the tale often enough."

"Raise the hatch and work the pulleys I've installed, and we have the finest service."

Phemie started for the proffered chair again but became distracted once more by the objects on the long table. "What are these?"

"Models for a steam engine I plan to build to run on a railway. Do you see, Phemie, how we could haul great loads from the quarry to the port? If I present myself to the duke as just one of the many McLaughlins in the area and show him my model, I believe he might provide the funds to build it, and hire me to see the project to its end."

Forgetting the meal himself, Leo went to the table and pushed a small contraption around on a circular track rimming the table. It was nothing more than a boiler on grooved wheels towing a coal cart and several wagons filled with pebbles. Leo pushed it along with a finger.

"Watch this." He took a candle and held it down the small stack of the model. A thin wisp of steam came out as he pushed the engine along. "A smoke pellet, you see, to make the model more believable."

Phemie clapped her hands. "How my little brother, Justinian, would have loved a toy like this. Truthfully, he still would, though he considers himself quite the young man now."

Leo frowned and stopped pushing the model along. "This is not a toy, but a demonstration of my invention. I've met Mr. Watt, the man who perfected the steam engine. He is quite elderly now, but he said my design shows promise. You see, it solves the problem of—"

"Our stew is getting cold, but I do want to hear more later. Come eat, Leo."

"Yes, I sometimes forget. If it weren't for my auntie hollering down the hole, I would miss many a meal. Please go first. I have only the one spoon, but fortunately, two cups."

He poured the ale and helped himself to the cheese and bread while Phemie took dainty mouthfuls of the stew. She left a large portion for him.

"Really, the Presbyterians fed me very well." She looked around the dungeon. "Is there a place I could wash after so many days on the road?"

"Yes, of course. In my bedchamber." He showed her into a cell and lit candles in sconces hanging on either side of a rather comfortable-looking featherbed.

"One of my mother's?" she asked.

"Most likely."

"Here." He opened a small trunk and took out a clean nightshirt. "After you wash, you might want to put this on. We shall see about clean clothes in the morning. The pitcher is full. They expected me back a few days ago and made preparations for my return. Take your time. I'll just close the door and give you privacy. But Phemie... afterwards, we must do the examination to ah...ascertain your purity, like it or not."

"I do not like it."

"We need to know."

"I do not see why."

"It is necessary because neither of us has any recollection of that lost day and night."

"You would think a woman would have some recollection of losing her virginity."

"Not under the circumstances. Please, make yourself comfortable." He pulled the heavy door shut and turned his back on the small, barred window.

~ * ~

First, Phemie made use of the plain white porcelain chamber pot under the bed. Rain began to patter in the pool blocking the stairs. She hoped it, and the stout door, covered the sound of her bodily functions, but wanted no delays, nothing to interrupt them once they started. She poured water into the washbowl and took up the cloth that hung from the side of its stand. Lathering a bar of common brown soap, she began with her face. Discarding her clothes as she moved down her body, she washed carefully between her legs and felt no soreness. Only her backside ached from the long days of riding. As she had no intention of fending Leo off, she unfastened the sheath holding her stiletto and laid it aside.

A comb made of horn, and a brush with half its boar bristles missing, sat on the stand. Using his shaving mirror to improve her appearance, she untangled her curls and brushed them to shining, then drew on Leo's nightshirt. Inhaling the clean scent of fresh linen after so many days, she felt like a bride preparing to meet her groom on her wedding night. Whether Leo knew it or not, she would have this night with him.

His nightshirt covered her to her toes and might have fallen off her small shoulders if it hadn't had a drawstring at the neck. The sleeves enveloped her arms well past her fingertips. She rolled them up and out of the way. The shirt emphasized the difference in their size, but she had no fear, given her petite mother and her brawny father, who managed more than well together.

In her bare feet, she padded to the cell door and peeped out the grill. "I am ready for my examination, Leo."

He had cleared the table of dinner dishes and was puttering with one of his inventions but put it aside and came to open the heavy door. Her full lower lip trembled, a skill she'd learned in childhood to get her way. He took her in his arms and held her tight.

"You must not be afraid. There will be no pain. I need only a quick glimpse."

"Oh, Leo. I must have some reassurance."

She stood on her tiptoes, clasped his face with her hands, and drew it down. He kissed her far longer and more thoroughly than he should have and now had a problem of his own, she noted. By lifting her up and carrying her to the bed, he covered his arousal.

"No need for alarm, my poor, trembling dove. Simply close your eyes and this will be over in a moment."

He placed her head on one pillow and took the other to put under her hips. He fetched a lantern to hang from a hook over the bed. Phemie lay very still. He raised the nightshirt. She opened her legs without being prompted. He parted her labia with his thumbs, probed gently with a finger. The slickness between her legs that appeared whenever they kissed eased the way.

"Phemie, the damage is done."

"I thought as much, Leo. I am willing to be your stolen bride and break the curse."

"There is no curse. But we should marry, unless of course, there has been someone else."

Her temper flared. She did have one but kept it well.

"Do you think a daughter of Lord Bellevue would give herself to just anyone!"

"I *am* just anyone."

"No, you are the Last Laird of Laughlin, and since I have been cheated of my first time, I would like to have it now."

"There will be no pain."

"I do not recall any the last time."

"We should wait to be properly married."

"Irrelevant now, I say. Leo, I am ready."

Put that way, he could not drop his trousers fast enough. With her still positioned perfectly upon the pillow and the need to be careful gone, he sank himself into her warmth, her tightness. She urged him on with a rocking of her hips. He stroked the place that would give her the greatest pleasure, and she surged upward, moaning and calling his name. He came in a burst that made him collapse over her small body. He'd possessed his stolen bride.

"Hold me, Leo."

Shielding his rather large privates with one hand, he snuffed the candles and the lantern and threw the rest of his clothes aside before covering them both with the bedclothes.

"There is no need for excessive modesty, my dear Leo. I shared a nursery with a multitude of brothers."

"The adult male is somewhat different."

"Indeed. I noticed your hair is redder below than above."

He held her, still gowned in his nightshirt, tight to his side. Rain poured harder, thudding like shot into the pool at the entrance.

"Leo, what if the dike overflows while we are down here?" She had no fear of him or the sexual act, and yet she fretted about a little rain.

"No problem at all. I've contrived a drain hole at a certain level to keep the waters from overflowing. Our bigger problem will be getting a clergyman to come out in the wet. Even if we do, he might refuse to let us wed without the duke's consent and feel obligated to notify your father."

"I feel sure you can solve any conundrum."

"Ever since we, ah—"

"Consummated our love for each other."

"Very delicately put. Yes. I've been considering how we might make our union legal. There is an ancient Scottish custom called handfasting that developed during a time when priests were few and distant. A couple stands before witnesses in a public place and, binding their hands together, pledge themselves to each other. It is still perfectly legal in Scotland, hence the popularity of Gretna Green for those who cannot get a license to wed."

"I've heard of it, a trial marriage for a year and a day."

"No, no. That man, Thomas Pennant in his *Tour of Scotland* book, had his facts all wrong. Handfasting is a solemn oath that two people will spend their lives together."

"Will we, Leo? I want no other."

"I no longer imagine life without you. Will you agree to take me as your husband on the morrow?"

"Yes, tomorrow I will become the bride of the Last Laird of Laughlin and the curse will be broken."

"Phemie, there is no curse."

"You live hidden in a dungeon, Leo. I think that is proof enough."

"What shall I do with you," he said with exasperation.

"I have an idea how we might pass the time." She laid one small hand over his heart and the other made its way boldly toward his privates.

Fourteen

"Damnation! The road to Castle Laughlin will be impassable tomorrow if this keeps up." The Duke of Bellevue gazed moodily out the window, though all he could see was the rain pouring into the blackness of the loch and a faint glimmer of the inn's lamplight on its surface.

"Worse places to be stranded than on picturesque Loch Lomond, Papa. Ah-choo!" Jason wiped his nose with a handkerchief and applied his spoon to a bowl of Scotch broth he hoped would clear his head.

"Write an ode to it, why don't you?' His father tucked into a sizeable piece of rare beef and sopped the juices with bread.

"I would, but my inspiration is rather clogged at the moment." He blew his nose again.

The duke's big hand shot out, and Jason drew back, expecting a small cuff for his impudence, but instead, those fingers came to rest on his forehead. "You are warm to the touch. Are you ailing, son?"

"Somewhat. Our ride in the wet yesterday, my exertions with the widow, and now this damp are taking a toll. I hope to feel better in the morning. Phemie's safety must come first."

The hand on his forehead moved to gently ruffle his hair, as if he were still the young boy who had taken a chill while hunting in the

Highlands. "You might not believe it, but I would not trade one of my children for another. If I am harsh with you, it is because I want to see you make your way in life, not spend it spouting verse and diddling women well past their youth. We will abide here until you feel up to the ride. If this physician has taken Phemie to Castle Laughlin or anywhere in the area, my people will surely know and have him arrested. But damnation, will this rain never cease!"

~ * ~

Voices woke Phemie. Leo no longer lay by her side. The dungeon should have been damp and chilly after last night's torrent, but exuded a pleasant heat. She entered the main chamber and found the stone floor warm to her bare feet. Some of the lanterns they had neglected to snuff last evening dripped little chandeliers of hardened wax, but others had been replenished with new candles. The cracked voice sounded from the great hall.

"Leo, I've brought your tea and oatmeal porridge. Are ye up and about yet?"

"Might be he has gone out if he does not answer," an elderly male voice suggested.

"I tell ye, old man, he has a woman down there. I heard them at it when I drew the dirty dishes up. She called his name quite loudly. They are probably still abed. About time he took some interest in the local lassies and got to work providing the next laird. Who knows how long he will last with the curse upon him and me with such a fondness for the lad?"

"Not any girl will do, old woman. Ye know that. My brother, Duncan, said he would be sure Leo found the right bride, and that was the purpose of his visit. Let's hope he swived a Longleigh female last evening."

Wiping his hands on a rag, Leo came from one of the cells. His pallid cheeks burned a shade brighter than Phemie's own warm blush.

"We can hear every word you say, Auntie, Uncle," he shouted up the hole.

"We—did ye hear him? We!" The old woman cackled.

"Send down a second bowl of porridge and another spoon, if you please."

"And who might that second spoon be for, nephew?" the male voice inquired.

Leo shot a look at Phemie. She nodded.

"Lady Euphemia Longleigh."

"Aye, aye! Duncan has managed it." A clatter on the floor above sounded like skeletons dancing on Allhallow's Eve. The laughter echoing in the hole had the same eerie quality.

"I believe I am the one who managed it. I was lucky to escape with my life—and my bride. After breakfast, I am coming up to arrange a handfasting. Now, would you send the porridge down? I am ravenous."

"At once! Ravenous, did ye hear, Sander? A good sign for a happy marriage, I think."

"He honors the old customs, too."

The pulleys began to creak as the tray descended. Smiling, Leo waited for its arrival.

"I rose early to take the chill off by lighting a fire in the Franklin stove. It's fully vented to the outside, so we shall have no smoke. What a marvelous inventor the American Benjamin Franklin was! Phemie, is something the matter?"

She'd gone from blushing bride to quite pale.

"The friend who drugged you is our gardener, Duncan?"

"I cannot deny it, your gardener and my great-uncle. Phemie, have you changed your mind about the handfasting? Speak now, and I will take you out of here and have them send word to your father of your whereabouts. That was my original intent until I discovered—"

"That I am no longer a virgin. Since you do not believe in the curse as everyone else seems to, is that your only reason for marrying me?"

"Hardly. You are an extraordinary young woman, fearless, intelligent, enchanting, a veritable Flora MacDonald, and far too good for your gardener's great-nephew. I never thought I would be able to keep you even for a short time. Despite the kidnapping, your dowry is large and your father influential. It need not prevent you from making a better marriage. Here, sit and eat. You've had a shock."

Delivering the steaming bowl of cooked oats and the teapot to the table, he poured a cup for her and doused both that and the cereal with cream from a small pitcher. "See, Auntie Mary has put some raisins in the porridge."

"Do not wait upon me like a servant, nor treat me like a child, Leo. Pandora would say men of the ton run off with opera singers and marry their mistresses often enough. Why shouldn't a woman have whom she will, be he the gardener's nephew, a respectable physician, or the Last Laird of Laughlin?" Her color had returned higher than before. "Arrange the handfasting."

Fifteen

When Phemie stepped from the tower and out onto the landing, the crowd in the courtyard cheered. A piper inflated his bag and skirled a tune. Wherever had so many come from at such short notice? To be legal, the handfasting had to be done in public. They would not lack for witnesses certainly.

Auntie Mary of the disembodied voice had turned out to be a wiry old woman with a great mop of white hair. She'd given over her best blue gown to the bride because they were of a size, "but ye fill it out much better than I, milady." The fabric smelled overwhelmingly of lavender. The women of the castle had seen she got hot water to bathe and dressed her black hair with white ribbons and yellow late summer roses from the rambling bushes planted by her own mother on the ruins to remind the duke of his wife in her absence. Oh, how she wished Mama could be here. What would she say to all this?

"Follow your heart. Marry the man you love as I did." But Flora's man was destined to be a duke. Would the duchess still give the same advice? She had wed Pearce Longleigh, the Indian warrior called Great Bear, with no certainty of ever returning to England. Yes, of course Mama would understand. Pandora would say her sister had become a romantic ninny. She dearly wanted both of them here.

Phemie descended the stone staircase and went to stand before the abandoned chapel built beneath it. Leo stepped from its dark interior with his great-uncle Sander, a small, wizened man perfectly matched to the ancient Mary at his elbow. She felt a momentary disappointment that her groom wore neither his trews nor a kilt, but only his well-brushed dark clothes and clean linens, his sunlit mane his only ornament in the rays of late afternoon. That the sun had come out at all and dried the flagstones of the courtyard, the household considered a good omen.

Sander McLaughlin took their hands and bound them together with a strip of the family tartan. Leo gazed at her with those eyes of bonnie blue and spoke.

"I declare before all those present that I, Leonidas Ian McLaughlin, do take Euphemia Longleigh to be my wife for as long as we both shall live. She is the bone of my bone, the flesh of my flesh. With my body, I do worship her." Leo raised their bound hands and kissed her fingertips.

Phemie determined to do even better. "I, Euphemia Dorcas Little Dove Longleigh..." She saw that slight lifting of his lips when she stated her full name, but at least he did not laugh. "Do take thee, Leonidas Ian McLaughlin, to be my husband for all eternity. I worship your body as well."

Laughter rose from the crowd. Phemie stood on her tiptoes and drew his head down with her free hand for a resounding kiss. The weird song of the bagpipe started up again and yellow rose petals flung by the castle women, so many that the bushes must have been plucked of every last blossom, fluttered down from the landing.

Sander McLaughlin held up his arms and shouted over the pipes as best he could. "Stop, stop, we have not finished."

The bagpipe deflated with a moan. The cheering stopped. The old castle steward handed something wrapped in the ancient plaid to Leo. Unveiling a claymore of fine workmanship, he placed it in the crook of Phemie's free arm. "I give you the sword of Ian McLaughlin to hold for our first-born son."

Rather awkwardly with only one available hand, he draped the plaid over Phemie's shoulder. "You are now a member of Clan McLaughlin."

The audience waited to be sure the ceremony had ended this time, but with a wave of Sander's hand, the pipes started up again, and the cheers grew in volume.

"To the great hall for a verra fine wedding feast!" Mary McLaughlin cried.

Thanks to the bounty of her father's land, they had venison and lamb, salmon, and the fish of the sea aplenty, summer fruits, plus a great deal of wine from his cellars and stronger beverages of a distilled variety made by the locals for their own consumption. Everyone seemed to have brought a cask or a contribution for the table. The castle's weekly supply of bread and baked goods disappeared at a rapid rate.

Lines formed for a reel, and Sander, unbinding the bride and groom, urged them forward to lead the dance. The participants were not nobles and gentry dressed in broadcloth, silk and lace, but quarrymen, herders, farmers, and fishers who danced with their wives and had more gusto than skill.

Breathless from the long dash down the row and much vigorous twirling, they paused to take refreshment. Phemie marveled, "Where did all these people come from so quickly?"

"As soon as we declared our intention, Uncle sent Ben Campbell, the understeward, down to the fishing village and then to the quarry to declare a half-holiday. He brought whole families in, using the mine drays, and picked up others at villages along the way. I swear if I wanted to declare to rebellion, Clan McLaughlin would gather in a trice."

"How wonderful!"

"No, how terrible. After the Forty-Five rising, little was left of them but widows and orphans, and their lands were forfeited to Lord Bellevue. That is why I have nothing to offer you today but myself, my profession, and my inventions."

"That will be enough for me."

A space cleared before the table where the bride and groom sat. Two men came forth, laid down crossed sabers from the arsenal the duke kept on hand, and declared they would perform the famous Scottish Sword Dance. Given their state of inebriation by that time, Phemie feared they would cut off a toe or fall and slice a buttock, but Leo reassured her.

"A McLaughlin who cannot hold his liquor is no Scotsman. Uncle Duncan says that often."

Sander felt moved to recite a wee bit o' poetry by Bobby Burns. A young woman sang a Gaelic song so plaintively that tears coursed down Phemie's face even though she could not understand a word. The toasts came fast and many:

"Here's to the heath, the hill and the heather, the bonnet, the plaid, the kilt, and the feather!"

"May we be happy—and our enemies know it!"

"*Slainte, sonas agus beartas*"

The last Leo translated whispering in his bride's ear. "He wishes us health, wealth and happiness."

"*Waverley*," Phemie murmured. "This could be a scene from *Waverley*. We might be Flora and Angus Mac-Ivor."

"I think not. They were brother and sister."

"Then Waverley and Flora."

"I hope I am never as vacillating as that idiot."

"But oh, the Highlands, the music and the poetry." She clasped her hands together and grew teary-eyed.

"Phemie, tell me, how much wine have you consumed?"

"Certainly more than Mama would allow me."

"It is time we left the party."

Leo stood, swaying slightly, a bit worse from all the homebrews he'd sampled in order not to insult any of their special concoctions, Phemie realized. How would he manage the twisted stairs in the tower to the bed chamber, and the expectation of the guests that he would carry Phemie across the threshold?

All eyes were upon him as he announced, "My bride and I are retiring for the evening. Please stay and continue to enjoy the hospitality of Castle Laughlin." He made a sweeping gesture with his hand as if this place did belong to him, and he shared his largesse, not that of the Duke of Bellevue.

Then much to her surprise, he tossed his little wife over one shoulder and headed for the door. Raucous laughter and shouting followed them out. The celebration spilled over into the courtyard. Courting couples who had sought the shadows in the long summer twilight paused in their own embraces to watch the Laird of Laughlin pass with his bride who, black curls dangling round her face and shedding rosebuds as they went, smiled happily from her perch.

Leo made it to the landing with no problem. Several guests applauded. He entered the tower, braced one hand on a wall and started upward. After a short pause before the solar, he assayed the flight to the duke's bedchamber. A string of guests followed behind, whether to catch them if they fell or to cheer them on, Phemie did not know. At the entrance, he kicked open the unlatched door, carried her inside and shot the bolt. Staggering, he deposited her deep in the featherbed hung with green velvet curtains held back with ropes of gold fringe.

"We are not going to the dungeon, I presume?" Phemie said with a giggle as she spread out her arms across the silk coverlet embroidered with the rampant golden lions of the McLaughlins.

"No. We shall spend our wedding night in the Master's bed."

"Papa's bed." Phemie freed a plump pillow from the cover and placed it under her head. "What's this?" she asked, tugging at a bit of lace that hung out from the edge of the case. She withdrew the sleeve of a garment, then the rest of it, a pretty nightdress embroidered with yellow posies, edged with lace and rather sheer. It smelled of attar of roses, her mother's scent. "And Mama's nightdress."

"I thought the duchess rarely came here."

"She doesn't. I believe Papa must keep this here for his own comfort when he is away from her. I always thought their affection for each other to be too extravagant and very embarrassing to their children...but now, I find myself wanting the same."

"You have it, Phemie. I will do better by you now than last night when I was much too hasty."

"You can do better?" A very gratifying thought.

"My bedroom skills might be rusty, but they are never forgotten. My father took me to a well-known courtesan when I was but fourteen to learn what he felt a gentleman should know about women." He paused, letting his mind catch up with his tongue. "I believe I ought not be telling my young wife this."

"It's quite all right. Mama took me aside before the season began and told me once I settled on a man for my husband and went to the marriage bed, I should not simply lie there like part of the mattress but must participate with enthusiasm in order to achieve the true bliss of the nuptial union. I had no idea what she meant until last night, but I do think I achieved it."

"That you did, Phemie. Um, a singular woman, your mother. A certain numbness in my nether regions will help me extend your pleasure. If you are ready?"

"Not yet! Turn your back."

He willingly indulged her and listened to the soft sound of her clothing being shed, the rustling of the bedclothes as she mounted the mattress. The last of the day's light still shone through the single deep-set casement window of the room.

"Turn around, my husband."

Phemie stood by the bed in what light remained with one hand pressed against the back of an embroidered lion on the spread. She wore her mother's nightdress, which revealed every soft curve of her body, the nest of black curls between her legs, the darkness of her small, brown nipples. No longer an angel, but a seductive nymph.

"I thought I'd rather not smell like your auntie when you disrobed me." She gestured to the simple blue gown thrown over a chair along with her stockings and undergarments.

"I believe you are your mother's daughter."

"I most certainly am. Come." She crooked a finger, and he went to her.

Leo knelt before her and ran one hand up the length of her leg, watching his progress as it skimmed her hip, and drew the light fabric up until he cupped a small, plump breast. He did the same with the other hand until the sheer gown raised to her waist. With his lips, he kissed the mound between her thighs. His tongue went deep into her cleft, and he lapped the dew he found there. She did not pull away or cry out "unnatural," but simply sank her fingers deep into his red-gold mane and said, "My lion."

Her thighs begin to quiver as if they could hold her up no longer. He rose up, his arms around her waist and laid her on the bed between the paws of the Laughlin lions. Casting his clothes, and his modesty, aside, he mounted her and set a rhythm long and deep. She cried out almost immediately. He slowed and went shallow but kept on as if determined to show her what the Laird of Laughlin could do here in the keep of his ancestors. Once she settled, he began to assail her again until, screaming his name, she clawed his back, and he raked the white ribbons from her hair. His release came soon after. He rolled to her side and held her close in the aftermath. When she shivered, he took her under the covers.

"Now, are you glad you took a Longleigh bride?" she whispered against his chest.

"I will never regret it."

Sixteen

Trembling and terrified, she woke with the dawn. Phemie bolted upright, trying to put the dream behind her. Her motion made Leo stir and blink at her with sleepy blue eyes.

"What is wrong, wife of mine?"

"The same nightmare where a great bear slays St. Euphemia's lion. The Longleighs believe a dream like this should never be ignored. I know Papa is on our trail. He is coming closer."

Smiling now, Leo reached for her. "Arrant superstition. Come back under the covers, and I will show you morning is as good as night for bed sports."

She slapped his hand away. "With my randy parents, don't you think I know that? The afternoon serves as well. No, we must go back to the dungeon and hide immediately."

"Not until we've had a nuptial breakfast above ground. Even if your father should arrive, we shall have warning, and no one here will betray us."

"It seems to me the history of the Highlands is full of betrayals. Consider what happened to Somerled. Leo, I am asking you to give me a wedding gift." She stroked his tawny hair.

"Whatever is in my power to grant."

"Promise you will flee if Papa comes here."

"This again. Surely I can reason with the man."

"Not before he kills you. If you run and hide, I will have time to explain and soften him toward you. We must consider that I might be with child. That will work in our favor, too, but I would like to have my baby know his father."

"After two nights together? I doubt that." He said it in the skeptical tone of a physician to a patient, which only irritated her further.

"The Longleigh women catch very quickly. Just ask the duchess, mother of ten. We worried so about my sister-in-law, Kate, because she took over a year to conceive. She did suffer a period of starvation, however."

"Yes, that would interfere with conception, along with other factors such as…"

Losing patience, Phemie said, "We don't need your diagnosis now. We must hide." She slid from the bed and started for the door in her urgency, entirely forgetting she wore her mother's sheer bed gown and not Leo's linen nightshirt.

"To please you, we will, but I suggest you get into your clothes first. I am certain the duchess must have had a dressing gown to go with that nightdress. Perhaps it is in the other pillowcase." He dared to jest.

He simply would not take her dream seriously. Phemie stamped her small foot, but it merely sank into the nap of Persian rug her mother had brought to take the chill from the stone floors. Leo came up behind her and kissed her neck.

"Let me help you out of that and into your wedding dress." He lifted the sheer gown over her head but found the curve of her naked back so alluring he continued his kisses down her spine to the juncture of her heart-shaped buttocks. From that position, he easily grasped her hips and placed his wife face down on the carpet.

"You know all bed sports needn't be done in a bed, and sometimes this position enhances the pleasure for both."

"I knew the first, but not the second."

"Let us see if the second is true."

By the time they finished and dressed, the sun had penetrated the courtyard below and complaints of sore heads and sick stomachs rose as high as their casement window. Coming out on the landing at the base of the tower, they saw Ben Campbell, the understeward, rousting hungover quarrymen from the places where they had dropped and herding them back to the drays.

"Holiday over. Back to the mine with ye." He added emphasis with a boot to the backside, his black eyes gleaming with the pleasure of it. Among the fair McLaughlins, he stood out like a single raven surrounded by white-winged seagulls. Seeing them, he gave a curt nod and a twisted smile, saying, "Milord, I can tell by the rosy cheeks of your bride, the curse is lifted. We have only to wait for good fortune to rain down upon us." Then, he raised another quarryman by his jacket collar and shoved him toward the wagons.

The fisher folk had prudently departed earlier, making their own way down the cliff to get their boats in the water with the coming of the sun. Getting rid of the fluids of too much indulgence, castle servants sluiced and swept the flagstones. In the great hall, others did the same, under the sharp eye of Auntie Mary. Still, she took the time to bring them their morning tea, eggs, toasted bread, and kippers from the castle's supply.

Barely had they finished when a commotion arose in the old bailey. Stepping outside, they watched a mud-splashed rider dismount and hand Campbell a message. Though all the mist and dew of the early morning had burned off, Phemie shivered.

"It's from my father, I am certain."

"Aye," said Ben Campbell bringing the missive to them. "It's the duke's hand and his seal. Addressed to the steward it is, but the old man is still abed with his elderly aches and pains and a big head. Now that ye are wed to Bellevue's daughter, ye might want to consider replacing him with a younger man, even though he be your uncle."

"That decision still rests with the duke or Viscount Laughlin. A laird is well beneath them."

"That even I know," Campbell said with a sharp laugh.

"Give me the letter." Leo held out his hand and Campbell slapped it into his palm. The address was written in a bold but inelegant hand and did bear the mark of the Bellevues. He slid a nail under the wax and broke the seal. Phemie leaned close and read along with him.

"All denizens of the castle and its districts are to be on the lookout for a dastardly scoundrel named Leonidas McLaughlin who might be the culprit in the kidnapping of Lady Euphemia. If found, the man is to be put under lock and key until he can be interrogated. A reward of two-thousand pounds is offered for the return of Euphemia and the capture of McLaughlin. Arrival delayed due the illness of Lord Jason but do expect us shortly."

"Should I arrest ye now, my liege lord?" Campbell asked with a smirk.

"No, I shall take myself to the dungeon. See my uncle gets this message. I would not have him taken unawares by the duke's arrival, whenever it might be."

"I'll take care of it." The understeward took possession of the sheet of paper and tucked it in his waistcoat.

"Phemie, you have your wish. We will go below and hide like Bonnie Prince Charlie in the cave of the Seven Men of Glenmoriston, though I believe thirty-thousand pounds was offered for his capture, making my reward seem rather paltry."

"Two-thousand pounds would tempt many to betray you, Leo."

"Och, the McLaughlins are loyal to a fault, if nothing else."

"Was Prince Charles Edward really harbored by brigands in a cave?"

"Absolutely, any port in a storm."

Leo led her to the dungeon entrance. He pulled on the boots and handed Phemie the lantern always kept lit when he was in residence. He scooped up his bride, waded into the dark waters, stepped over the dike, and set her gently down. Moving around the chamber lighting oil lamps and candles, he joked, "My auntie says I've used up the castle's entire illumination budget since my arrival, and the duke will be wroth about it next time he comes—which I suppose will be soon."

"Papa can afford it. He simply won't like the expenditure." Phemie stared, as if seeing the place for the first time. "While highly romantic, entering this way is very inconvenient. If my father, sword, and pistol in hand, should come over that barrier, you will have no escape."

"I do have a bolt hole. My ancestors had a trapdoor built into the dungeon floor. They tunneled through the rock to a sea cave. My great-grandmother made her escape from there. It's under the table and rug."

"I'd be surprised if Jason doesn't know of it. He and Joshua explored this place thoroughly."

"I'm sure they do, but remember, the place appears to be flooded. You need not worry, Phemie. We are safe."

"Then, do I have your promise you will leave if you are in danger?"

"Where would you have me go?"

She pondered a moment with a hand to her chin. "To the cave of the thieves, where Bonnie Prince Charlie took refuge. After I have pacified my family, I will meet you there."

"My darling, you do not know your Scottish history well. That cave is clear across Scotland on the other end of the Great Glen, a very great distance."

"No matter, I will find you. You must move the table aside and have the hatch readily available for your escape. You should pack a bag now with whatever funds you have on hand, a change of clothes and your physician's instruments, and place them beside it."

"Phemie, you are a delightful blend of the practical and the fantastical, but really, I'd rather be doing more interesting things at the moment. We have a great deal of privacy in the dungeon, and day or night does not matter here." He stoked her black curls, wound one around his pale finger, drawing her near, and bent for a kiss.

Two small hands held him back. "Do what I ask now, or there will be no more of what you want."

"Did you learn this from your mother, too?"

"She did mention that most men have only one desire when it comes to women, and so they are easily led by their—urges."

"Not the term she actually used, then?"

"No. The sooner you prepare for your escape, the sooner we can move on to what we both want to do."

With a sigh heavy in frustration, Leo moved aside the massive table holding his inventions and rolled up the carpet to expose the iron ring that raised the trapdoor. He got his medical box and sat it down with a pronounced thud by the hatch. Rooting in the trunk at the foot of the bed, he carelessly thrust items of clothing into a sack and dumped it next to his instruments. A purse of coins and currency retrieved from a cranny in the wall clinked down beside the rest.

"There, are you satisfied?"

Phemie came to him and pressed close. "No, but I soon will be."

Seventeen

The first of the youthful lookouts scrambled down the side of the lichen-spotted boulder and raced fleet as the deer that used these faint trails cross-country to the nearest village. "The duke comes!" he shouted and gave a push to the boy who was to carry the warning next in the relay.

The second boy's father, a gamekeeper, stayed his son for a moment and asked of the first lad, "Are ye certain?"

"It's as you said. No man is as big nor black horse so large in all of Scotland except for our dray animals. Young Lord Jason rides aside on a more spindly sort of animal."

With a swat to his offspring's rear, the gamekeeper sent his boy on his way. "Go fast as ye can and warn the laird."

So it went until the last of the runners, a lanky lad with the reddish-blond hair and blue eyes of the McLaughlins stumbled into the old bailey and cried his message to the steward. Sander hobbled to the oubliette in the great hall and raised the wooden seal. He interrupted a lecture on railroads.

"You see, Phemie, the grooved wheel runs on the iron rail as shown in the model. I think we shall need three wheels on each side to distribute the weight of the quarry rocks rather than the usual two. The course of the rails must be carefully chosen because the engine does not have sufficient power to pull the load over tall hills. The rails shall have to be pounded into the ground to prevent any upsets, but our quarrymen have the strength to do so. The speed of transport alone will save…"

The glow on Leo's face when he spoke of his inventions was surpassed only by the heat in his eyes when he looked at Phemie in bed. She'd listened patiently to his plans for the boiler and engine, the couplings for the ore carts, and the problems of keeping up a head of steam. Though she still thought his model would make a charming toy for children, she did not say so at this point, and expressed her disappointment that carriages could not be attached to the engine to transport people.

"Far, far too dangerous for now, my love," her husband said. "But someday that will come to pass."

How refreshing that a man believed a woman could understand every word he said, no matter how complex. The light in his eyes faded when the words sounded in the dungeon from above. "The duke comes, and Lord Jason with him. Lie quiet as ye are able."

They hadn't spent the entire week below ground but dared not stray too far from their sanctuary. At night, they emerged like fey creatures and took the old plaid out to spread among the dry, stubby heather plants beneath the late summer moon. They made love to the sigh of the sea in the firth and added their own cries to the calls of the night birds.

Just yesterday, Phemie had insisted on descending the treacherous steps to the cave in order to check the seaworthiness of the small sailing vessel hidden there. Leo had used the reliable little boat often when he visited the castle in childhood, always when the duke was not in residence. The village fishermen had taught him how to sail. He told his bride how he'd imagined himself to be Somerled, Lord of the Isles, as he skimmed over the waves, experiencing a perfect sort of freedom. Uncle Sander kept the craft well caulked and the sails mended.

Lifting Phemie into the vessel, he pushed the boat down the sand bank the waves of the firth had created in the cave and rowed out them out into the narrow inlet. Raising the sail, they went for a run across the water and jested that if the duke should see them from the cliff above, they would simply keep sailing until they found refuge in Ireland. The time for jesting had come to an end with Sander's harshly whispered words.

Not long afterward, they heard the clatter of iron horseshoes on the stones of the courtyard and the steward's quavering voice welcoming the duke back to the castle and inquiring about his journey and Lord Jason's health. They doused all the lights in the dungeon, but one they shielded lest her father see any reflection on the water.

"Turned out to be merely a stuffy head. It impeded his poetical outpourings for a while is all. Son, take the horses over to the stable. What's this, the dungeon still not drained? I have no wish to smell stagnant water during my stay. Who knows what miasma might arise from it?"

"So sorry, Your Grace, but the pump is broken."

They must be standing right by the entrance. The sound of her father's gruff voice made Phemie want to cry out that she was safe and well—and married, but she kept her peace.

"Well, this is the least of my worries. I have a kidnapping scoundrel to hunt down and kill as I would any wild beast that carried off a child for his consumption."

Phemie's pulse beat hard in her neck. She whispered to Leo, "You see."

"Papa!" Jason's lighter voice called. "Bosworth is here in the stables."

"Explain," the duke boomed.

She could imagine her father in full threatening bear mode towering over the frail, elderly steward.

"Why, Your Grace, we found him in the courtyard after that heavy rain, no trace of how he got here. I recognized the old boy at once as your former mount. We have given him the best of care."

"Proof positive that Leonidas McLaughlin is the man we seek and is hiding nearby. What sort of thief returns a horse and keeps my daughter?"

"I'm sorry to say I do not know, Your Grace, but perhaps a better man than you assume."

"A kidnapper of young women is the foulest creature to walk the earth."

Phemie pressed close to Leo. He squeezed her hand in the darkness.

"Yes, Your Grace."

"Have hot water brought to my chamber and a bottle of port opened and placed in the solar. We have had a long and dirty ride and need a bit of refreshment to stay us until supper."

"I am so sorry to report our last shipment of wine did not arrive, Your Grace. However, I do have a wondrous selection of Scotch whiskies for you to sample."

"With some nuts, cheese and crackers, that would not go amiss. I will speak with Ben Campbell about organizing a search for my daughter, also."

The voices moved away toward the tower, and Phemie let out a breath she did not even know she'd been holding. Leo spoke before her.

"All right, I do agree it will not be easy to make your father see reason in this situation. Still, cowering here does no good. Tonight, I must carry you out. Go to him and say I've released you unharmed—more or less. Then try to explain the kidnapping was unintentional on my part, and I have done all I can to rectify it by taking you as my wife. If he receives that news well, call out for me to reveal myself."

"Leo, you are a dreamer. I feel our time together will not last long. Come to bed with me, beloved, one last time."

He quirked a smile at her. "You are too loud when you cry out and will give us away."

"Not if you smother my cries with your kisses. Please, Leo."

Like most men, he was easily led to the bedchamber.

~ * ~

The duke finished his ablutions and donned the hunting tweeds he left at the castle. In the time he took, some castle lackey had polished his boots and left them on the landing. He brought them inside and sat to pull them on. All in all, the castle staff pleased him. They had plumped the featherbed and covered it in fresh linens smelling of lavender.

In the process, some well-meaning maid had discovered Flora's naughty nightdress and laundered it, thus destroying her scent. A pity. He would have to bring another on his next visit. He might even invite Flora and not his sons. She deserved some respite from the trials their children thrust upon her. He could not imagine the extremity of her woe, sitting at Bellevue Manor waiting for some word of Phemie. At least, he had the solace of taking action.

He went down the tower stairs to the solar where Jason, similarly attired, lounged with a tot of whisky already in hand. His son's nose, still red on the tip, dripped a bit, but clearly, the boy was well enough to enjoy the liquor.

"You cannot fault the Scots on their spirits, Papa. I feel better already."

"No, they do this very well." The duke filled his own glass and sniffed the contents with appreciation before drinking. He helped himself from a tray of cheese and crackers, nuts, and dried fruits. "Do not overindulge, however. We begin the search for your sister tomorrow. He must be hiding her nearby, since he left the horse. The gall of the man to bring her to my own lands."

"As a McLaughlin, he might think of this as his land. Consider that, Papa."

"I had nothing to do with taking it from his family."

"I believe you've said that is what all the white men claimed when they cut down the forest to farm on the Shawnee hunting grounds."

"The Scots and the Shawnee do have that in common, along with a habit of stealing women," the duke acknowledged.

"Let us not forget it worked both ways in the borderlands. I've often thought I should write an idyll about fair Rose of Laughlin."

Before the duke could reply, a scratching came upon the solar door.

"Enter."

Ben Campbell came, his hat in hand, and bowed before his master. "Ye wanted to see me, Your Grace."

"Yes. Send word to the huntsmen and have them gather as many men as they can to search for my daughter tomorrow morning. Come along yourself, as I am sure you know every cave and hiding place."

"Aye, I do." Campbell's black eyes shifted around, never looking directly at the duke.

"Have you any idea where the culprit has taken her?"

"I might, but I have some other matters to bring to your attention. The old steward is failing. I think when ye go over the expenses, ye will notice a squandering of wine and candles. He can no longer keep track, and people take advantage. Now if a Campbell were in charge, the McLaughlins would not dare, as we have always been their overlords, no matter their supposed connections to the McDonald clan."

"And the Campbell to do the job would be you, Ben?"

"Aye."

"I will have a look at the books before I go and give the thought some consideration, but the place seems well-enough run except for neglect in pumping the dungeon."

Campbell swallowed and stared at the tips of his brogans. "I been thinking ye might be very grateful to the man who finds your daughter and brings this Leonidas to justice."

"Yes, two-thousand pounds grateful." The duke put down his drink and waited for the man's next words.

"Would that gratefulness include the castle stewardship as well?" Now Campbell's black eyes met Longleigh's.

How the duke did despise a traitor who would turn on his kin, but they had their uses. In the case of his daughter, he had no qualms about making deals with this one. "Possibly," he answered.

"Well then, ye should know old Sander is the great-uncle of this Leonidas, who fancies himself the Last Laird o' Laughlin and good enough for your daughter. He held a handfasting for them not a week ago."

Jason Longleigh rose from his indolent pose and went to the chest where they had left their armaments. Methodically, he began checking and charging the weapons.

"Where are they now, man?" The duke's explosive question made the chamber ring.

"Why hidden under your very nose in the dungeon."

"The place is flooded."

"A ruse, Your Grace. Only a small dike holds the water in, but I would go in there with stealth. Leonidas might shoot ye dead or do harm to your daughter if ye come at him too quick, he is that kind of man. Best to take him by surprise and kill him at once."

"Certainly. See that the steward and his wife are locked away lest they give warning, Campbell."

"My pleasure, Your Grace."

The duke strapped a sword over his tweeds, not caring how ridiculous it looked and Jason did the same. Each took a pistol and followed Campbell down the twining staircase.

~ * ~

Leo sat buttoning his trousers on the side of the bed. He drew his shirt on over his head and stood to tuck it in. Phemie, made lazy by their exertions, wore only his nightshirt for a covering and showed no inclination to rise and dress properly. He fastened his somber black waistcoat and shrugged into his jacket, leaving his neckcloth dangling.

"Are you sure you want to put on all those clothes? I will only have you out of them after our supper. I plan to eat as I am, possibly in bed as well."

"You tempt me, but we should sit at a table like civilized people this evening and wait for dark so I can put you above to speak to your father. Once you have explained our situation, we will have many nights to spend together. Come now, don't protest."

Leo lifted her effortlessly from the feather mattress and deposited Phemie, kicking and wiggling just for show, into one of the rush-bottomed chairs. They'd left but a single lantern burning, and now he lit a candle from it to illuminate their dinner table. The sound of the oubliette cover being lifted signaled their meal.

"You see, just in time to prevent Auntie from hearing anything but our growling stomachs."

Mary did not draw the tray up to fill with food. Instead in a shrill whisper that sounded as if she'd lowered her head well into the hole, she said, "Leo, ye've been betrayed by Ben Campbell. He's locked Sander in the top of the tower and now seeks me. Ye must hie for the hills, take to the heather like McLaughlins afore ye. Quickly, the duke is in the courtyard and armed with sword and pistol. Flee!"

They heard next the noise of a scuffle and the shrieks of his aunt. "Run, Leo, run!"

"Do it. Raise the hatch," Phemie urged. She shoved the purse into his waistcoat and threw the old plaid over his shoulders. "To keep you warm."

Leo opened the trapdoor, flung the sack of clothes over his shoulder, and seized his medical kit. Phemie pressed a hasty kiss to his lips, and he began the descent just as water displaced by a large body entering the pool sloshed over the lip of the dike too quickly for the drains to carry it off.

She closed the hatch and dragged the rug over it, then blew out the flickering candle and stood on a chair to douse the sole burning lantern. Her father approached. She knew it by a simple law of physics and the amount of water the duke's mass displaced as he came on to slay her husband.

~ * ~

Pressed against the wall on either side of the dungeon staircase, Bellevue and his son descended into the dark water soon topping their boots. Away from the main path used by McLaughlin, slime slicked the stones. The duke missed a step but held back his curse as a small wave raced to the edge of a barrier and spilled over. He'd alerted the villain, not that the screams issuing from the throat of the old woman had not.

Instead of stepping over the dike, he crouched behind it, caring not how sodden his clothes became. Jason did the same. Both raised their pistols and peered into the inky chamber. A white form that might have been the ghost of a former prisoner floated in its middle.

The duke raised his pistol, sure he drew a bead on McLaughlin. His son knocked his hand aside as he fired.

"No! It's Phemie."

The shot ricocheted off the stone walls, and the pure white figure plummeted. No longer concerned with Leo McLaughlin, the two charged over the barrier in an instant.

"We need light," the duke barked.

Jason saw a small glow escaping from the doors of a cast-iron stove in one of the cells where he'd played as a child. He made his way toward it and tripped over a scuttle but righted himself before he put a hand on the hot metal or shot off his own foot. Opening the doors released enough light for him to find a candle and ignite it with a burning coal. He turned to find his father cradling Phemie in his huge arms.

"My Dove, my Little Dove, I've killed you!"

"Um, no, Papa. Your shot startled me. I fell off the chair and hit my head. Nothing but a small bump, you see." She placed one of his hands on her forehead.

"Where is the villain, Phemie?"

She closed her eyes to hide the lie he would see there. "I do not know. He left some time ago."

Jason kicked at the rug, making the mythical beasts on its surface ripple. "I remember a hatch being right about here." He shoved the carpet aside and pulled on the iron ring. Far below, they could hear footsteps still descending.

That quickly, the duke deposited his daughter in a chair. "After him!" He snatched Jason's still loaded pistol from his son's hands.

"No, no, let him go! He did not harm me."

Phemie tugged her father's arm, but as if she were as light as her namesake dove, he flung her off and lowered himself through the trap. Jason remained behind and made his way to the stove where he stood drying his clothes.

"What, don't you want to kill Leo, too?" Phemie asked with a small catch in her voice.

"First of all, Papa will desire that honor. Secondly, I am beginning to suspect a Romeo and Juliet sort of tale here. I am always on the side of the lovers. I suggest you put on some clothes. I hear a crowd gathering above, and I have had enough romantic close calls to know you do not wish to be found either half-dressed or naked in a situation like this. I swear, Phemie, I've taken a chill to save you, not to mention making other sacrifices, and now I find it's all for naught. I do hope I won't develop an inflammation of the lungs as well."

Phemie nodded and turned to the bedchamber to don the only gown she had—the blue wedding dress. She'd barely gotten into her undergarments and dropped the dress over her head when the echoes of another shot exploded from the open trapdoor. She ran to the hatch and listened to a single set of footsteps ascend.

"Leo is unarmed," she said bleakly.

"Fool," Jason muttered. "Did you not warn him about the Longleighs? I had hoped for a happy ending."

"I did. He thought Papa would listen to reason."

"Only on a good day with Mama there to stay him, though she probably would have told him to go ahead and shoot, since this Leo ruined her perfect daughter."

"I am not perfect."

"As I know, having been a victim of your childish pranks."

The iron gray head of the duke appeared at the top of the secret stairs. He heaved himself into the dungeon and set his pistol carefully on the small table.

Phemie, hand to her heart, asked, "Papa, what have you done to my husband?"

"Nothing! The cowardly blackguard ran away. I managed only to put a ball through the sail of his boat. Never fear, I will have Campbell send McLaughlin's description to every town across the firth. We will capture him yet."

The duke paused as if just taking in what his daughter had said. "He is not your husband, no matter what he has done to you. A handfasting is legal only in Scotland, and we are taking you home to England."

"Unfair! You and Mama married in the Shawnee manner, as did Grandpapa to Full Moon Woman. I see no difference," Phemie argued.

"We were married by a Methodist preacher, also."

"Again, not recognized by the Church of England or Uncle Roderick."

"Your mother was a widow, and I past my majority. We were able to make such decisions, while you are still a child who wed without my consent."

"Leo is a physician and older than you when you married Mama. I am eighteen now and know my own mind. Address me as Lady McLaughlin or I will never speak to you again." Phemie folded her arms under her bosom and thrust out her lower lip.

"Brat," Jason remarked.

"The same goes for you, brother."

"Now, Phemie. You have been unhinged by your ordeal." The duke opened his arms to her.

Forgetting her promise not to speak to her father, she answered, "I did not suffer an ordeal. I had an adventure equal to any in *Waverley*."

"Jason, remind me to burn that book when we return to the Hall. It has addled her brain. Come, my Little Dove. Let me carry you out of here. I'll have Campbell drain the pool and clear this place of all foul memories." The duke dashed Leo's model steam engine to the floor. Scattering its carts and pebbles and chips of coal everywhere, it fell unharmed on the disheveled carpet.

Phemie dropped to her knees and cradled the object. "Don't you dare harm Leo's contraption. He is a brilliant engineer. Mr. Watt said so."

The duke raised a foot to squash one of the tiny, six-wheeled ore cars that had rolled his way. "Stay, Papa," Jason called out. "I know little about such matters, but they do say steam is the coming thing. I'd look the plans over before discarding them. They may be of some use."

"Thank you, Jason." Phemie rescued the cart from beneath her father's boot and began gathering the pieces of the train in her skirts.

"My pleasure, Lady McLaughlin," her brother answered with a mocking bow.

To her great surprise, her brawny father got down on his knees before her and took her face in his large hands. "My Little Dove, this man might be a genius, but I do know he is a coward who left you ruined and abandoned. I will do all in my power to fix this."

"I bade him leave, Papa, knowing your tendency to act before thinking."

"A real man would not have listened to you."

"He is gentle, a healer and an inventor, not like you. Give my husband a chance."

The duke's hands dropped and his expression hardened. "No one harms a Longleigh and gets away with it."

Phemie's lips trembled and her big brown eyes filled with tears. She held that small steam engine like a beloved infant in her arms. "I want Mama."

"As do I, child. As do I.

Eighteen

Sander and Mary McLaughlin stood in the storage room at the top of the keep. As frail as the two dried moths that had hatched in old plaids and failed to find their way out, still they did not tremble before the Duke of Bellevue's roar. The elderly couple clasped hands and met his burning black eyes.

"Tell me where this Leonidas McLaughlin has gone."

Sander answered bravely and truthfully enough. "I doubt he knows himself, Your Grace. He wasna reared in the Highlands, but only came to visit us now and again."

"Yet you harbored this villain who would harm my family. You squandered my candles and fed him my food." The duke waved one thick finger at them as if they were his children.

"Leo did earn his keep. He birthed half a dozen bairns and saved some ewes during the lambing, not to mention setting the broken bones of several quarrymen. All he asked was a place to build his wee machines. He intended to present his steam engine plans to ye for the betterment of the estate."

"He kidnapped and ravaged my youngest daughter."

"Och, no, Your Grace. I mean he did take her, but he did the honorable thing and married Lady Euphemia before the entire clan."

"I would add the ravishment was mutual from what I overheard," old Mary said, clamping her gums together as the duke turned his glare upon her.

Quickly, her husband intervened by directing that grim, black stare back to himself. "As for the wine shortage, I did think ye would want your daughter to have a grand wedding feast when she wed our laird. He is a minor nobleman of sorts, ye know."

"I know what a laird is! I simply did not think they existed anymore except in Mr. Scott's fervid prose."

The duke lumbered about the chamber. The elderly couple did draw back a little when he passed, as if fearing a swipe of his mighty paw. True enough, if he chose to knock their old noggins together, both would die. They fixed their eyes on the portrait of Ian McLaughlin gathering cobwebs in a corner and drew strength from it.

"Let me explain, Your Grace," Sander ventured. "We have a belief that the McLaughlins will not prosper until one has stolen a Longleigh bride—as an ancestor of yours once took our finest lady."

"A physician, a man of science, agreed to this?"

"Only under the influence of drugs and drink, I am sorry to say."

"No excuse for a gentleman. What am I to do with you? You served me well for many a year and now this treachery. I should have you deported at the very least, but you would never survive the journey. As it is, I dismiss you without a pension. Get off my lands and never let me see your faces again. Ben Campbell is steward now."

"McLaughlin lands," Mary muttered.

Her husband moved in front of her to absorb any violence, but the duke continued to pace. "I wouldna do that, Your Grace. Campbell is seen as a Judas to the laird. No McLaughlin will work for him."

"Employment is scarce in the Highlands. I am sure they will manage to overcome their scruples."

"Not exactly what I meant, Your Grace."

"This discussion is ended. Take your belongings and see you are gone by morning."

The duke left the old caretakers and made his way to the solar where Phemie sat, carefully packing Leo's plans and models fetched from the dungeon into a box for transport to Bellevue Hall. He watched her for a moment—dainty and curly-headed like her mother, and now just as bold. Where had his sweet, biddable daughter gone? He might have expected such defiance from Pandora if she had any interest in men, but not his Little Dove. She should be crushed by her experience, and yet here she was, spine stiff, wrapping each of the curiosities in cloth as if they were made of Sevres porcelain.

"We leave in the morning. You will ride Bosworth. He is gentle enough. The servants have found a sidesaddle and a riding habit from the last century, no longer stylish, but it must do."

Phemie, holding to her vow not to speak unless addressed by her proper title, remained silent, but she did nod her head to indicate she understood. She settled the last object in the chest and stood to face her father.

"I have sent a messenger ahead to notify your mother, but you know she will not be content until she holds you in her arms. You will sleep above in Jason's chamber tonight. He will share mine."

Again, she nodded, then swept past the duke to climb the stairs to that room.

~ * ~

Mary and Sander, making their way carefully down the worn, crooked steps, encountered Phemie on the landing. "The duke has put us out with no pension, and I have lived here all my life, Lady Euphemia. So has Sander, except for the time he went away for his schooling. What shall we do?"

"Have you any place to go?"

"Aye, we've a daughter in Glasgow, but she lives with her daughter, a son-in-law and our three great-grandchildren. We will add to the crowd and the number of mouths to feed. I'd thought to end my days at Castle Laughlin, but that is not to be. Still, we are a tough and thrifty lot and will manage." Sander squeezed his wife's hand.

"You are my people now. I have told Papa he must address me as Lady McLaughlin." Phemie tossed her curls and raised her chin, even though the duke two flights below her could not see her defiance.

"He dinna strike ye, child?" Sander asked with concern.

"Heavens no! Papa would never hit a woman. He simply ignores or overpowers them. After I return home, I shall enlist the aid of the duchess. She will see you get your pension and reconcile my father to the marriage. Leave your direction and have faith in me. Leo and I will return here as man and wife."

"You see, old woman, the curse is broken as my brother Duncan said. We will have our laird back again and prosper. Blessings be upon ye, Lady McLaughlin."

Giving her their bow and curtsy, the aged couple tottered on their feeble way. Phemie entered her bedchamber to find the voluminous riding habit spread out on the bed. The bodice was low-cut and edged with yellowing lace. The small waist made her glad she had a tiny form, or a corset would most certainly have been called for. At least, the color was a becoming dark green.

The accompanying hat made her laugh. It resembled descriptions of the chapeaux her mother had worn when young. Large enough to cover a high, powdered wig or her own mop of curls, it sported a black ostrich feather and a dotted veil to protect the rider's complexion all the way down to her chest. Perhaps seeing her dressed in the fashion of his youth would soften her father and even make him laugh.

She moved the clothing aside and lay down on the bed. Leo—was he safe? Would he go to the cave that had harbored Bonnie Prince Charlie and wait for her there or simply vanish to avoid her father's wrath? Plenty of ships set sail every day hauling Scots to Australia and Canada where they hoped to find prosperity. Doctors were welcome anywhere.

She pushed the antique gown aside and lay on the bed. More tired from the tribulations of the day than she knew, she fell asleep, and with Leo safely away, did not dream of bears and lions. Phemie woke to find daylight gone, a cold supper tray, and a locked door. So, Papa feared she would flee to join Leo. No, she would bide her time and enlist her mother's aid. If that failed, she had the remainder of summer and all of autumn to make her escape to the cave near Inverness before the onset of winter.

They departed in the early morning after an unsatisfactory breakfast of runny eggs, salty kippers, cold toast, and lumpy porridge.

Phemie was unsure if the kitchen staff had performed poorly out of sympathy for the former steward and his wife, or because their efforts were no longer being overseen. Perched atop the amiable Bosworth, she soon had her answer. As the duke rode past, men doffed their caps and bobbed. Women dipped a quick curtsy, but both sexes reserved a deeper obeisance for their Lady McLaughlin who rode behind her father and before Jason, as if she might bolt back to the castle at any moment and would have to be stopped. She heard her brother's chuckle, but he gave nothing away.

On the fine main roads, they made excellent time, though Phemie was aware her father tempered his pace with the knowledge that she did not ride as well or with as much stamina as Pandora. People did gawk at her costume. One would have thought Lady Godiva was passing by naked. She came to appreciate the veil that guarded her privacy, even more so when they rode in through the gates of Bellevue Hall at last, and found not only her mother and Pandora waiting, but two of her suitors.

Because of old family ties, these young men could not be shooed away or held off until grouse season. Lord Butterworth's amiable and chubby heir quickly suppressed the smile that parted his thick lips when he saw her strange outfit. Giles Moncton's slight and charming by-blow with the actress, Fanny LeFevre, merely quirked an eyebrow. He would have made an excellent actor had his father not inherited the title upon the death of an older brother and raised him as a gentleman. Usurping a footman who got in their way, both rushed forward to help her from her horse.

A boot well-placed by Reginald LeFevre sent his heavier rival stumbling, and he slid to Bosworth's side with all the grace and aplomb of his mother in one of her breeches roles when she acted the man so convincingly. He offered an elegant, gloved hand to help her dismount from her high perch.

"Thank you, Reg. There was no need to trip Bertie, however," she said, for she'd known the both of them for years. They had tried unsuccessfully to court the Longleigh twin daughters and failed. Now only she and Pandora remained. Neither wanted her sister, but she so wished they did. They were doomed to be disappointed again.

"Setting a new fashion, Phemie?" young Lord Bertrand asked with his round face beaming between the parentheses of long, dark side whiskers.

"Rather wearing an old one," her mother said as she came to her daughter's side and embraced her. "Wherever did you get my old riding habit? Ah yes, I must have left it behind in Scotland many years ago. How delightful you thought to surprise me by wearing it home from your short sojourn in the north."

The duchess raised the veil. "Yes, I see the Highland air has restored the roses to your cheeks after such a strenuous season. Come inside and do tell me of your travels with your father and brother."

Ah, so they were to pretend before the guests that nothing at all strange had happened. Her father had sent a missive ahead explaining the circumstances, and her mother had created this lie. Phemie longed to be alone with her mother and Pandora, who glowered from her place on the steps. Both were strong women who could give her the support she needed. Still, she gave Reg and Bertie one of her beguiling bowed smiles.

"I am fatigued from days on the road and covered in dust. Allow me to refresh myself. I will see you both at supper."

Her suitors made way, and the duchess and Pandora closed ranks behind her across the checkerboard marble of the foyer and up the gilded staircase to the bedchamber she shared with Panny. Calmly, Lady Flora sent the maid for warm water to wash off the dirt of travel. As the door closed behind the woman, she hugged Phemie tightly.

"My poor child! At least you are returned safely. The servants are forbidden to say a word about the incident and the search for you. We have put down the rumors by saying you went to Scotland for your health. Now, you can tell me anything that happened without fear."

"Oh, Mama, do not be so distraught. I went to Scotland a maiden and return a married woman. Leonidas McLaughlin is surely the most gentle, intelligent, and inventive man that ever existed and a Scottish laird as well." Phemie clasped her hands over her heart.

"Inventive? How so?" the duchess asked with great curiosity.

"I mean he invents marvelous steam machines, and I have brought some samples home with me."

Pandora slammed her hand against the inlaid armoire that held their clothes. "I cannot believe you allowed yourself to be seduced by one of the treacherous male gender, let alone the head gardener's nephew. Where was your stiletto? Why did you not thrust it between his ribs as he slept?"

"Leo meant to take *you*, but I said you would never have suited him. Do not be jealous, Panny."

"Jealous! Your head has been turned by all this *Waverley* rubbish."

The duchess held up her hands. "Girls, girls, enough. The question is, why did this Leo, whom you describe as kind and intelligent, take you at all?"

"He was under the influence of drugs and alcohol at the time, Mama."

"I am not comforted as to his character."

"Really, he is no degenerate and only takes a dram of Scotch whisky now and then. I so wished the both of you could have been there for our handfasting at Castle Laughlin. The entire clan gathered to see me become Lady McLaughlin. Leo presented me with the family sword, the one hanging over the fireplace in the great hall, for our first-born son. We had a great feast with piping and dancing and singing after the ceremony. But oh, Papa has dismissed the old steward and his wife for their part in it, and I am worried about my people."

"A spurious, illegal act! You are not truly married, Phemie. You are not Lady McLaughlin. You have no people except the Longleighs. You have been deceived," Pandora insisted, leaning close to her sister's face as if to drive all her points right into an addled brain.

"I can assure you I am married, very much married in every way, Panny."

"Well, I no longer wish to share a chamber with a married woman."

"Nor should you, now that Phemie's status has changed. I will assign you another and have your belongings removed," the duchess replied.

"You see, Mama believes I am truly married. She understands."

"More than you truly know. My child, you will face many obstacles, and the greatest of these will be your father."

~ * ~

Ordinarily, he would not discharge a servant in the drawing room with his wife and daughter sitting on the settee to observe, but the Duke of Bellevue felt he had a serious point to make. No one trifled with his family, especially his most young and tender daughter. Duncan Gardener stood before him hat in hand, the only sign of humility and acknowledgment of his station in the life he'd given to his lord. Otherwise, he stood as straight as his old bones allowed and declined to lower his fierce blue eyes or his old, white head.

"For your deceit in claiming unknown brigands took my daughter and slowing my rescue, you are deprived of your cottage and salary and any further aid from the Longleighs. If you should ever show your face at Bellevue again, I shall shoot you as a trespasser. Do you understand, Duncan Gardener?" The duke's deep voice thundered around the room and shook the fragile vases on the mantle with its force.

"Aye, but the name is Duncan McLaughlin and proud of it. I will have my say before I go. I did this for my clan and to protect its leader. Leonidas McLaughlin is a fine young man and a laird to boot. He is a sight more useful than many sons-in-law and most of the nobility, too. Why, isn't it said a man should never travel abroad without taking along a Scottish physician? I tell ye, his contraptions will make him rich one day. My great-nephew is every bit worthy of Lady Euphemia."

The duke's hand slapped to his side, but prudently, his wife had asked him to discard his sword before entering her drawing room. He would not have killed the impudent servant, perhaps merely marked him in a permanent sort of way. Raised by the Shawnee to admire those who showed defiance in the face of death, he had some respect for this elderly man who had delved in his park for so many years and now would not bow down to him. He understood clan loyalty as well. Was he not a member of the Bear Clan and always would be, even if he never ventured to America again?

Behind the duke's broad back, Phemie's soft voice sounded. "Leo *is* worthy, Papa, and I love him so."

He turned around with the quick reflexes of a big man who still practiced regularly with a saber. He shook a thick finger at her like a weapon. "Sit and be silent, daughter!"

With her countenance far from contrite, Phemie did resume her seat next to her mother. How alike the two women were: both so lovely and curly headed, so deceptively feminine and fragile on the outside, each incredibly strong-willed within. His wife spoke in that beautiful lilting voice she used in her most charming moments.

"Dearest, I know you seek to spare our daughter from dishonor, but by dismissing and threatening people right and left and leaving them without means, do you not encourage them to share the story with any who will listen, not to mention pay them for the information?"

"They will not speak on pain of death."

"I doubt that means very much to the elderly. Not to mention that Duncan is my head gardener and a very fine one indeed. Could we not retain him and swear him to secrecy about the whole incident? The household still believes Phemie was abducted by a stranger and, out of love and loyalty to her, they will not say a word to damage her reputation."

With the decision still floating in the air between the duke and duchess, a tap sounded on the closed door. Busby, their butler, presumed to turn the knob.

"A messenger has arrived from Castle Laughlin, Your Grace. He delivered this letter." Not a single muscle on the butler's face betrayed that he had most likely heard every word of his master's loud tirade as he held out the missive on a small, silver tray.

The duke took up the offering and broke the wax seal bearing the image of the keep and rampant lions, the same one he had handed over to Ben Campbell along with a bank note for the reward the new steward had earned. The ormolu clock with a bronzed goddess holding the dial ticked in the silence as he read.

Glancing at the two women awaiting what he had to say, the duke dismissed them. "Ladies, you may go."

"What is it, my darling? You know I am no frail flower that must be protected from the realities of life. Did I not see my own father slaughtered by your kin? This could not be any worse." Still, the duchess unfurled her fan and cooled herself in preparation for more bad news.

"Phemie, return to your chamber."

"As Lady McLaughlin, I have every right to know what has happened at the castle." She remained seated by her mother.

"Very well, I will tell you as you are now so very grown up. Ben Campbell left for Glasgow soon after us to cash the banknote for finding the man who kidnapped my daughter."

"Humph, finding. He knew vera well where Leo hid all along, the traitor," the gardener dared to say. The duke silenced him with a black look.

"Someone hung Campbell by his heels and gutted him like a deer not far from the main road. His killer stuffed my banknote with the word 'traitor' written across it into his mouth."

"No more than he deserved," the bloodthirsty old Scot remarked, but the news had set Phemie to trembling.

Her father showed no pity. "Now do you understand that you do not live in a romance novel, Phemie, but in a harsh world where actions have consequences, often unpleasant ones? It seems I am in need of a new steward," he said without inflection. "If you will set aside this nonsense and cease calling yourself Lady McLaughlin and a married woman, then I will reinstate the old couple and retain your mother's gardener. You will resume your life as an eligible and unsullied young woman, never saying another word about what happened in Scotland. If you do not agree, I will continue to hunt Leonidas McLaughlin no matter where he has gone and make you a widow. More blood will be on your hands."

"Pearce, really, must you be so cruel?" His wife knew he had it in him to be so, but he had long suppressed his darker nature for her.

As for Phemie, his Little Dove murmured, "For Leo's sake, and that of my people, I will be silent." She turned her head and wept on her mother's breast.

Nineteen

Docking on small islands and sleeping in the boat, Leonidas McLaughlin had to admit he'd enjoyed the long sail to Loch Linnhe. Since his father's death, he'd spent all his years on study, hoping to restore the family fortune with his inventions, and working as a physician to meet his needs. Now he experienced an extraordinary sense of freedom unknown since his youth. Thanks to Phemie's foresight, he had clothes to protect him from the weather and money enough to purchase food. He swore he could still sniff her lingering scent on the old plaid he used as a cover each night. If she were here, all would be perfect.

While he'd fled for an age-old reason—stealing and seducing the daughter of a duke out for his blood—Leo appreciated the irony that he now steered his boat into the sea lock of the new Caledonian Canal, a modern marvel of engineering surveyed by the great James Watt himself and engineered by the admirable Thomas Telford. He would go as far as he could using the new waterway that aimed to connect all the lochs of the Great Glen from Ft. William to Inverness and so make it possible to sail across Scotland from the North Sea to the Atlantic. When he reached the area still under construction, he would sell his small craft and seek other transportation.

In the meantime, he could enjoy watching the double locks at Corpach close behind his craft, fill with water and lift it to the next stage of his voyage. He traversed Loch Lochy and Lock Oich and the canals joining them, but as all good things must come to an end, he eventually came to the work area and had to dispose of his boat.

Ever mindful that he did not know how long he would be hiding in a cave, he took the time to offer his medical services to the project engineer and pick up some extra cash by treating the workers for various ailments. To his surprise, most of them were not Highlanders, but Irishmen brought in to complete the task. As Leo amputated a crushed finger and pulled a splinter from another man's eye, the supervisor rattled on about the unreliable Scots who vanished from the job to cut peat, help with the lambing, or dig their potatoes.

Several days later, his pouch plump with added money, he traveled overland to the next loch, took passage in a ship along its length until he reached the next phase where the canal had not yet been cut. Here, the Highlands remained pristine with misty mountains rearing up in the distance, and lakes of such depth and murkiness they seemed to have no bottom. How Phemie would adore these places! The earth was torn where the canal thrust its way eastward, but that would mend with time. Certainly, steamboats would traverse the distance as some now did on the River Clyde. He would bring his wife to marvel at both the miracle of engineering and the beauty of Scotland. The Caledonian Canal would open the heart of the Highlands, no longer hidden and remote, to the world.

Leo paused again to admire the amazing eight locks being built at Neptune's Staircase in Banavie before moving on finally to Inverness where he inquired the way to the cave once inhabited by the Seven Men of Glenmoriston who harbored Bonnie Prince Charlie after Culloden. More than one person offered to guide him, blessing in same breath the name of the unknown author of *Waverley* for bringing on the tourists. Not wanting to admit he planned to stay in the cave, he paid instead for written directions and made his way there on his own. Thomas Telford, the architect of the canal, had left his mark on this place as well with a fine bridge spanning the waterfalls that crashed into Loch Ness.

But once up into the hills, Leo might have been going back in time, breathing air so cool and fresh as he hiked out of the glen. Evergreen trees exuding their piney scent spiked into the blue sky, and the River Doe cascaded musically into the valley. The cave had a wide mouth and its own gravelly stream, not an unpleasant place to camp in the summer, though he had his doubts about the winter. All in all, his haven was a much more comfortable hole in a rock than the one where he'd come awake and found Phemie pointing a knife at him. The thought filled him with her loss. He spread the plaid on a dry and sandy spot and built a fire to toast some sausages he'd brought along in a knapsack full of provisions. Water would be no problem for certain.

Once he'd eaten, he went to sit on a large rock and watch the sun descend. A golden eagle catching the last light on its wings wheeled by, returning to its roost for the night. If only Phemie were here to enjoy this view with him. When darkness came, he returned to the cave and settled into the plaid for the night. Sleep eluded him for some time as he wondered exactly how long it would take to reconcile the Duke of Bellevue to his daughter's marrying her kidnapper, but at last he closed his eyes.

~ * ~

A voice woke him, not Phemie's, though he dreamt of her. Leo sat up, still wrapped in the plaid. Yesterday's exertions had kept him asleep far past the rising of the sun. The voice, deep and heavy with a Scottish brogue, came closer.

"And so valiant Roderick Mackenzie took the identity of the Pretender and was captured and killed in his place, while the Prince hid here in this vera cave with the Seven Men of Glenmoriston. Some might have called them thieves, but I say they were loyal Jacobites. They dinna give up Bonnie Charlie, nay even for the thirty-thousand pounds placed on his head for a reward. Feel free to look around, ladies and gentlemen. Get ye the feel of the place."

Leo stood and flung the plaid over his shoulder as two men and two women dressed for a country outing gawked at his camp site. Their guide, a rather runty fellow despite the size of his voice, pushed his way between them.

"Who are ye?" he demanded. "Ye canna stay here on sacred ground. Ye'll ruin the tourist trade what's just got going good."

Leo made a brief bow. "Your pardon. I had no idea this was not a public place."

"And a bloody Englishman, too. Be gone wit' ye." Though Leo towered over the man, the leader of the group glared at him with dark and beady eyes set on either side of a beaky nose like a bantam chicken challenging a much larger white Leghorn rooster.

Offended, Leo answered, "I am the Last Laird of Laughlin, Leonidas McLaughlin, M.D."

"Are ye now? Say something in the Scottish tongue."

He had no Gaelic, only a few words, but did his best to impress the little man. "Och, hoot mon, I am vera pleased to meet ye all. *Slainte, sonas agus beartas.*"

The women tittered and the men smirked, but their guide took on a considering look. "Step outside and let me see ye better." Leo obliged him.

"Ye have the height and hair o' the McLaughlins, sure enough. Viking blood, ye know," he informed his group.

"Direct descendants of Somerled," Leo added, feeling this might gain him some respect.

"Aye, tell them that story, lad."

Leo sat down on the rock where he'd watched the sunset. The two couples gathered near and listened respectfully, as if he were some ancient bard, to the same story he'd told Phemie under the stars. He threw in whatever Scottish words came to mind to enhance his credibility. When he finished, one of the visitors to the cave gave him a small gratuity he was not too proud to accept under the circumstances. It seemed he would have to pay for a lodging place while waiting for Phemie. What a ridiculous situation he had gotten himself into simply because he could not let her go.

"A majestic Highland eagle to the left," the craggy-faced guide directed, and his tourists rushed to the edge of the declivity to observe its flight. "A pair of eagle feathers in a Scottish bonnet means the man is a chieftain or was in the olden days."

Leo left his rock and went into the cave to gather his belongings into the knapsack. The Scotsman followed, probably to make sure he truly meant to go.

"Nicely done with the tale, lad, but ye need to work on your accent. Let me introduce myself...Brodie Urquhart." He shook hands hard like a small man trying to prove a point. "I have the concession for tours to the cave and canna allow another to intrude on the making of my living. There is little enough work here about. Still, if ye are not camping here for a lark, I might take ye on as my assistant. I'd let ye live here in the cave, provide meals, and a proper costume to impress the guests. Whether ye are a laird or no, the guests will be thrilled to meet ye as one. What do ye say, lad?"

Leo held out his hand and shook Urquhart's wizened little claw like a man with an uncertain future. "I would be most happy to give it a try."

~ * ~

Brodie Urquhart made the trip up the mountain early the next morning before the dew on the grass had turned to mist. He had no tourists in tow, but did carry a sack he dumped with a clank at Leo's feet sticking out of the plaid.

"Up wit' ye. We must see how the costume fits before the tourists finish their breakfast at the inn and get ready for the hike."

Leo sat up and poked the bag with his toe. "I don't suppose my promised meal is inside, too."

Urquhart rummaged in a poor specimen of a sporran with most of its fur worn off dangling in front of his privates and drew out two large, brown lumps. "Scotch eggs and all the water ye can drink." He gestured to the stream in the cave and the rushing waters of the Doe.

Leo bit into the breaded, sausage-encased boiled egg with the grease of its frying congealed on the outside. "I don't suppose you could supply me tea or coffee and a pot to make it?"

Urquhart shook his head and addressed the cave in general. "It's luxuries he wants and not a bit o' work he's done yet."

"I assure you I will do my best." Leo wiped the grease off his lips with the back of his hand, which gave him a reminder about his appearance. "Perhaps I could borrow a shaving glass and razor."

"Nay, let the beard and hair grow. The ladies will delight in the color, and the wilder ye look, the better. Done eating then? Try on what I've brought ye."

"Turn around."

"Oooh, and modest as a wee lassie, ye are," Urquhart mocked, but he did leave the cave.

Leo upended the sack and exchanged his garments for what it held. There appeared to be more armaments than clothing. The shirt, vest and short jacket presented no problem, nor the tartan stockings held up with elaborate garters. The sturdy brogans pinched his large feet, and the kilt—there was no getting that right. No matter which way he turned or tugged it, his long drawers showed.

"I say, Urquhart, I cannot get the kilt right. Should it not be longer?"

"Ye need only buckle it on, man. 'Tis not like the old ones that needed folding." Exuding exasperation, the guide reentered the cave and let loose with a loud guffaw that echoed back from its dark recesses. "The Last Laird o' Laughlin knows not what a Scotsman wears under his kilt."

"Shorter drawers?"

"Nothing, he wears nothing beneath his kilt."

Leo felt his accursed blush rising under his beard and spreading all the way to his temples. "Perhaps you might supply me with shorter drawers. The alternative is immodest, unsanitary and—drafty."

When Urquhart finished laughing and wiped the tears of mirth from his eyes onto a sleeve, he said, "We canna disappoint the ladies, now can we? Partly they come hoping to see beneath a kilt. Off with the drawers, if ye want to keep the job, Leo. Hang the sporran on the front of your belt to give some warmth to your privates, then."

Leo did both. In such an isolated place, how else could he survive until Phemie came? The sporran was a magnificent thing made of tasseled badger fur and large enough to provide some protection from the elements like a big muff. It put Brodie Urquhart's worn bag to shame. Speaking of shame, Leo protested, "I am a tall man, and this kilt is certainly too short. Why, it exposes a full four inches of my thigh."

The guide stepped back from shoving a brace of antique pistols into the belt of the costume. "Aye, not many lassies will try to look under a kilt, but not a one will take her eyes off your hairy thighs."

He picked up a small knife in a sheath and slid it into Leo's stocking elaborately embroidered with thistles. "Here, laddie, your *sgian-dubh*. No wearing a kilt without one." Urquhart adjusted a bonnet adorned with two eagle feathers on his new employee's head. "I dinna bring a plaid, as ye've brought your own."

"Could I not wear trews?"

"I tell ye when visitors come to Scotland, it is a man in a kilt they want to see. Your targe and claymore, your lairdship." He handed over the small, round shield and a sword far less magnificent than Ian McLaughlin's weapon.

"I feel ridiculous."

"A good thing ye do not look it. Aye, the men will be envious and the women will swoon when ye walk from the cave. Your cue will be 'and behold the Last Laird of Laughlin,' and ye come forth brandishing the sword and tell a few tales. I'll allow ye an hour for that, then we herd the lot o' them up the crag for a nice picnic with a view of the Highlands. How does that sound?"

"I think it would be prudent to call me something else."

"Lyin' were ye?" Urquhart's bushy eyebrows rose.

"No, I merely prefer to remain incognito—in disguise, that is," he elaborated, when his new business partner seemed puzzled.

"Well, ye won't be the first or the last rascal to hide in the Highlands. Is it murder, money, or a woman who sent ye here?"

"I'd rather not say."

"Suit yourself. Practice that brogue now. Ye may keep any coins they offer and end o' the day I'll split the take twenty-sixty."

"A paltry amount for sleeping in a damp cave and making an ass of myself."

Urquhart considered. "Thirty-seventy, then, more if ye do well. It's to be roast beef sandwiches for the picnic. I will be back with my tourists afore noon."

Leo nodded. He watched the guide, nimble as a goat, scramble down the hill. Picking up his plaid, he went to sit on his rock, tucking in the blanket to keep his chilled organs warm and setting aside the sword and shield until the sightseers arrived. If being a physician, inventor, and laird failed to impress the Duke of Bellevue, he doubted if his current employment would. Ah well, if Longleigh came at him again, at least he would be armed to the teeth.

Twenty

Phemie kept silent, far too silent. Reg and Bertie, who had used their family connections to get the jump on her other beaux, inquired of Jason if his sister had been taken ill, she was so unlike the merry and mischievous girl they had known for years. Without answering yea or nay and assuring them he had enjoyed their jolly good company, he hinted they had best go home and try again next season when all would be sorted out. Reporting to Phemie, he urged her to, "Buck up. Love conquers all things, as the immortal Virgil wrote." She thanked him wanly for getting rid of two suitors her father would prefer to Leo.

However, Reg and Bertie gave way to the phalanx of grouse shooters who sought both sport and a large dowry. Taking breakfast early and gone all morning with the duke, they returned with revolting piles of bloody birds, and all wanted her to survey and praise the biggest bag, the largest of the cocks, the most unusual victim of their shotguns. The display turned her stomach, as did many things lately.

She often napped away the afternoons, and her Mama allowed this as long as she appeared for her supper and whatever entertainment the evening offered. Then under her father's eye, she was required to make light conversation, engage in charades, or play the piano while at her side Pandora plucked a harp more like the goddess Diana aggressively releasing arrows than an angel in heaven. No matter what the result, her beaux applauded enthusiastically.

Pandora, now ensconced in their eldest sister Thalia's old quarters fit for a princess and very much not to her austere tastes, came back frequently to her old chamber and sat with her sister, making her smile as she cursed the knots and tangles of her embroidery just as if nothing had changed. Showing regret for her former harshness and noticing the dark circles under her sister's eyes, she asked Phemie if she would rest better if they shared a bed again.

Phemie replied, "I want Leo," and for once, Panny did not berate her but stayed the night and held her when she cried.

When she found Phemie hunched over her washbowl losing all she'd eaten the night before, Pandora exclaimed, "Dear Lord, I hope you did not catch consumption in that drafty Scottish dungeon." By then, she'd heard the entire story, sharing secrets as they always had in privacy. Only here could Phemie speak of her husband and although Panny disapproved, her sister did listen.

"The dungeon was quite snug, thanks to a Franklin stove. Do not fear for me. Remember when we found Mama vomiting and thought she would die, but our nurse told us that was the way of women who were going to bring a new little angel into the world? We both thought it very mean of God to make our mother suffer so." Phemie poured water from the pitcher into a porcelain cup and rinsed her mouth.

"Especially when the angel turned out to be another brother, Justinian, who had no wings at all. I was five and you four. How greatly disappointed we were."

"I wish Justin had come home for his school holiday instead of going to Thalia's place. I want to show him Leo's steam engine." She placed a hand towel she had recently embroidered with a thistle pattern over the mess in the basin to contain the odor until her maid arrived to carry it away.

"Freakishly bright as he is, he would understand every bit of it," Pandora continued obliviously. "I suspect he prefers our eldest sister's home because her children are nearer his age than Jason. He can play the big brother instead of the baby of the family with no fear that Papa will drag him from his books to participate in manly sports, though Thalia's husband is likely to do the same."

Phemie assumed the smile of a Madonna on the day of the Annunciation and waited for her usually acute sister to reach understanding. When Pandora continued to reminisce about their brilliant little brother, she folded both her hands across her stomach. Panny stopped in mid-sentence.

"God in heaven, you are with child! Does Mama know?"

"I believe she suspects. She has been through this ten times and more, if we count the ones that did not take."

"You must tell her at once. She might know what to do about it if it is not too late."

"She wanted all her children. How would she know?"

"Do not be a simpleton, Phemie. Married women talk amongst themselves. Since I am considered a likely spinster, they hardly curb their tongues when I am in the room. Not everyone wants a large family. Midwives know ways—"

"I want my baby. He is the next Laird of Laughlin. Please tell no one. I plan to hide my condition as long as I can. The fashions favor me."

Covering her nightdress still damp on the shoulder from Phemie's tears with a dressing gown, Pandora pulled the sash tight. "For your own good, I will tell her if you will not."

~ * ~

Closing the door on Phemie's wail, she stormed down the long, drafty hall like a gale in the making. At her mother's bedchamber, she gave the door a sharp and prudent rap. While she assumed her father had gone out at dawn with the hunters, one never knew. He might need a moment to slip back into his own room through the adjoining door. Due to their rank and for appearances sake, they maintained separate beds, but were always to be found together in one or the other early in the morning.

"Enter," the duchess said. She sat at her dressing table, a cup of tea and a selection of flaky rolls easily within reach. Her maid was arranging her pale blond curls for the morning.

"Mama, may I speak to you privately?"

Taking in Pandora's state of undress with her long, black hair flowing out from under her nightcap to her waist, her feet bare and her expression wild, the duchess flicked a hand and sent the maid away. Another Pandora crisis, her expression seemed to say.

"Now what? A good cause needing immediate funding? A tenant's wife beaten by her husband the previous evening and now crying at the back door?"

"This has nothing to do with me," she told her mother automatically. "Phemie is *enceinte*."

The duchess cast a desperate glance at that discrete door in the paneling, not quite closed, leading to her husband's chamber. "Not so loud, child!"

Too late. That door crashed back, and the duke filled that entrance with his massive body. "How long have you known, my dear?" he asked, in a tone not nearly so considerate as usual.

"Phemie has not said a word to me."

"Yet you have allowed her to loll in bed instead of taking exercise as you have always demanded of your daughters. Surely, her maid reported any of the usual symptoms."

The duchess stood, her petite form unbending, and confronted her husband. "I suspected but did not know for certain."

"When were you going to tell me, Flora?"

"When the right time arrived, of course."

"And that would be...?"

"When you acknowledge that Phemie is just as married to her laird as I was to a Shawnee warrior."

"I did not steal you from your father's estate in a drunken, drug-induced haze. The earl placed you in my care."

"And you rescued me time and again." The duchess produced a tender smile, perhaps hoping to temper his reaction to the news with old memories.

Pandora's eyes shifted from one to the other. What had she done—exposed Phemie and caused a rift between her parents? If only she had contained her passion for truth this single time. While the

Longleigh offspring often jested about the overwhelming fondness the duke and duchess exhibited for each other, she hated to see that spark gone from her father's eyes, replaced by a flat and frightening darkness.

"I intend to rescue my daughter as well." The Duke of Bellevue crossed the room in a few long strides and exited to the hallway. Pandora and her mother hastened after him as servants moving about their morning duties dissolved back against the walls as if they were furnishings that saw and heard nothing. Their lord opened Lady Euphemia's door without a scratch or knock, and the duchess on his heels closed it quietly behind them after Pandora slipped inside.

Phemie had gotten into bed again. She sat propped by pillows with the covers pulled up to her chin. Her large, brown eyes seemed to fill her face, but her chin stayed resolute, and her small mouth remained stubborn.

"I will not take any noxious potions to bring off my child or allow you to foster him out to a tenant."

For just a moment, Pandora, who had rushed to her sister's side, saw the hurt in her father's eyes caused by his daughter's disgrace, or perhaps he was more wounded by her distrust. Whichever, his stern, unrevealing Shawnee face dropped into place before he spoke.

"The child is after all a Longleigh and will be raised as such. Flora, which of our daughters is currently *not* breeding?"

"Pandora, of course."

"She will be of no help."

His words stabbed rather keenly. She *had* been no help, only made matters worse for Phemie.

"There is no telling with the twins. They lead such irregular lives. Iris is too far distant for me to know, though that might be a good thing. Thalia was not increasing at the end of the season."

Pandora marveled how her mother appeared to know exactly where her father's thoughts were going. She found Phemie's hand cold under the covers and squeezed it gently, giving what comfort she could.

"Very well. You will write Thalia and explain the situation. She is to give out hints that she is carrying a child due in April. Is the month correct, my darling?"

The duchess nodded and moved to Phemie's other side. She, too, took her daughter's hand and chaffed it lightly to chase off the chill of fear.

"We will take Euphemia to Yorkshire where she will have the baby. Thalia shall claim it as her own and raise it with her others."

"If her husband does not agree?"

"Thalia has given him two boys and a girl already, and I have given him my eldest daughter. He owes allegiance to me. This one is not likely to inherit, but he or she will be raised in an earl's household. Phemie will be its doting aunt."

"As will I," Pandora proclaimed. "It will be the most adored of Thalia's children."

"You must take into account Thalia's nature, dearest. She does love society and entertains frequently when at the country house," the duchess prompted.

"Not this year. She will be enduring a difficult pregnancy. Her sister, Euphemia, will be at her side to help with the household and the other children. As a Longleigh, Thalia will do this for me."

"I am certain she will, but haste is not necessary. Phemie will not show for some time. I propose we go on as usual. In mid-October, we are expected to attend Sir Guy's wedding at a place called Ferry Grange, a harvest home sort of festivity. It is best if Phemie is seen celebrating her childhood friend's happiness to allay any suspicions."

Pandora sniffed. "Yes, Guy finally found a girl as simple and optimistic as he is. Snaring a heredity knight is a great step upward for the daughter of a mere squire."

"Bella Stilwell is a very pretty young lady and most mild-natured. Not only do they suit, but I believe theirs to be a love match. I introduced them, you know. I saw immediately she would be perfect, and the poor boy did need my help in finding anyone. Besides, the girl's mother comes of better stock than one might suppose."

The duke's low growl interrupted their women's talk of weddings and matchmaking. "I do not care how this is done, so long as it *is* done. Make the arrangements." He turned, his broad shoulders very square, as he strode from the room.

Phemie whimpered, "How can he be so cruel when he was the kindest of fathers to his girls?"

"Child, you do not know the meaning of cruelty. You, his Little Dove, wounded him more deeply than you will ever know. Yet, he has devised a plan that will allow him to call your baby his grandchild. Believe me, he will not soften on this. It is best we all comply."

Pandora conjectured, "What if the child is born with red hair?"

"Oh Pandora, you always see the worst in every situation. We will simply pray the infant resembles the Longleighs."

"Or else Thalia will appear to be an adulteress and her very blond husband a cuckold."

"Enough! We'd best start mentioning at Sir Guy's wedding that Thalia's husband had a red-haired grandfather, and we wonder if that trait will ever show up in her children."

"What of the family portrait gallery full of fair-haired men?" Panny countered.

"His mother's father, then!" The duchess threw up her hands as she so often did when dealing with her daughters.

There, she had coaxed a small smile from her sister with her exasperating questions and comments. Pandora vowed to do all she could to assist Phemie since she had brought their father's wrath crashing down on that small, curly head.

Twenty-one

"That's my girl. Allow your vivacity to shine. Accept another dance from Bertie to keep up the pretense," the duchess urged Phemie from behind her fan.

Over the top of its folds, she regarded the lovely if slightly plump bride, Bella, gazing at her groom with wide and rather vacant blue eyes. The yellow curls beside her ears fairly jiggled with her joy at wedding Sir Guy. His round, pleasant face shone with an equal amount of adoration. Phemie knew her mother congratulated herself on another very satisfactory match.

"If Bertie cannot tear himself away from the remains of the wedding feast, he will soon be as stout as his father," Phemie answered. She sighed as she watched the happy couple.

"Yes, all the Butterworths have been portly men, but so very good-natured. You might consider him in reality once this is all past."

"Mama, would you have considered another if Papa had not come for you?"

"You are not me," her mother evaded. "And Leo has not shown himself."

"At my request."

Instead of Bertie, the bride's tall brother, John, bowed before her and drew her into the long line of the country dance. Playing her role, Phemie favored him with a girlish giggle as they romped away. She noticed Pandora conversing with Lucia, the family spinster and elder sister of Bella, in one corner of the large structure where they had come to celebrate after Sir Guy said his vows in an ancient and moss-covered Romanesque church nearby. Did Panny, obviously trying to be kind to one unfavored by marriage, realize that her beauty simply made Miss Stilwell's long face and strong jaw appear even more plain? The old maid, well into her twenties, did have luxurious brown hair and startling ice blue eyes, but favoring her father and brother, she towered over most men at the gathering and so often went in want of a dance partner.

Pandora, no matter how harshly she drew back her shining black hair, allowing no ringlets or fringe, could not diminish her looks. Yes, her complexion was dark, but those high cheekbones, those arched brows over snapping dark eyes, still drew the masculine eye, along with an alluring figure, fuller than Phemie's own—until recently, that is. Phemie glanced down at her enlarged, bobbing breasts dewy from the exertion of the dance, and when she looked up caught her partner doing the same. His identical icy blue eyes immediately took an interest in the garlands of autumn flowers and colored leaves bedecking the rafters.

Mrs. Stilwell had reiterated her pride in her annual Harvest Home and her thought to combine it with the wedding celebration so many times, the duchess had to assure her over and over that the idea was so very clever to put an end to it. Indeed, Phemie agreed. She found herself enjoying this less formal affair, even if the fat, greasy hams and rich, roasted geese roiled her stomach and required a great deal of dry bread to quell. Indefatigable local musicians supplied rollicking music to dance off the currant-studded puddings and abundant fresh apple and custard tarts. As Mrs. Stilwell said, no one ever went hungry at Ferry Grange. By her own size, she proved that.

Phemie swore the woman had borrowed every chair in the parish to provide seating in what was essentially a great storage barn, well-cleaned of cobwebs and agricultural filth. The duke and duchess being of the highest rank to attend were immediately directed to two Gothic throne-like seats begged from the bishop who had been prevailed upon to perform the marriage. It seemed Mrs. Stilwell did have some connections. The duchess was not one to sit, however, and mingled with both high and low. Jason lounged in the over-sized chair and conversed with their father. Not on the alert, he found himself required to ask the next dance of Lucia Stilwell when Pandora led her over and forced an introduction. He at least had a few inches on the homely woman.

The dance came to an end, and the musicians paused to revitalize themselves with hard cider and beer. Her escort returned her to her mother, who stood with Pandora watching Jason attempt conversation with Miss Stilwell, a woman who, judging by her expression, had no interest in poetry or men with lace at their sleeves. His dark, handsome looks did not unnerve her nor gain him any admiration.

"I find Lucia Stilwell has a great deal of character. Can you not find her a match, Mama?" Pandora said.

"She has a tongue as sharp as yours, I have heard, but she hasn't the appearance or the dowry to make up for it. Still, I will set my mind to the task. She presents a challenge to my matchmaking abilities," the duchess replied.

"Oh, if only you would, Your Grace." Mrs. Stilwell had crept up on them followed by a servant holding a large green wine bottle wrapped in a clean white cloth. "More champagne?"

The duchess held out her empty glass and accepted the bubbly. While casks of ale and cider flowed freely and punchbowls of fruity drinks for the young abounded, the mother of the bride did parse out her wines to the more prominent guests.

"I will need to know more about your daughter, if I am to make an attempt."

"Oh goodness, well, Lucia does love small children and is very interested in good works. She takes especial care of our blind vicar."

"You see, she does have character," Pandora insisted.

"Character is seldom of interest to eligible men. Come, walk with me and give me more," the duchess said, stepping away with the rotund

Mrs. Stilwell and the wine porter following closely. "We go from here to Yorkshire where I might find someone for your daughter—if you have no objection to red-haired men. They run in my son-in-law's family."

"While I do find red hair vulgar on a woman, I am sure Lucia would have no objections to it on a man, any man of modest rank, any man." Mrs. Stilwell's own faded blond sausage curls wobbled vehemently beside her small, pink ears as hope blossomed for her daughter. She trotted alongside the more vigorous duchess.

As her mother and Mrs. Stilwell moved out of hearing range, Pandora shook her head sadly. "Why must marriage always be our goal? Mama is doing her best for you, and I suppose we ought to do the same by alluding to red-haired men in Yorkshire whenever we can. Well, no champagne for the Longleigh spinster and her sister, I notice. Lemonade, Phemie? You look as if you could use some, but you also seem to be having a wonderful time. I am glad to see you smiling again."

"First of all, never refer to yourself as the Longleigh spinster. You have just turned twenty, and I simply know that one day someone like Leo will sweep you off your feet before you reach Miss Stilwell's advanced age."

"Heaven forbid!"

"Secondly, I am having a wonderful time. Once these festivities are ended, we are on our way to York, not far from Hull, which is a river port and all rivers flow to the sea."

"Yes?" replied Pandora to this obvious statement. "I thought you hated the idea of having to stay with Thalia."

Phemie lowered her voice to a whisper. "Not anymore. I have conceived a plan to escape and join Leo in Scotland."

"That is not all you have conceived. Would you make a further mess of it?"

"In York, we will not have the Armstrong boys dogging our every step to the dressmaker or to church or prowling the grounds as if Leo were going to lead a hoard of howling Highlanders across the border. They have never gotten over our eluding them at Gretna Green and remain overly vigilant. But our brother-in-law will lower the guard, seeing me only as a foolish, harmless girl."

"Which you have never been, despite those sweet ways of yours— until you met Leo, of course."

"Panny, I am counting on you not to betray me again. Do I have your word?"

Pandora nodded, knowing what the word of a Longleigh meant.

"I mean to disguise myself as a humble, pregnant woman and take passage to the coast. There, I will set sail for Inverness and meet Leo at his hiding place. Afterward, we will go abroad. He has the means to earn his living as a physician, and I am sure I can learn to cook oatmeal and keep a house."

"Phemie, Phemie, Phemie. Do you not realize that you are still a very pretty girl and a big stomach will not prevent any lower sort of man from taking advantage of you? You cannot travel so far alone and in your condition."

"Then, I shall ask Jason to escort me. He will love the idea of traveling in disguise on a grand adventure."

Pandora snorted as she so often did at ill-conceived ideas. "He would if Papa did not hold his purse strings. If he helps you escape, he will be selling his verse for a pence on street corners to earn a living. Papa will cut him off just like that."

She made an unladylike gesture of a throat being slit with a very sharp razor. It drew some attention, and she turned her sister toward the lemonade and strolled off arm in arm. As they approached the punchbowl, she cocked her head near Phemie's and gave the audience a glittering smile as if they shared a pleasant jest. Several young men returned it. Not wanting company, she immediately put on one of her daunting frowns, warding them off.

"Phemie, I will do it. I will be your escort."

A pleasant country woman stuffed into a maid's uniform for the day poured two cups for them. Phemie drained hers before replying.

"Panny, you forget you are a beautiful woman and not in..." She moved away from the punchbowl and the woman behind it. The music started again, and they both paused to watch Jason lead Miss

Stilwell out with a look on his face as if he had eaten the bitter fruit in their beverage. "My condition," she concluded. "Two young women traveling alone would be in no less danger from unwanted attention."

"I would not be going as your sister, but as your brother. If Reg's mother can play a breeches role, then so can I. After all, Grandpapa could act when he wished to, and I might have inherited his talent. I find this as challenging as Mama does matchmaking."

Phemie saw her sister's eyes light, and her face take on a fascinating animation at the thought. Men who had been attracted by her smile and then repelled by her frown started toward her again. One was able to close the distance before Pandora could resume a sour lemon expression. She had to accept his offer to dance, but like Jason, did not have to enjoy it.

As her escort led Panny away, Phemie began to consider the offer. Her father would hardly throw Pandora out on the streets for defying him if he had not done so to her. He protected the women in his family, but did expect his sons to earn their way by pursuing a profession, and that, he willingly financed. Hence, Jason's pretense at studying law when he would rather be writing. Still, Jason might offer some help if he thought he would not be caught. Panny would need men's clothes and perhaps some tutelage in masculine ways. Yes, it could work.

Several gentlemen tripped over themselves to reach the pretty young lady now standing alone, a duke's daughter with a huge dowry. Little did they know what else she would bring to a marriage. Phemie bowed her lips and accepted the first who asked her to dance.

Twenty-two

Battle Hill, the country seat of the Earl of Danelagh, sat well above the flood plain of the Vale of York. Despite an attempt in the past century to soften its appearance with larger windows capped with ornate carvings, it still retained the look of an unassailable fortress much like a rock that had been draped in velvet cloth. Thalia said the same of her husband, Godric Erikson, whom she pricked when he became too imperious by saying, "Should I simply call you God, then?" She'd wanted a man who could stand up to her father and yet be a bit like him, and had gotten that. The trouble was he also stood up to her. Most of the time, they lived congenially and she referred to him as Rick.

The stately couple, both quite tall, stood dwarfed before the massive doors of their home as they watched the duke's carriage climb the hill. The black vehicle with the ducal crest flanked by four riders progressed past the barely discernable remnants of an ancient hill fort and a still stout Roman lookout tower, then over a stone bridge spanning the crescent-shaped pond, all that remained of a moat. Put to use to build a stable and outbuildings, the outer walls were long gone.

Despite its forbidding appearance, Phemie knew the four wings formed a square around a generous courtyard with a deep well that visitors persisted in sullying with coins to gain wishes. She had some coins to spare. Even if Thalia and her husband were completely unaware of her scheme, escaping Battle Hill would not be easy with its clear view of the valley and single set of outward doors. All others opened into the courtyard. The earl kept the gray stone walls free of vines, the base bare of bushes as if, Thalia said, they might be attacked at any moment and could not allow the enemy any advantage. The duke admired that in his son-in-law. After all, only a century and a half had passed since the place served to repel an attack by the Roundheads. Napoleon had been contained for now, but one never knew when a fortress might be needed.

Truly, the stark grandeur of the place revealed Castle Laughlin as the paltry ruin it was. Ah well, she did not want a husband like the Earl of Danelagh. He suited Thalia, ten years her elder and possessed of imperial airs, but she now preferred a gentler man sort of man—Leo— and a smaller home filled with loving people.

Thalia had ruled the nursery amongst the first five of the Longleigh children—James and Iris, Clio and Calliope, and herself, nicknamed Queenie by their eldest brother. James, though the first born, had allowed her to boss the rest out of complete indifference. He simply ignored her edicts when he disagreed with them. When she had married away from home ten years ago and the others had gone to school, the second half of the tribe—Joshua, Jason, Pandora, Euphemia, and little Justinian—had come into their own—their own sort of mischief their mother said. They'd excelled at plotting and planning. That gave Phemie hope.

The carriage rocked to a stop, and a footman jumped down to extend the steps. Thalia and Rick moved to greet the Longleighs. This close, the smaller doors cut into larger ones that once guarded the entrance to the courtyard were easily visible. Each possessed a huge brass knocker in the shape of a fist, but no need for them today. The boy who kept watch in the Roman tower had scampered to the house as soon as the duke's coach began the climb.

Danelagh handed his mother-in-law down and offered her a broad smile that softened the faint crescent-shaped scar borne on one side of his face. He bent to kiss her still-fair cheek. They might have been a mother and loving son, both with white-blond hair and gray eyes, except his bold features had no delicacy.

Thalia bent to hug Phemie as she stepped down, holding her so tightly she mingled her own black curls with her those of her sister. She whispered in her ear.

"Oh, poor Little Dove seduced and abandoned. Never fear, your shame will be our secret."

Phemie bunched her gloved hand much in the manner of the doorknockers. How she wanted to deliver Thalia a good solid clout. Pandora had often done so in childhood when their eldest sister became too overbearing, but never Phemie or Justinian whom Thalia had doted upon and called her dear little poppets. Usually, Thalia referred to Pandora as the Little Beast or a dozen other uncomplimentary terms.

Phemie struggled from Thalia's grasp, but her sister kept on, increasing her volume only slightly to be heard over the disturbance of men, the duke and Jason amongst them, dismounting with a jangle of armaments. "You shall have your own wing where you may stay out of sight. If anyone comes to call, I will take to my bed with a pillow beneath the covers and complain of my condition until they are chased away. I do hope we have a girl. Helena would so love to have a baby sister."

Pandora had come close enough to hear. "You were not so thrilled when I was born."

"From birth you were a fractious child who would not be cuddled or cosseted, which was not my fault. Always trying to keep up with the boys. But Phemie has always been a lamb and her child will be one, too, I am sure."

"Stop!" Phemie stamped her foot and raised her voice for all to hear. "My child will be the next Laird of Laughlin as I am married to the current holder of that title. I will not have it any other way."

Silence fell over the group. The escort of Armstrongs looked off toward the blue smudge of York distant in the valley, as if they had no idea she'd spoken. Her father's bronze complexion went a shade darker, and her mother's fair face paled. Jason smirked, and Rick by his side frowned, the scar on his cheek turning a forbidding red. Pandora's head swept from side to side as she mouthed, "No, no, no." Only the black coach horses continued to shift, making their harness creak. Finally, the duchess, her fan open and waving like the wings of a hen whose egg had been stolen, moved to Phemie's side and took her elbow.

"Nature decides—and God, of course," she said. "Thalia, show us to our quarters. Your sister is overwrought."

"I am not...ouch!"

Pandora had delivered a quick pinch, an old signal to keep one's mouth shut, whether confronted by the duchess or their school's headmistress.

"I suppose I am fatigued. Forgive me my crazy words. Thalia, I appreciate all that you are doing for me. If I might go and have a lie down now?"

"Certainly. I am often temperamental when I...Think nothing more about it and do come inside." Thalia led the way.

Servants opened the doors as they came, the chief among them, Bascom, the butler who had the build and face of a medieval torturer unsoftened by his formal wig and black and gold livery. As children, exploring forbidden sections of Battle Hill, Bascom often routed Josh, Jason, and their little sisters and sent them shrieking as he played the role of monster to the hilt. Phemie suspected the man had a soft spot for children as he'd never reported their antics to Danelagh, just scared the dickens out of them and made their adventures all the more delicious. Now, he would be her jailer in reality, as Bascom would never conspire against his master.

Their party entered what had once been a deep portal and now served as a foyer with a large arched window edged in colored glass providing a view of the courtyard that Thalia had converted to a walled garden. An oil lamp worthy of a Gothic cathedral hung from a chain in the ceiling to provide illumination at night. Archways bored through the original masonry allowed access to the house, right and left.

"I do wish Rick would allow a rear entrance for the servants, but he simply will not agree to it. Better never to leave a back door open, he says. So, we must take deliveries here and trundle everything across the courtyard to the kitchen. Very inconvenient," Thalia explained as she did every time the family or anyone else visited. Thus far, her criticism bore no inroads in her husband's stolid determination.

Two steps up to the right, they passed without benefit of a hallway from chamber to chamber filled with sculptures of ancient warriors and yielding nymphs, portraits of stern blond men and their statuesque wives, one striking painting of the Spartans dying at Thermopylae done by Iris' husband, and gilded cabinets full of curiosities to the staircase built into the right angle of the wing. The men dropped behind to examine a new display of antique weaponry, but the ladies continued upstairs to a long corridor of closed doors.

A brisk walk brought them to the rear of the house where Thalia threw open the entrance to a large room with a view of the distant moors. An enormous bed with hangings of light blue brocade and gold fringe dominated the chamber. Every piece of furniture glittered with gilt and writhed with decorative curlicues...French elegance within a fortress.

"I've been told Rick's great-grandfather kept his mistress here across the entire courtyard from his wife's quarters."

"Are you implying...?" Phemie began, even though Pandora standing in the rear of their tall sister kept shaking her heard.

"No, I am not! This suite is as fine as mine. You have both a large dressing room and a bathing chamber to yourself. Please, Phemie, let me help you in your time of trouble. I had the devil of a time convincing Rick. Helena is three, and he thinks we should be starting on another of our own right now."

"How do you do that—have a child only every third year?" Pandora inquired.

"With discipline, forbearance, and imagination, and now we must employ those measures for another whole year and more," Thalia snapped. "I would be happy to discuss it further with you once you are engaged."

"I do think it would be more interesting and useful to know now. If Phemie had known—or Mama."

"You would not be here," Thalia countered.

"Enough, the both of you!" the duchess said as she did so often. "Of course, I know such things, but your father and I share an uncommon passion not easily set aside. Dear me, I should not be speaking of this before an innocent."

"If you are referring to me, please continue," Pandora suggested with a wry smile.

"She has always been so forward and contrary," Thalia huffed.

The arrival of several burly footmen, big enough to be bodyguards to the king, arrived bearing the baggage and put an end to the conversation. Her boxes were few. No need for party finery this visit, and the necessary gowns would be contrived as she increased. Thalia's arm swept round Phemie's shoulder.

"Since you will not be out and about very much, I thought you would appreciate the larger space and the prospect of the hills. The stairs at this end of the hall go down to the courtyard garden. We get a full extra month's use of it with the walls warming the plants. Why, I still have late roses in bloom. Feel free to use it at any time. We do want you to be comfortable here. I won't be far away in the family wing whenever you need me."

"Might Panny stay with me? There is ample space, and she would be a great comfort to me."

Pandora's smile grew wider and was accompanied by a slight nod. The other women would assume she merely enjoyed Thalia's irritation at the request.

"I have a chamber prepared for her between Mama's and Jason's that is entirely suitable for her short visit."

"Could she not stay longer?" Phemie allowed her lower lip to tremble. She'd used this skill to great effect as a child when discipline was in order.

"I'd be willing to remain through the holidays, perhaps even until spring. If Phemie wants me to sleep with her, why that bed is certainly big enough for two—or three or four." Pandora watched her eldest sister's brows rise half the height of her forehead.

"Why must she always be so provocative, Mama?"

"That is simply our Pandora. Certainly, you have my permission to remain if Thalia will have you, but you must be on your best behavior."

Phemie thought she detected some relief in her mother's countenance at the thought of several months without Pandora's company. All the better for their scheme. Pandora's smile had changed to one of pleasant compliance, always a bad sign, and the duchess frowned. Phemie took a turn at slightly shaking her head as if to rearrange her curls, and Panny switched to her usual thin-lipped expression.

"I swear to be of all the help I can to Phemie and will attempt not to vex Thalia. The last I cannot promise."

"Give it your best try, Panny. Might as well have her boxes brought in here, then. We shall remain a week to see Phemie settled in before returning to Bellevue Hall. Bless you, Thalia, for what you do for our family." The duchess raised on her toes to kiss the burnished cheek of her eldest daughter.

~ * ~

Wearing only their shifts, Phemie and Pandora lay gazing up at the painted canopy of the immense bed. Zeus, in the form of a great yellow bull with a wild gray eye rimmed in red, was making off with the Princess Europa across the sea accompanied by a bevy of Nereids and horn-blowing Tritons.

"That bull looks rather like all the blond, brawny Eriksons in the portrait gallery," Panny remarked.

"I believe that was the intent of the artist, a compliment to his patron."

"Imagine having to look up at that night after night while some big Danelagh earl sweats over you. How does Thalia endure it?"

Phemie turned her head to smile knowingly at her maiden sister. "Actually, the joining of a man and woman can be quite transcendent."

"Are you going to tell me or not?"

"It's hard to explain, Panny—like all of your being concentrating into one small hot point and then bursting and expanding to fill the entire universe."

"Prettily put, but not of much help. As it is, I keep expecting the fourteenth King Louis to enter and expect us both to service him."

Phemie poked her sister in the ribs. "You are so naughty."

"The product of too liberal an education, some would say. But we are here to plot, not to rest or admire art. Best to get it done while Mama takes her turns in the courtyard with Thalia and assumes we are recovering from our travels."

"She already suspects, as you are never fatigued."

"Then she is turning a blind eye. Phemie, you must cease being defiant. Sweet compliance will make them drop their guard."

"I am sorry about that. My emotions are in turmoil because of my condition, I think." She smothered a huge yawn with the back of her hand. "I am tired much of the time, too."

"Heaven forbid I ever find myself in that way. We must act quickly before Jason returns to London. We need men's clothing adjusted to fit me, and he is our best source."

"He will be reluctant to part with anything. Papa is rather strict about his tailoring bills."

"Well, he has no valet to give his castoffs to, so why not us? We will alter them as needed to fit me."

"We, Panny? You know I will have to do most of the work."

"My contribution is the planning. I am thinking it would be wiser to take a coach than go by inland waterways to Scarborough, no, Hull. It is a larger port and trades with Scotland. We must devise some fabrication to get there. Thalia is not likely to allow us to go alone, but Jason is free to come and go as he pleases. Perhaps he would book an advance passage for us to Inverness. Then, we have only to get there on time. A story, but what story? Something that would gain Thalia's approval and allow us to escape Battle Hill."

Phemie did not answer. Her eyes had closed, and her bosom rose and fell with the soft regularity of sleep. Let her baby sister rest, then. Pandora rolled from the center of the vast bed to the edge and got up. Her mind would not let her lie still, and she wasn't in the least tired.

Moving quietly to the wardrobe where one of Thalia's maids had placed the simple day gowns she insisted upon, the ones a woman could don without assistance, Pandora selected a frock. She drew on her undergarments, gartered her stockings and put her feet into soft slippers before dropping the gown over her head, trying its sash in front, and maneuvering the bow around the back. Hanging down and in disarray, her straight black hair got no more attention than a few stokes of the brush and a ribbon to tie it back. Plenty of time to have this daily annoyance dressed in time for supper. She crept to the door of the suite and let herself out.

In the long corridor, she went to one of the windows that let light into the hall and looked down on the courtyard where her mother and Thalia still strolled, taking fresh air and exercise and well bundled against the autumn chill in the air. Her father, who had ridden most of the way, took his rest on a bench and relaxed with a pipe and a flagon of wine by his side. Rick, the late afternoon sun making his blond hair gleam from above, kept him company.

Thalia's children, nine-year-old Axel, six-year-old Piers, and little Helena played tag among the potted shrubs and trees. She noted the boys allowed the small girl to catch them. Josh and Jason had never done so for her and Phemie, and that had made them stronger, faster, and more determined. Good then, somewhere Jason was alone, and she thought she knew where.

Pandora made her way downstairs, past the closed doors of the long, narrow ballroom and through the ornate galleries and foyer to the family wing. Sure enough, she found her brother in the library, a comfortable room with its small collection of books attesting to the fact that the earls of Danelagh preferred action to intellect, another reason the duke favored Rick. Jason sat in a comfortable armchair before a small fire using its light and that of an oil lamp to illuminate the small volume he held in his hands. He barely glanced up when Pandora entered and took a seat in an armless ladies' chair across from him.

"Interesting reading?" she asked.

"Byron's *Corsair*— it's all the rage, but simply a thinly disguised version of his misspent youth and dislike of humanity, except the female portion, that is. I do admire his use of cantos, but I could do as well if only Papa would sponsor my publications. Thalia has made some attempt to bolster the selection here, but the pickings are rather slim. She does have that blasted *Waverley*. Wonderful lyrical prose, but I regret what that tale has done to Phemie."

"Would you like to see Phemie happy?"

"Certainly. She is the only one in the family who has never mocked my poetic ambitions, except Mama, of course." Using one long finger to keep his place, Jason closed the book. "What are you about, Panny? I see the gleam of scheming in your eyes."

"First, I must have your word as a Longleigh not to repeat anything I tell you."

"Serious indeed. Go on. I am intrigued."

"Phemie wishes to rejoin her Scot. He hides near Inverness. I propose to help her."

Jason quirked one black eyebrow, an expression he cultivated and used often, much to her annoyance. "After you betrayed her condition to Mama and Papa?"

"I want to make that up to her. In order to accomplish this, we will need a suit of men's clothing and someone to book us passage north from Hull. We will also need a plausible story to get away from this place. We are counting on you—and your creative talents." Pandora waited for the compliment to take effect.

"A viable tale is no problem for me, but money for your travels, no. You realize I am always somewhat short of funds and with Papa rich as Croesus, too."

"Mama has given Phemie a sizeable purse for confinement gowns. We propose to use that."

"Good, good, now explain the need for masculine garments."

"Considering Papa's temper, we did not want to involve you directly, but a young woman must be accompanied by a male family member aboard ship. I propose to take your place as her brother on the voyage."

Now both of his brows rose, this time without affectation. "Dangerous, Panny, very dangerous."

"I will have my stiletto much more conveniently located in my waistcoat, and I propose to pack a pistol."

Jason's expression did not become any less skeptical. "In a woman's hands, the last would be more useful if you simply conk a man over the head with it, not to mention having the resolve to pull the trigger."

"You believe I would lack resolve?"

Jason looked into her eyes, and she knew what he saw. "You, Panny? No, you would blast away and accidentally kill someone standing nearby."

"Drat that Mama believes a woman's hands should never smell of gunpowder. You must give me some lessons before we leave."

"That would be very amusing to be sure. We might get it by Papa, since his zeal to protect his daughters is high right now. But you say you need a plausible reason to go into Hull without Thalia. I can think of only one idea that might appeal to her—getting you married off to some unsuspecting man."

"Nonsense! Papa says I may remain unmarried as long as I wish."

"Don't you see, Panny, it's the same as Mama admiring my poetry. Neither would say anything else. Of course, they want you to marry. Now, let's conjecture that you did gain a suitor during your last season, one whom Papa might not approve, say an officer in the king's navy who has worked his way up the ranks and has no other social status or source of income."

"Ridiculous. Papa would adore a self-made military man, and we could live on the interest from my dowry."

"Very well, that is not reasonable then. Suppose we say you met only briefly before he shipped out, and now having some shore leave has come to Hull to seek you out."

"I like that idea, a man unafraid of the sea, a bold sailor who has fought Napoleon's fleet. But why wouldn't he simply come to Battle Hill?"

"Too in awe of the Earl of Danelagh to present himself?"

"Oh, I would have nothing to do with a man cowed by nobility."

"You make this difficult, Panny. Fine, he suffered a wound battling the Americans, as we are done with Nappy and is recovering in Hull. He begs you to come to his side so he might see your face again to affect his cure. One glance of sympathy from your dark brown eyes, one touch of your soothing fingers to his fevered brow, and he believes he will be cured." Jason laid his own free hand palm outward across his forehead and swooned deeper into his armchair like a languishing invalid.

"I like it! What is his name and rank?"

"Captain, no Lieutenant Josiah Weatherby. We must not give him too high a rank or else he would not need a wealthy bride, and captains are too easily traced. The navy swarms with impecunious lieutenants."

Pandora tried, but failed to keep the disappointment from her face. "He is courting me for my dowry, not out of love?"

"Trying to be realistic, Panny. You are the most sensible of women and possess not one ounce of romance. I never thought the concept would wound you."

She stiffened. "I am not wounded. I would simply prefer he have some affection for me."

"So be it. His letter begging you to come to Hull will be a masterpiece of longing."

"How do we get Phemie there?"

"Simple, she and I will escort you, since Thalia must begin feigning her difficult condition. Reluctant to resume my law studies, I will linger behind after our parents return to Bellevue and so be free to act as chaperone, though the poor chap will hardly be up to any seductive moves in his grievous condition."

"Avoiding your studies—entirely believable. I commend you, Jason. You might be able to turn this into a novel someday."

"As if I would lower myself to that from worshipping at the high altar of poetry." He flicked open his book and returned to reading *The Corsair*.

"So sorry I suggested it. How vulgar that you might earn some money with your writing. I will tell Phemie the entire plot. Bring us the garments for alteration as soon as possible—and do not forget my shooting lessons."

"Tomorrow," he replied, without even looking up.

Twenty-three

Jason dumped the heap of his lesser garments on the bed and took a moment to admire the artwork under the canopy. He deemed it, "*most inspiring*" before taking a seat on one of the spindly chairs far too delicate to support his long frame and wide shoulders. He reversed his seat and straddled it, dangling his arms over the blue brocade backrest, and watching as Pandora picked over the donated garments.

"Couldn't you do better than this? We shall have to travel second-class."

"All that I have with me to spare. Papa believes an aspiring barrister should dress somberly."

"But not shabbily." Pandora held up a jacket. "The cuffs are frayed and the buttons cut off. Did you give them to your tailor for reuse?"

"They were gold. I'm afraid I lost them in a game of chance. Surely, you have others in your sewing boxes."

Phemie took the coat and examined it. "We shall have to cut several inches off the sleeves and turn the cuffs regardless. Brass buttons will have to do." She picked up a somewhat soiled black waistcoat. "Far too fitted for your figure, Panny. If I put a panel in the back, there will be room for your bosom, but we will have to plump up your stomach with a pillow to make the rest of you match. I'm afraid my fictitious brother is going to be a tad chubby."

"Then, you must walk like old Lord Butterworth, shoulders back, and lead with your belly. Tuck in your chin to make it double and practice a waddle as if supporting your weight." Jason jumped up to demonstrate his impression of one of the duke's best friends and had his sisters doubling with merriment.

Phemie blotted tears from the corners of her eyes and returned to perusing the garments. "The trousers must be shortened. I'm afraid they will be snug in the rear, but the tails of the jacket will cover your bottom. I suppose a fat man would have a wide bottom in any case."

"Exactly." Jason seized two small cushions from either end of the settee in the sitting area and, ducking behind a changing screen, reappeared with both shoved down the rear of his pantaloons. His tails split comically over his now broad hind cheeks. He dropped his handkerchief to the floor and mimed Lord Butterworth's attempts to pick it up, again with the bulk of his stomach getting in the way. Laughing, his sisters fell back on the bed.

"How wonderful to hear laughter coming from this room instead of nightly tears," the duchess said as she cracked open the door.

Hastily, Phemie flipped the bed covers over the clothes and sat atop them. She folded her hands in her lap and assumed the most innocent of expressions. "Jason was amusing us by aping Lord Butterworth."

"Do not make mock of dear Butterworth. He is a fine man, if rather portly, and came to my rescue when I needed it. Put the cushions back, Jason."

"Yes, Mama." He slipped behind the screen and removed his padding, plumped the cushions, and returned them to their places.

"I do appreciate your trying to make Phemie smile, but consider some other way. What, the maid has not made up your bed today? I must speak to Thalia about the sloth of her servant. Just because you are tucked away in this wing, does not mean they can neglect you."

Hating to have the maid reprimanded for her deed, Phemie said, "Oh, she did come and do her job, but I felt weary and climbed back under the covers."

"Very well. Do come outside and walk in the courtyard. You need fresh air and exercise as well as rest. Why, the Shawnee women had no trouble giving birth. They worked in the fields until the child came. We do coddle ourselves too much, and that accounts for so many deaths in childbirth, I am positive."

Her children had heard this too many times to count, the girls and even the boys, to their eternal embarrassment. Jason moved toward the door.

"Come, Jason, walk with your sisters instead of holing up in the library again."

His expression immediately changed from mortification to amusement. "I have a better idea. Pandora has expressed a wish to learn to use a pistol. You are invited to observe her lessons."

"As she has many times before. I will not have it. The Duke of Bellevue's daughters are surrounded by footmen, bodyguards, and brothers. They have no need to learn weaponry."

"None of that helped save Phemie. I want to learn to defend myself, Mama." Pandora did not need to feign her enthusiasm for learning a masculine skill. Yes, she had asked before and always been denied.

"I will confer with your father about this."

"You know he will allow it. After all, he gave us knives and lessons in using them," Pandora insisted. "It is you who have prevented us from learning."

"Haven't you said the frontier women of America knew how to use a rifle? I'd wager the Jacobite, Flora MacDonald, could use a pistol, too." Phemie added her support.

"It is a grievous thing to kill a man, even when necessary. I would never have my daughters know that feeling."

"Mama, you took the scalp of the man who tried to molest you! I have always admired that tale," Pandora reminded the duchess.

"Truly, I simply cut off his queue as your father so often points out when I am telling my story. All right, you may have your lesson, Panny, but not Phemie. Guns do have a kick, and I won't have her injured. Wear your plainest clothes. Heaven knows if the scent of the gunpowder will ever come out."

All three of her children grinned in triumph.

~ * ~

The Earl of Danelagh provided the weapons from his considerable arsenal, a servant to reload, and a clanking sack of empty wine bottles. He guided his family by marriage to the level space inside of the old hill fort and had his man set bottles along its rim. The duchess sat in the chair provided for her and opened a parasol, even though the day was overcast. Thalia kept her company, but Phemie had declined to watch the spectacle. She claimed she had promised to mend a stack of clothes for Jason before he left for London. If only Papa would allow him a more generous allowance for apparel. Putting in a word was the least she could do for his help.

The men selected pistols from the array laid out on a folding table and discussed weight, balance, and range before reducing the targets one after another to glittering, green shards in the grass. Thalia and the duchess applauded their perfect marksmanship. The servant cleared the low wall of jagged remnants and set up another row of bottles.

"There, you see how it is done, Panny. Assume your stance, hold out your pistol steadily, and squeeze, not jerk, the trigger. Give it a try." Jason selected one of the lighter weapons and offered it to his sister.

Dressed in a snug jacket so threadbare it should long since have gone to charity except for her pride in scorning new clothes, Pandora stepped up to the line the men had drawn in the dirt. She tried to imitate their sideways stance, but her bonnet obscured the view. She pulled at the ribbons with her free hand and pitched the hat behind her. Her hair drawn back in its accustomed bun would present no problems.

"Panny, your complexion!" her mother exclaimed. "You are so dark already."

"There is no sun, and I do not plan to bask, Mama."

She planted her feet wide beneath her skirts and tried again. The gun weighed more than she'd anticipated and dipped in her grasp. As one, the gentlemen called for her to raise it up and hold it steady. Still, the weapon bucked badly when she shot and sent her back a few paces. The ball slammed into the earthen wall. Aim higher, her audience said, as if that weren't obvious. Two more attempts failed, with shots going wide or diving into the ground. Oh, the frustration. A woman should be able to do as well as a man at this...she simply should.

Jason stepped forward to address the problem. "I do not believe a sideways stance benefits as you have more before and behind than a man."

"Are you saying I am fat?"

"No, actually I was rather giving you a compliment on your feminine form. Face front and hold the weapon with both hands."

She did and was gratified by an explosion of glass. "Bravo, Panny," her father cried.

"But a man would not shoot this way."

"No matter, as long as you hit your target when it comes to defense, child. All a matter of practice, really. If your mother had not been so against it..."

"As if Pandora weren't unfeminine enough," Thalia commented.

Pandora swung round and pointed the still smoking pistol at her sister, who backed away shrieking. Jason disarmed her. "Oh, for God's sake, it isn't loaded anymore. As I said, once you have fired, a pistol makes a better club than anything else. Try a few more shots, Panny."

She destroyed four out of six of her targets, but her shoulders were beginning to ache slightly. "Thank you, gentlemen, for the instruction. I believe I will go assist Phemie with her sewing."

"You handle a horse better than you ply a needle," Thalia sneered to get revenge for her fright.

"And proud of it!"

"Ladies!" their mother intervened.

Pandora scooped up her discarded bonnet, slapped it on her head and started up the hill to join Phemie, the sister she loved and would do anything to make happy. As she strode away, she heard Jason say, "That reminds me. I believe I will go into Hull in a few days' time and see if I can find any bargains in woolen goods. My tailor charges such exorbitant rates for fine cloth."

The duke commended his son's unexpected thriftiness and offered to foot the bill. The men resumed their target practice, slaying one glass enemy after another. Pandora kept walking away to hide her satisfied expression. The plans were proceeding most smoothly, even if she did shoot like a girl.

Twenty-four

The duke applied a manly blow to Jason's shoulders and admonished, "Apply yourself to your studies, son."

The duchess embraced Phemie and kissed her cheek. "I will return when your time draws near and see you through your travail, a woman's most dangerous time."

"I am not afraid. I believe we have more in common than you think, Mama. I know I will have an easy time of it."

"Pandora, you are in Thalia's home. Give her no trouble." She wagged a finger at her contrary daughter, then drew her in for a farewell kiss. Thalia, Rick, and her line of grandchildren all received the same. Because he never could resist doing so, the duke put his hands around his wife's small waist and lifted her into the carriage. She slapped at him with her fan and giggled in delight. His black eyes gleamed like a satyr's alighting on a nymph in the woods.

"Since we have so much room in the carriage, I believe I shall ride with my duchess. Bring my horse along," he directed one of the Armstrongs. He joined his spouse, closing the curtains on the far side of the vehicle even as she waved goodbye out the other window. They were off, best of all taking the guards with them.

"They will be at it before they reach the bottom of the hill," Jason remarked.

"Yes, I have always admired your parents' ardor," Rick said, nodding his blond head with approval.

"Because you did not have to grow up with it. Well, I am off to Hull in search of some bolts of superfine cloth. I shall return tomorrow to enjoy your hospitality for a few more days before departing for London."

"Yes, do put off the inevitable as long as you can, Jason," Thalia pricked.

"Thank you for your kind invitation to stay." Words being his forte, he ignored her sarcasm and turned it his way. Mounting his horse, he tipped his hat to the ladies and admonished, "You must carry on without me for a while." Down the hill he rode and turned in the opposite direction from his parents' route.

"I believe we will go to Phemie's suite and apply ourselves to some sewing," Pandora announced.

"Again? I expect you'd rather have a morning ride. Feel free to choose any mount in the stables, Panny, since you did not bring Dark Star, the mare you took away from me years ago by pleading with Papa for my Dark Fire's foal. If I am to give up riding and all society, the least Phemie can do is keep me company. I have a very pleasant fire going in my sitting room, and the light is perfect for needlework."

Phemie folded her arms under her bosom and hung her head. She pinched her inner arm even harder than Pandora had and thanked heaven for long sleeves that did not show the bruises. When tears filled her wide brown eyes, she raised them to Thalia's equally dark orbs.

"I-I want to make some gowns for my babe—for the new infant. Oh, I cannot bear the thought that I will rarely see him." She rushed into the house.

"There, she is upset now. Let me go and calm her. We will both join you in your sitting room once her tears have passed." Leaving the row of confounded Eriksons behind, Pandora raced unladylike after her younger sister.

Once in the isolated safety of their chamber with the door securely locked, Pandora fairly shouted with glee. "Well done, Phemie. With Jason gone to arrange for the letter from my pathetic suitor, we must have our final fitting of my costume."

Without waiting another moment, she went behind the dressing screen and took the garments from a small trunk. The trousers fit snugly, especially in the rear, but were now the right length. The shirt had ample room and needed extensive tucking in. Expanded across the back with a swath of light blue brocade cut from a hidden fold of the curtains, the waistcoat spanned over her breasts, but the addition of a pillow evened out her semblance of a portly figure. She closed the brass-buttoned jacket over the vest and found the sleeves to be a good length, even if the shoulders drooped like the work of a poor tailor. Coming out from behind the screen with her neckcloth dangling, she went to the mirror to tie it in a simple knot.

"I wish Jason had let us keep the lace edging. I'd like to appear slightly prosperous."

"He claims he needs it for his own use. Try the boots and see if you can walk naturally with the stockings stuffed in the toes." Phemie handed over a pair of well-worn boots down at the heels that one of the servants had shined to best of his ability.

Pandora drew them on and took a turn pacing with her hands locked behind her back as a man might do, but never a lady. "What do you think?"

"Well, your dark complexion works in your favor. No one will notice the lack of a beard. With gloves and a proper hat, I think you will do very well as a man. We should pad out the shoulders, though, to make them seem broader. Jason did not need the help."

Pandora assumed a wide-legged stance with arms akimbo. "Trousers afford such freedom of movement, no mincing along encumbered by skirts. Do my buttocks appear too big?" She attempted to see behind her where her coattails split across her hips.

Phemie allowed only the smallest smile to escape. "No, I'd say they are very fetching. No wonder Reg's mother is so popular in her breeches roles."

Pandora touched the black hair bundled at her nape. "This will have to go. We must whack it off!"

"No, oh no! Your silken hair is one of your best features, Panny. I won't allow you to sacrifice it."

"Our sister, Iris, cut hers when she went spying against Napoleon."

"Yes, and it has never come back to its former glory."

Pandora continued to argue. "Iris prefers to keep it shorter for her travels with her husband to exotic places...far less bother. Mine is only a tangled nuisance most of the time. Imagine never having to brush your hair one-hundred strokes every night again. Think of the time saved. Men are so fortunate."

"They do have shaving and beards to contend with, you know."

"So I shall have the best of both worlds—short hair and no beard."

"Absolutely not. We will braid it into a queue."

"A very long queue. Won't that seem strange?"

"I've seen sailors with very long queues. And we will double it up, too. You will merely seem out of fashion like Papa. Here, allow me."

Phemie moved behind her sister and took down the mass of fine, straight black hair falling to the waist. Swiftly, she began braiding down its length. Doubling over the braid, she fastened it with a black bow. "There, that will do."

"It looks far too unwieldy. People will notice and laugh."

"Only women are mocked for poor hair arrangements. As a man, you are immune and allowed to do as you wish."

Pandora perked up immediately. "Yes, that is so. I suppose I can manage it."

"Why don't we leave it in the braid to save time? In just a few days, we will be on our way to Scotland!"

"We'd better go sit with Thalia the rest of the morning to appease her."

"Then let me pin the braid up around your head." Phemie's fingers were already working to unfasten the ribbon and rearrange her sister's hair. "Be careful not to muss it when you change back into your gown."

Not wanting to endure more fussing with her hair, Pandora did take care. Shortly, they were on their way with their sewing boxes to Thalia's sitting room down the set of stairs that took them to the courtyard and over to the family wing. They entered the pleasant room with its floral décor and cozy fire. Their eldest sister sat, a portrait of contented domesticity, sewing by the window which let in the morning light from the courtyard.

Thalia pierced the cloth with impeccable small stitches despite a scar crossing her right palm. Supposedly, she had been wounded slaying a Moslem with a blade. They both knew the story, had read the flattering book entitled *Life in the Harem and a Daring Rescue from the Hands of the Turks* written by a former servant, but doubted every word of it. Thalia was far too proper to kill anyone. Most likely Rick had done the deed and given her credit. Heaven forbid anyone should ever write such romantic rubbish about her younger sisters.

Thalia's little daughter played at her feet with empty wooden spools which she attempted to thread onto a long string of red yarn. Whatever else could be said of Thalia, she was a loving mother and spent time with her children. She looked up from embroidering the neckline of a small gown for Helena.

"Ah, there you are. A new hairstyle, Pandora? How very nice to see you taking some interest in your appearance."

"Where are the boys?" asked Phemie as she took an opposite chair and opened her box.

"With their tutor for the morning. Let me see what you are working on."

"Mama gave me several pieces of soft flannel cloth to make into little shirts. She thought it would help me pass the time. See, I've drawn a pattern of lions around the neck and will fill them in with red floss."

Thalia laughed and shook her head at her sister's inexperience. "Oh my, no. Babies are forever puking and spitting and drooling. Their clothes must be boiled frequently, and the red will run in the process. Best to keep the day-to-day garments simple. However, I have some delicate lawn that we could gather into several layers and garnish with lace at the hem and cuffs to make a christening gown. We could devise a tiny cap and embroider it with pastel flowers. You could put more on the yoke. Wouldn't that be wonderful, your gift to the child from its loving aunt?"

Phemie's eyes filled again, and she had neither pinched nor pricked herself. Staring down at the lion pattern, she managed to say, "I think flowers would not do for a boy."

"Well then, we will simply go with the lace and some white-on-white design that could be used for either sex. Pandora, what is your project?"

"As you said, a simple shirt." She held up a piece of red flannel already cut into shape.

"Let me see it. Something seems wrong. Ah, you've sewn the neck hole closed. You must rip it out and hem the edges."

"Damnation, how can I concentrate on making a shirt when women are always yammering when they sew?"

Little Helena's bright gray eyes, uncannily the same as Lady Flora's, fixed on her aunt's face. Her tiny pink lips formed the word, "Damnation." The child repeated it three times to fix it in her vocabulary.

"See what you've done, Pandora, corrupted my daughter. Never, never say that word again, Helena. It is unladylike."

"Damnation!" the child crowed, throwing spools into the air.

"Papa said it in front of his children, and we have turned out perfectly well." Pandora insisted.

"*That* is a matter of opinion." Thalia rose and tucked the little girl under her arm. Black curls tumbled over the small, defiant face. "If you persist, we must wash your mouth with soap."

"Damnation," Helena said again as she kicked her heels to get down. Her mother carried her from the room.

Pandora enjoyed the moment with an amused smile on her face. "I've never cared much for children, but I think I like this one. She has a will of her own. Still Phemie, are you sure you want to abandon this safe haven for your baby? Thalia will bring it up well and in a far more orthodox way than we were raised. I mean, what if we cannot find Leo?"

Phemie's brown eyes had cleared, and she stared at Pandora with that stubborn look from childhood.

"Leo will be at the Cave of the Seven Men waiting for me. You shall see. Thank you again for helping me get there."

~ * ~

They waited in the courtyard long after the walls had begun to lose their heat and the sun had sunk toward the western horizon. Phemie wrapped her shawl more tightly. Pandora, in lieu of pacing, made several vigorous laps of the area. At last, they heard a horse advancing at a light canter up the hill and rushed to reach the front entrance. Each opened one of the small doors and tumbled out before a servant could assist them. They met Jason partway down the lane.

"Such an enthusiastic welcome," Jason remarked. He dismounted and led his steed by the reins.

"Do you have the letter?" Pandora pressed.

"Of course. I paid a scrivener to write it out from my dictation lest Thalia recognize my handwriting. Your berth aboard the *Selkie* bound for Inverness in two days' time is secured under the names of Porteus and Iphigenia Crowe. I inspected the vessel personally as it sat at dock—very seaworthy."

His preening a bit over his handling of the matter goaded Pandora into saying, "Never having been to sea, how would you know?"

"But I have associated with sailors and bought them many a tot of rum to glean their stories for my poems. Actually, the same inducement works when one wants to find a reliable captain and a good ship. How I wish I were going along on your little excursion. These wretched wars with the French and the Americans have kept me landlocked. Now my sisters go to sea whilst I wither in London trying to force my eyes to read page after page of legal text."

Phemie patted his arm sympathetically. "Your time will come for adventure. But such names, Jason. Why not simply John and Jane Smith?"

"Boring, and no one would believe it. Smith is the name an eloping young couple would use, and we wouldn't want anyone to think that. We are about to have company. Pandora, your letter. Prepare to be overcome." Jason removed the missive from his waistcoat and placed it in her hands.

Holding the hand of her younger son, Thalia came toward them. Axel, the elder boy, raced to meet their group. "Uncle Jason, Uncle Jason, did you bring us a present from Hull?"

"I found several things of interest in Hull, but first you must do me a service." He lifted his younger nephew into the saddle and handed the reins to Axel. "Lead him carefully to the stables, walk him until he has cooled, and you shall have your gift."

Thalia beamed at the good uncle. Her children were ever her weakness, as they all knew well. He leaned closer to her ear. "I thought it best to give Pandora time to compose herself."

"Whatever for?"

"I encountered an acquaintance in Hull, one of Sir Samuel's younger sons who makes his way in the navy. He, in turn, informed me of another person of interest, a sailor recovering from battle wounds. We paid a visit and asked if we could do anything to speed his recovery. Only one thing, he said. Carry my letter to Pandora."

"A sailor speaks of her so familiarly?"

Jason nodded. "A young lieutenant whom Salisbury introduced to her last season. I believe Pandora was quite taken with him, but he was bound for America within a few weeks. Now he says he regrets never having made his intentions clear."

Thalia's face displayed her incredulity. "He had intentions toward Pandora and she did not rebuff him like all the others?"

"I think not. Only look at her."

Pandora stood, one hand clasped over her heart, the other holding the letter. Her head bent, flushed from quick pinches to her cheeks only Phemie observed, as she read the words her brother had written from her fictional suitor.

> *My Dearest Pandora—since you gave me*
> *leave to address you so,*
> *I sit in Hull, an invalid, a victim of a*
> *bombardment. Knowing myself unworthy*

*of you, I could not speak before I ventured
forth hoping to gain fame, fortune, and
advancement in my naval career through the
taking of American ships. Alas, I have not
succeeded, though should I live, I have some
expectation of sharing in the profits from the
sale of the vessel that, in the conquering, led
to my sad condition.*

*Still, if I should pass from this earth
without telling you of my deepest regard, my
most sincere love for you, I would be in Hell
for all eternity even if the Lord God himself
should place me in Paradise. I beg of you to
come to my side so that I might draw strength
from a single touch of your hand and feel
once more a lock of your silken, raven hair
betwixt my fingers. The fire of your dark eyes
will warm my soul once more and, perhaps
persuade it to remain within my mortal form.
I cling to life awaiting your visit.*

Yr most Admiring and Adoring,

Josiah Weatherby,

Lt. His Royal Majesty's Navy

Pandora raised her eyes to Thalia's. "I must go to him." She made a gesture as if she meant to hide the letter in her bodice, but her sister snatched it away.

Thalia skimmed down the single page. "My, this is most ardent and intimate. Lieutenant Weatherby writes a very firm and elegant hand for a man on his deathbed. Are you certain his wounds are so grave, Jason, or is that too indelicate a question to ask? I would not have Pandora lured to Hull and her affections taken advantage of by a poseur after her dowry."

"I, um, assure you the lieutenant is in dire straits. He's lost some limbs. Salisbury had to write for him."

"More than one limb?"

Jason scrambled for an answer. "Ah, yes. His right arm and—and a foot which has left a festering wound. He will never dance again—if he lives."

"Pandora, are you sure you wish to encourage this man who will be crippled all his life if he survives?"

Pandora lifted her head and set it at her most defiant angle. "Do you think me so shallow that I would cower from a hero's wounds or have any less affection for him because of them?"

"I would never accuse you of being shallow. You are so deep men cannot fathom you. I suppose this might be your only chance to mar... to see Lieutenant Weatherby again. If you are set on granting his desire, we shall take my carriage to Hull first thing in the morning. I am sure my dear friend, the Lady Pillsbury, will offer us accommodations for our stay."

Alarmed, Phemie blurted, "But you are supposed to be in a delicate condition and very ill. Our plan will come to naught if you go to Hull as if nothing were wrong."

"I suppose you are right."

"Never fear, dear Thalia, I shall escort her and see her safely to and fro." Jason expanded his arms in a generous gesture.

"To further confuse people, I will go also—to provide Panny with an understanding female companion and to show nothing is amiss with me," Phemie extemporized.

"But Phemie, you shouldn't be exposed to such a sight. What if the baby should be born without a foot or arm?"

"How can you believe that old wives' tale when we live in an age of science and enlightenment? If it will make you feel better, I shall stay outside the sickroom."

"Do that for me. However, I insist you stay with Lady Pillsbury. I will pen a letter immediately asking her to extend you hospitality."

"No need, sister dear. A reputable inn sits very near where our valiant sailor lies abed. I stayed there on my visit and will pay for the lodging," Jason volunteered.

"I have no idea which amazes me more—Pandora's unexpected suitor, or your willingness to part with any of your allowance, Jason.

Far be it from me to quash any of your better impulses. Have the maid pack your belongings for a short stay. Panny, do take something stylish. Even a dying man would prefer to see a lady in a fashionable frock. Go prepare then."

Thalia clapped her hands as if urging on reluctant children. Jason, Pandora, and Phemie jumped to obey. The young women held up their skirts and raced up the hill. Jason easily outdistanced them with his long, trouser-clad legs.

Thalia called after them. "Go with more decorum, ladies."

Pandora sniffed at her sister's command. "If I wore pantaloons, I could beat Jason."

"I doubt it, as you are not as tall. Do you think Thalia has always been so strait-laced and proper? We were very young when she married," Phemie asked.

Jason leaned in the doorway gloating over his quicker arrival. "We were all raised in the same family, so I doubt it. What is it Mama says—that propriety comes when one has children and must set an example?" Gallantly, he opened the door for his sisters and let them pass first.

"I am following Mama's example, but she will not like it," Phemie laughed.

"Certainly, Thalia has secrets. One day we will find them out, and she will never be able to flaunt her superiority over the second five Longleighs again. Until then, we must simply enjoy making a fool of her." Pandora reached the second set of doors to the family wing and practiced her masculine role by bowing and opening them with a flourish for Phemie and Jason to pass through before the astonished footman standing guard could do his duty.

Twenty-five

"We've done it, escaped from Battle Hill!" Phemie and Pandora linked arms and danced so wildly about their chamber that those below at the Viking's Head Inn must have assumed a party was in progress, and they were not invited.

"Oh, the gratefulness of Thalia's coachman when we told him we would not need his services because we intended to walk to our destination, and he could have a few days to visit family in Hull. Then into a hackney coach to reach this place with only the carriage horses boarding at the more respectable inn." Phemie grasped her sister's hands and spun with her in a circle again. "I am on my way to Leo!"

"Quiet, do you want to be tossed out and have to find another place so late in the evening?" Jason fussed.

"As if a rumpus would be noticed here so close to the docks. What a deliciously awful place. I do adore the grisly painting of the beheaded Viking hanging above the entrance." Pandora settled into a chair that wobbled under her weight.

"Vikings had a low popularity in the area, but the place is expedient, as you leave on the morning tide. I shall sleep by your door, though I suspect from all the noise, the proprietor thinks I have taken the room to cavort with two shameless doxies."

Phemie eyes sparkled at his statement. "Leo thought I might be mistaken as his light lady when we traveled through Scotland. I believe the idea bothered him, but not me."

"I am seeing a side of my baby sister I've never suspected—nor wished to see. But it is good you are joyful again. Panny, I will step out and allow you to assume your masculine garb. You might need further directions."

Pandora opened their one small trunk and took out the men's garments she had added after the maid finished packing for both of them. She had also rooted out her own clothes and stuffed in extra for Phemie. Ever practical, she'd also added a set of sheets filched from Thalia's linen closet as Mama always said better to travel with one's own bedding, considering the unsanitary state of many inns along the way. Observing the sway-backed bed the sisters would share this evening, it seemed a prudent choice.

She had her costume on in minutes and called Jason to enter. "Ah, men's clothing, so much easier to assume if not too particular about a tight fit or an elaborate neckcloth arrangement."

Phemie claimed the single chair as Pandora strutted about the room, putting on a show for her brother. She opened the sewing box brought along on the pretext of needing something to pass the time and took out the little shirt with the lion pattern drawn around the neckline. Defiantly, she threaded her needle with red floss and began to fill in the figures with a satin stitch by the light of a guttering tallow candle.

"I do not care how carefully it must be washed!"

"What is that you say, dear sister?" Pandora inquired in a deepened voice.

"The garment for my son. Thalia said the red would run in the wash."

"I know nothing about such female matters. Do as you wish." She flicked her hand in disdain.

Jason threw back his head and laughed. "You make a splendid man, Panny, but I must suggest a few refinements."

He took the sewing scissors from Phemie's box and tugged free a lock of black hair on either side of her face from the long braid she had let down but not bothered to double over and tie. Two quick snips and he smoothed down the short ends beside her ears.

"There, this gives you some semblance of having side whiskers if you glue them down with pomade. A bit of grime applied to the chin will help disguise the lack of a beard. I am sure we can find some grime around here. You should also have a watch for your pocket and a walking stick. I offer you mine." With a courtly gesture, he held the items out to Pandora.

"I cannot take the watch. Papa gave it to you to make certain you did not miss any important judicial sessions while you study to be a barrister."

"I assure you, having an accurate timepiece will never force me to arrive on time at any boring place I do not choose to be. I can always ask the hour of Joshua. Besides, I have a less costly watch that runs fifteen minutes slow and affords me with the best of excuses. Twist the head of the cane."

Pandora did, and with glee, drew out a hidden sword. She took a few cuts through the air with the blade, narrowly missing Jason's right arm. "Now this I truly can use!"

"Try not to injure yourself or others unnecessarily. Panny, these items are only on loan. I will expect them back when you are safely returned from Scotland. I do mean that. Take care."

Catching her off-guard and almost getting nicked with the sword in the process, he embraced his wayward sister, coming in contact with her soft pillow stomach. "Now that's an odd feeling. I suggest you bump into no one. They will think you very out of condition and take advantage of your weakness. Damn it all! I should be the one escorting Phemie."

Pandora shook her head. "Papa would treat you far more harshly than me. I hope you have your story concocted about our escape."

"Never fear, my imagination seldom fails me. By the time I return to Battle Hill, our parents will be far enough away to make a fast return difficult. I fear poor Lieutenant Weatherby must succumb to his wounds, and you, Pandora, deranged by grief over losing your only chance to marry, have run off with Phemie to help raise her child in some distant land."

"My only chance to marry? I could have proposals if I wanted them." Such an odd statement coming from Pandora in her masculine attire made the others laugh, a light moment badly needed.

Phemie rummaged in her sewing box and delved a pouch from the very bottom. "Here, take the money Mama gave me for gowns to pay for our passage and this fine establishment." She gestured at the dingy gray walls and the stingy dormer window letting in chilly puffs of autumn air around its loose frame.

"Keep it for your own use. I paid with the funds Papa gave me for cheap woolens. I should be the one going with you."

"You kept nothing for yourself. Do not worry, all will be well, Jason," Phemie said with feeling.

"God, I hope so."

Twenty-six

They stood by the railing in the dim morning light as the *Selkie* pointed her figurehead of a half-naked woman emerging from the body of a seal toward the mouth of the estuary. The figure of Jason waving farewell, the lace at his cuffs limp with the damp, merged with the light drizzle accompanying them to Scotland and disappeared.

The young woman standing next to Phemie inquired, "Who was that handsome young man bidding you farewell? Your intended, perhaps? He seemed most bereft."

Phemie answered the overly familiar questions instead of ignoring them. They had agreed to keep to themselves and lie low, and, to Pandora's chagrin, here she was befriending this intrusive girl with the lank brown curls and misty blue eyes.

"No, he is my brother, a poet who feels very deeply. I travel to Inverness to meet my future husband with Porteus, my other brother. I am Iphigenia Crowe.

"Oh, I do see the resemblance between them. Both are dark, though the other is so tall and...this brother is more....Gladys Hotchkiss, so delighted to meet you. So pleased to have the company of another woman on the voyage and a gentleman, too. Perhaps I will find a husband in Scotland."

Judging by the eager bobbing of her head, it took very little to please Gladys. Each nod should have been accompanied by the spring of the long curls beside her pleasant, unremarkable face, but the wet air had turned them stringy. She twined one around a stubby finger as if trying to restore it. A dollop of moisture accumulated on the edge of her bonnet and dropped down on her equally stubby and slightly red nose. Flustered, the young woman bit her chapped lips and searched frantically for her hankie.

Gladys had the desperation of a girl who had failed to find a match her second or even third year out of the schoolroom. Pandora had observed this panic to please often enough at Almack's, though Miss Hotchkiss would not have qualified for that exclusive husband hunting club, judging by the quality of her clothes and her lack of aplomb. Probably she'd been shipped off to Scotland in hopes of finding some prospects there. It was one thing to choose spinsterhood within the safety and comfort of a ducal mansion, and quite another to be set unwillingly on a middle-class shelf. Pandora's heart went out to her.

"Allow me." She presented Gladys with her own handkerchief made masculine by the ripping off of lace and picking out of floral embroidery, a well-developed skill due to her many sewing errors. She might have presented Miss Hotchkiss with the rarest of orchids from the reaction received.

"Oh, how extraordinarily kind of you, Mr. Crowe. How can I repay you?" Gladys dabbed delicately at her red nose.

"By sitting beside me at the captain's table and sharing your conversation." The words were out before Panny considered them. She'd only meant to give the girl some self-confidence, but by the lighting of hope in those watery, blue eyes, Pandora knew she'd done much too much more. No gentlemanly way out now, for the moment.

"Grandfather, do come meet the Crowes, Porteus and Ip-ah-phagia. They are also bound for Inverness," Miss Hotchkiss cried out eagerly, betraying at the same time a total lack of a classical education.

Phemie corrected gently, "Iphigenia, after the woman who was to be a virgin sacrifice for the Greeks before they sailed to Troy. Please, simply call me Effie instead."

A spare elderly man of lofty if stooped height, his thick gray hair bushing out on either side of his tall hat and with vigorous side whiskers turning white framing his gaunt face, made his way along the deck to their group with the aid of a stout, knob-headed cane. Showing his hearing was still sharp, and his tongue sharper, he acknowledged his granddaughter's new friends with a curt bow and a flat statement. "A pity your parents cursed you with such a heathen name. Virgin sacrifice, indeed."

"Grandfather is a Presbyterian minister who leads a congregation in Inverness," Gladys explained, as an embarrassed flush bloomed on her cheeks. "I am to spend some time with him. Perhaps you and your fiancé might come to call on us—and your brother, too." There it was again, that faint tinge of hope.

"Ask for the residence of the Reverend Andrew Hotchkiss. My church and my sermons are well-regarded in Inverness."

Even though they had not been properly introduced, Phemie answered courteously, "A pleasure to make your acquaintance, Reverend Hotchkiss." With a slight smile, she continued, "Actually, my parents are not at fault. My brother named me."

"They permitted that?"

"He did not appear so much older than the two of you as he stood on the dock," Gladys said, clearly picturing the striking poet by the faraway look in her eyes.

Pandora deepened her voice all she could. "Jason was a precocious child, learned Greek at an early age and so impressed my parents, they allowed him to name his baby sister. However, his talents are wasted composing poetry and chasing after sponsors for his work."

"Jason Crowe? I have never heard of him," Reverend Hotchkiss stated.

"Precisely. A young lady such as your granddaughter should avoid such romantic characters and consider more substantial men who would allow her the freedom to do good works." Pandora wondered if she sounded as pompous as most men and thought she did.

"Such as yourself, Mr. Crowe? How do you make your way in the world?" The old man appeared to see right through her manly disguise. His eyes flicked from the gold watch chain draped across the soft belly to the shining but shabby boots and the lethal walking stick.

"Why, um, I am a wool factor. I travel frequently in Scotland gathering wool and a—selling it to spinning mills for a tidy profit. No sense in wearing new boots to muck about on sheep farms, eh?" Jason was not the only Longleigh who could spin a tale.

Phemie pressed her fingers to her lips and turned to gaze at the water for a moment. Regaining her composure, she said, "I believe the weather will clear by afternoon. Until then, I think we should be sure our trunks were delivered to the proper cabins and get out of this dampness. It cannot be good for the lungs. I look forward to seeing you both at dinner. Come, brother."

She held out her arm and, after a moment's hesitation, Pandora offered hers for support. They made their way across the deck and down the steps to the cabins. Both entered the same room and as the door closed, Phemie flung herself on the boxed-in bed and allowed her laughter to ring. "A wool factor! However did you come up with that?"

"What else does Scotland have but sheep? If Jason had been less stingy with his garments, I might have aspired to something higher. As it is, I look as if I buy my clothes from a secondhand clothier." Panny tossed the hat that completed her costume onto a wall peg. The edge of its brim had lost its curl and gone soft from repeated wearing.

"I believe Miss Hotchkiss will overlook your outfit. She seems very taken with you."

"Nonsense. She is mooning over Jason standing in the mist with his woebegone expression plastered on his face."

"You advised her to seek a man of substance—like you. Oh, Panny, what have you done? I never thought our voyage would be so amusing." With her hands holding her belly now showing the very slightest of curves, Phemie giggled until the tears ran down her cheeks.

"If I can make you laugh, I do not mind that the joke is on me. Now to get through dinner without becoming engaged."

~ * ~

Miss Hotchkiss kept her promise to sit beside Porteus Crowe when they dined. Her grandfather, across the table and next to Phemie, provided a lengthy blessing for the meal, giving thanks for the plain, sustaining food and asking for fair weather and a safe voyage for all aboard. Once he raised his head and opened blue eyes far more perceptive than his granddaughter's, the preacher never took his gaze from the face of her potential suitor.

"Did you pass a good morning, Miss Hotchkiss?" Panny asked, posing the most innocent question one could ask outside of the state of the weather.

"Grandfather and I read the Bible in our cabin."

"Gladys has a solid Sunday school education, young man, and can both read and write a plain hand and do her sums," her grandfather added. "Women need little more education than that. More leads them astray, gives them unseemly airs and opinions."

No words were more likely to ignite Pandora's temper, except a defense of slavery. Phemie put a hand on her arm to stay the explosion. None came.

Instead, her Pandora answered smoothly, "I would value Miss Hotchkiss's opinion in any matter. If I found her to be ill-informed, I would endeavor to steer her gently to another conclusion, sir."

"You would?" the subject of the masculine conversation said, dropping her spoon abruptly into a bowl of oyster stew and splattering the top of the table to top as well as herself.

"There, you see, giving consequence to their opinions only flusters the female mind," the old man asserted. He raised his own spoon and sucked up the milky broth and a plump oyster.

Having brought along a large supply of her own poorly hemmed efforts, Pandora offered Miss Hotchkiss another handkerchief as she could not find her own once more. As Gladys scrubbed at the splotches on her gown, Phemie said, "Never fear, I do not believe the soup will stain, and if it does, I know a receipt for spot removal."

"That is exactly what I mean. Women should confine themselves and their conversation to the topics of hearth and home. I can see your sister is a well-bred young lady who would never encroach on the purview of men." The reverend gave Phemie an approving nod.

Pandora observed Phemie's quickly quelled outrage. Even if their mother did try to make them into perfect ladies, their opinions had always been welcomed, and their intellects indulged within the walls of Bellevue Hall. How confining and dreary to be Miss Hotchkiss.

Panny smirked. "Let us say you have but a short acquaintance with my sister." She let that statement lie, however, and returned to eating her stew.

Other gentlemen took up the conversation, speaking of their experiences at various stops along the way for the edification of the less well-traveled women. In other words, little of substance was said for the remainder of the meal.

The ladies retired from the company. The men stayed behind with their port and pipes and talk of politics and war. Pandora more than held her own in knowledge of the subjects as she read the newspapers avidly and had never been prevented from doing so. As for port, the wine was quite sweet, and she rather preferred it to sherry. No reason on earth that men should keep it to themselves, as far as she could see. At first, she declined an offer of a pipe of tobacco and instantly won the minister's approval, which immediately compelled her to accept a cigar from the captain.

"My brother, Joshua, prefers them to a pipe. I must keep an open mind and give it a try." After a few puffs, she indicated she thought she would enjoy the smoke more in the open air and excused herself for a stroll on the deck. There she found Phemie and Gladys walking arm in arm.

"Are you ill, Pan—Porteus?" Phemie asked. "*Mal de mer*? You have turned quite green, yet the sea is very quiet tonight."

"Cigar," she answered and tossed it over the side.

Miss Hotchkiss applauded that decision. "Grandfather says tobacco is the Devil's weed."

"In that, he might well be right."

Not long after Pandora's decision never to accept another cigar, Reverend Hotchkiss came seeking his granddaughter. "I thought you had returned to the cabin, child."

"Truly, I felt in need of exercise, and I had Effie's companionship the whole time, and then Mr. Crowe's company."

"Time to go below again and say our evening prayers."

"Yes, Grandfather. Effie said according to her itinerary we shall dock at Scarborough to take on more goods. There is a splendid promenade along the cliffs that we might enjoy. Could we go ashore, all of us?"

"If my rheumatism is not acting up, I will consider it. Good evening, Miss Crowe, Mr. Crowe." With his thick, black stick thumping on the deck, he herded his granddaughter before him like the Good Shepherd guiding his flock.

Pandora leaned her arms on the railing and allowed her rump to protrude in a deliciously masculine way while Phemie stood beside her with hands folded. Both contemplated the dark bulk of the land mass off to the left, and the stars growing in number as the light faded.

"I do believe I enjoy the sea and would like it even more if Mama had not kept us from learning to swim. All the boys were allowed. Sometimes, I dream of drowning because I would not be able to save myself."

"She feared for our modesty and our complexions, but you know nothing of the sea until you have skimmed across its surface racing before the wind in a small boat as Leo and I did on the firth. With Leo at the tiller and sail, I never worried about overturning. This coastal vessel is plodding along compared to that experience."

"I do envy you. Imagine what it must be like on the open sea crossing the wide Atlantic. I know I shall never smoke another cigar, but I would like to go on a great voyage."

"Someday you might, fighting off privateers as Flora MacDonald did."

"Yes, I can see myself doing that."

"In the meantime, we must help poor Gladys Hotchkiss. She is most desperate."

"No surprise there, but do not expect me to marry her."

Phemie shook her head, making the ringlets around her face bounce in a manner men found adorable. "No, but you can continue to pay her some attention to restore her confidence. Her mother passed away a year ago leaving her in the care of a stepfather with no good intentions. He made little attempt to find her a husband and indeed, tried to force himself upon her."

"Shocking."

"Yes. She wrote her grandfather, who came to take her away, but as you can tell, he is quite the old tyrant. She fears she will remain his housekeeper and caretaker in old age and never wed. Her mother, it seems, bore her out of wedlock. The reverend arranged for his daughter to marry an older man of his acquaintance who lived in Hull to contain the scandal. They had no issue, but the stepfather still declined to adopt Gladys. He was to provide a small dowry, but now that will not come to pass."

Pandora straightened. "You learned all this on a short promenade."

"Women do confide."

"Not in me."

"You make most women feel silly and shallow and their concerns too light."

"Well, nearly all are, but this is more serious. I would gladly run the stepfather through if I had the chance."

Phemie took her hand and squeezed it. "You always tried to protect me at school."

"But I could not save you from Leo."

"I thank heaven you did not. He is my true love. No, all I am asking is that you pay some attention to Gladys and try to bring out her good points. She is sweet and uncertain, but has good domestic skills and some more delicate accomplishments, thanks to her mother's efforts. The other men aboard might take notice and consider her. Please help her to shine."

"You have my promise on that."

~ * ~

The reverend's rheumatism did not allow him to accompany the shore party on their excursion up the cliffs, even though they took transportation from the dock. At first, it seemed he would deny his granddaughter the pleasure, too, but Phemie, in that sweet way of hers, convinced him that Gladys would be safe in the company of the Crowes. They looked in at the spa with its healing pools of water and enjoyed the delightful gardens and wonderful views from the south promenade.

Trying her best to bolster the girl, Pandora complimented Miss Hotchkiss on her rosy cheeks brought out by the spanking breeze and how nicely she had arranged her hair—as it should be, since Gladys and Phemie had spent a great deal of time primping in the cabin before the excursion. As she'd paced the deck waiting to depart, she experienced some of the impatience men must feel while women wasted time on their appearance. Still, Phemie had improved Miss Hotchkiss quite a bit in a very short period with the tiniest bit of powder to cover the redness of her upturned nose and the merest touch of lip rouge to enhance a very pretty, if chapped, mouth.

In the hackney on the way back to the ship, Gladys brought up the subject of the old ballad about Scarborough Fair and asked if Mr. Crowe knew it. Of course, Pandora did. She had not been favored with her mother's light soprano voice possessed by all the sisters except her and Iris. At school, she had always been forced to sing the alto parts and often been obliged to take the male role in duets because of her lower range. Phemie declared her sister's voice was rich and strong, small comfort when the other girls giggled.

"Yes, I have sung it a few times."

"Might we present it for entertainment this evening as a fitting end to such a fine day?"

"I do not think…"

"Porteus would be happy to join you in a duet. He has a very good voice," Phemie rushed to say.

"Mama saw that I had some lessons. I would not shame you with my performance."

"I am certain your voice is lovely," Phemie said as she alighted from the coach, Pandora having jumped out first to assist both the ladies.

They all linked arms with Pandora in the middle to walk the short way to the ship. She did not feel the actual snatch, just a light tug as her watch chain left its buttonhole. Seeing only a portly man encumbered with two women, the thief, an underfed urchin of the docks, had overestimated his skill and underestimated the speed of his victim's reaction. He sauntered away, tucking his prize quickly out of sight into an inner pocket of a loose, shabby jacket.

Dropping both arms, Pandora spun and unsheathed the blade hidden in her cane. Only the pounding boots behind him caused the boy to pick up speed after a quick glance over the shoulder. Pandora bore down on him, leading with the blade. The small thief slipped out of his jacket just as she reached him and slashed the tip of the sword through the fabric. He scooted down an alleyway, leaving his impaled coat behind for Pandora to retrieve the watch as well as several men's handkerchiefs. She left the jacket draped over a barrel and returned to the women.

"There, I have saved Papa's watch and gained some fine handkerchiefs as well," she jested.

Miss Hotchkiss, her usually vague blue eyes sparkling, gushed, "That was so thrilling."

"Yes, it was exhilarating."

"But why did you leave the jacket and not pursue the boy?"

"The lad will have need of the coat. The poor turn to thievery because they have no other choice. If free education were more prevalent, it is my belief that crime would decrease."

Gladys handed over the hollow cane she had picked up from the ground and observed as Pandora replaced the blade. "You are both valiant and charitable, Mr. Crowe. Grandfather would say a thief is preordained to die on the gallows. As for the poor, surely they have done something to deserve their low lot in life."

"We do not choose our parents."

"Yes, I am all too aware of that. But you will sing with me tonight?"

Phemie gave her such a look that Pandora found herself saying, "It would be my greatest pleasure."

~ * ~

That evening at dinner everything about Miss Hotchkiss gleamed: her lackluster curls now treated with some kind of feminine concoction Pandora had never used nor needed; her blue eyes that sought those of Porteus Crowe time and again; her gown embellished with an inset of silver lace straight from Phemie's trunk. Phemie knew the way of such things almost as adeptly as the duchess. Naturally, Gladys's animation when she told of their small adventure in Scarborough added to the glow of her face under the gently swaying, gimbaled lanterns illuminating the dining table.

The other men did take notice, especially a merchant of some forty years who thought to mention he had been widowed in the past year and left with three half-grown children.

A bit gray about the temples and no less stout than Porteus appeared to be, he asked, "Why did you allow the street rat to escape? You should have run him through. One less petty thief to grow into a greater hazard."

"When I first turned, I thought I pursued an adult perpetrator. Seeing the small size of my quarry, I only meant to prick him and have my watch returned, which did come to pass. This close call might force the lad to consider other ways of making a living."

Both the merchant and the reverend said, "Ha!" simultaneously.

"I believe Mr. Crowe showed a great gentleness of heart." Considering her grandfather's glare when she spoke up, Gladys put on a brave show herself. She plunged on while her courage remained up. "In honor of our visit to Scarborough, Mr. Crowe and I have prepared a small after dinner entertainment for all of you."

One or two of the company seemed out of joint to have their port and pipes delayed, but the captain said he welcomed the diversion and several others chimed in to encourage Miss Hotchkiss to rise and perform her song. Reluctantly, Pandora stood, too, ready to do her part. They'd had scant time to prepare and had only agreed that she would sing the first verse, he the second, she the third, and then combine their voices in the last chorus. And so they began:

Are you going to Scarborough fair?
Parsley, sage, rosemary and thyme
Remember me to one who lives there
He once was a true love of mine

Tell her to make me a cambric shirt
Parsley, sage, rosemary and thyme
Without no seam or needlework
Then she'll be a true love of mine

Tell him to find me an acre of land
Parsley, sage, rosemary and thyme
Between the salt water and the sea strand
Then, he'll be a true love of mine.

Are you going to Scarborough fair?
Parsley, sage, rosemary and thyme
Remember me to one who lives there
She once was a true love of mine.

"Bravo, very charming," said the captain, retired from the king's navy but unable to give up the salt sea. "Entertainment aboard ship is always welcome and especially when so well-performed."

"Humpf," said the reverend. "The tune is from an old Scottish ayre and speaks of fickleness in love. Could you not find something more appropriate, Gladys?"

Miss Hotchkiss's elated smile at the captain's comment winked out like the stars at dawn. The rest of her faded as well, a light extinguished. She excused herself so the men might have some time to themselves and hurried from the room. Phemie, not bothering with polite phrases, went after her.

Pandora wanted to leave as well but forced herself to stay as smoke rose to the rafters and glasses clinked. She declined the offer of another cigar but could not escape an invitation to play chess with Reverend Hotchkiss while the other men indulged in their vices, or so the minister implied. She played well enough, though Phemie was the true master of the game. Only Justinian could best her baby sister among the family, and he had shown himself to be a sort of prodigy. She made these remarks as each moved their pieces on a small table inlaid with the pattern of a checkered board.

"You have a great many brothers, Mr. Crowe."

"I do, four in all."

"Are each as peculiar as you?"

"I beg your pardon?"

"You, sir, have the complexion of an outdoorsman, but hands near as soft as a woman's."

"My trade does take me out of doors a great deal, and the handling of greasy fleece acts as a balm to my hands." She made a move calculated to end the game quickly.

"I observe you are beardless and have a voice somewhat high for a man. Did you, perhaps, suffer an accident that might make you unable to perform marital duties? I ask only because you are taking a deep interest in Gladys."

Pandora stood and clothed herself in outrage. "If you must know, my grandfather was some time in the American colonies and fathered a child on a Shawnee woman. If knowing I carry the blood of a Red Indian in my veins offends you, I withdraw all interest in your granddaughter. As for my voice, I have known men with higher who are completely natural. I bid you good-night." She moved her queen. "Checkmate."

"Sit, sit. We are all God's creatures. A man must protect weak-brained females who would bestow their affections on the first man who pays them any attention." The reverend's knotted, arthritic fingers set the chess pieces back into their starting positions. "Church of England, are you?"

"Yes." Cautiously, Pandora resumed her seat and moved a pawn.

"I do question how any thinking person can engage in a set of religious principals devised to allow a king to divorce." Challenge issued.

"I have often asked myself that."

"Then, your mind would be open to other beliefs, purer in origin, not dominated by papist forms of worship."

"I am open-minded on most subjects, but adamant about one, the abolition of slavery."

"There we do have common ground."

"Which goes hand in hand with equity for women."

"We part ways again." Hotchkiss seized her pawn and set it on his side of the table. "Do you make a good living as a wool factor? Is it a lucrative trade?"

"I do very nicely. I have twenty-thousand pounds at my disposal."

True enough, the amount constituted her dowry. How Mama would fuss over this crass revelation or even the previous discussion of religion. But then, men among men said what they pleased, or at least, she thought so. Pandora moved her knight carelessly and immediately saw her error. The reverend's sharp, blue eyes glittered—with cunning or with avarice, she could not tell.

"Then, I give you permission to court my granddaughter. Check and mate."

"I-I am honored." No, no, she should have said she was not at liberty to marry. "We are even now, and so I bid you good evening."

Hotchkiss smiled with teeth as long and yellow as the old stallion, Bosworth. "Sleep well, Mr. Crowe, now that you have my blessing." He opened the drawer beneath the table and meticulously set each piece in the place where it belonged.

Pandora made for Phemie's cabin as fast as she could, relieved when she found her sister alone reading a small volume of Mr. Scott's *Marmion*, purloined from Thalia's library and packed to pass the time on the journey. She took a ladder-backed chair from its pegs on the wall, threw herself into it, splayed out her legs and put her face into her hands.

"Whatever is wrong, Panny? I thought you were enjoying your life as a man."

"Reverend Hotchkiss has given me permission to court Gladys. A trap...I fell right into it."

"You were only to give her some attention and arouse the interest of the other men."

"I know, I know."

Phemie considered her sister's masculine posture. "Are you sure this was a mistake and not something you secretly wish? Could it be you are like Countess Rushmore who prefers women to men? If so, I would try to understand."

"No, heavens, no! I simply want the same rights as men, to have my ideas taken seriously, to wear trousers if I damn well please because they are so comfortable and convenient, and to say damn if I wish—but I do not want to marry a woman or be a man."

"Then I hope you will find a man who will respect your opinions, fight for your rights, and love you just as you are."

"Unlikely, since I am practically engaged to Miss Hotchkiss."

"Never despair. We are Longleighs, and the Longleighs are nothing if not inventive. We will kill this courtship—without crushing Gladys."

Twenty-seven

Jason Longleigh sat in a straight-backed library chair while the duke in full Great Bear mode paced before him. He often thought of his father by his Indian name, since it suited the man so perfectly. Well, at least he had survived the initial interrogation by Godric White Hair, a sobriquet he'd devised for his brother-in-law and thought to use in an epic poem centering on Vikings. His mind wandered, composing a few lines as Papa roared and ranted.

The duchess fluttered in the background, though he knew very well she was not the fragile social butterfly many supposed her to be. She reached out one small, delicate hand and stilled the beast in his tracks. "Please dearest, allow Jason to tell his story from the beginning. We might learn something. Cursing over his letting Phemie and Pandora escape does no good at all."

The duke waved one of those big paws of his and said, "Talk."

"As I told Rick, we put up in a respectable inn. Pandora insisted on flying at once to Lieutenant Weatherby's bedside. Phemie and I went with her, of course. He had worsened greatly since I last saw him. Oh, oh, the stench from his rotting limb! I can smell it still." To add to the drama, he pinched his nostrils for a moment before going on with his tale. "But Panny was stalwart and would not leave his side nor let go of his remaining hand."

"Yes, Pandora would not be put off by any such thing," the duchess agreed.

"Deep in the night, his soul departed for God's realm even as my sister held him in her arms. Wailing and weeping, she threw herself upon his cooling corpse and could not be parted until dawn."

"Our Pandora did that? Seems unlikely," the duke said. "Whatever else, she has always shown good sense. I'd rather expect she would call the undertaker and arrange for a sturdy lead coffin to contain the effluvia like the one we ordered for Kate."

The duchess tapped him with her fan. "Our daughter does have tender womanly emotions, deeply buried, but still there, I am sure."

"Arrangements were made for Weatherby's burial and, by that time, evening had come again. We were all greatly exhausted. After seeing my sisters to their chamber, I admit I slept long and hard well into the next morning. By that time, they had vanished, called a hackney, taken their small trunk and were gone. Since I had given Thalia's coachman leave to visit relatives while we sat with the lieutenant, I had to send for him before rushing back to Battle Hill to tell of their escape. It is my thought Phemie played upon Pandora's distress to convince her to run away to another country where the two could raise the child together. After all, Panny's last chance at marriage surely died with Weatherby."

Satisfied with his rendition, Jason slung a casual arm across the back of the chair, thought better of it and instead wrung his hands together on his lap. He had given the girls a good head start and could do no more. His brother-lyn-law entered the library, which now seemed even more cramped, filled with two such hulking men. Yes, he himself had the height and broad shoulders of the Longleighs, but the more graceful form of the Evertons, his mother's people, Jason thought. Again, his mind wandered to Viking sagas.

"The document you wanted has arrived, Bellevue," Danelagh said and handed it over to the duke.

His father, never much of a reader, took the volume to a table, sat and began paging its contents with great concentration. His mother peered over the paternal shoulder. The soft sound of pages turning, the crackling of a lively fire burning, should have been comforting to him, but Jason's unease grew greater the longer they read.

"What have you there of such intense interest?" he asked.

Rick, standing in the doorway with his huge arms folded across his wide chest, smiled in exactly the same way Jason imagined a Viking lord might have just before he drove a battle axe into an enemy's skull. "The *Navy List*," Danelagh answered.

His head began to throb as if his brother-in-law had actually struck the blow. Double damnation! Why had he not remembered the Royal Navy had chosen this year to publish a complete listing of all its members, their ranks, and stations?

"No Lieutenant Josiah Weatherby to be found in its pages," the duke replied. His mother stalked over to his seat and waved her often stinging fan before his nose.

"A very pretty and affecting tale you told, but did you think I would take no notice of any man Pandora failed to scare off these past two years, no matter how short the acquaintance? I would have done anything in my power to see such a fellow remained safely ashore. Now, where are my daughters?"

"Safe, I am sure, Mama."

"How can you be certain?"

"Because I put them aboard a ship myself and saw that Pandora went armed with knife, gun, and sword. I can say no more. I have given my word as a Longleigh not to betray them. Do what you will with me. I have come down on the side of love and always shall."

"Now that is our Pandora," the duke said with some pride.

"You can drive burning splints under my skin, and I will not tell you where they have gone," Jason swore, a little jealous of the praise for his sister.

"Phemie has gone to Scotland to be with her Leo and nowhere else. They must have agreed on a meeting place before you drove him off, my dear." The duchess tenderly touched her husband's arm. "Try to remember I was so determined to have you, I followed you all the way to America. She truly is my daughter.”

“So like you, I do not want to give her up to this rascal. How do I know he will take care of her and the babe and not simply run off again? We must find her.”

“Let your mind be at ease. As soon as I sent a rider to recall you, I dispersed my men to question at every hostelry and stable in Hull that might rent a conveyance. Others went to the docks. A young lady as pretty as Phemie does not go unnoticed, even if plainly dressed and cloaked. Word arrived with the *Navy List*. She boarded the *Selkie* bound for Inverness in the company of a stout, dark-visaged man. That is the part I find most troubling. What has happened to Pandora?” Rick unfolded his arms and moved to loom over Jason in a most threatening way, his big, pale fists clenched at his side.

“I believe we will find the dark-visaged man to be Pandora. The last duke had a penchant for acting—in disguise to be sure. Some of my children seem to have inherited that unfortunate predilection.” Bellevue went to stand beside Danelagh, forming a very formidable wall before the errant son.

Godric Erikson—just the kind of son Pearce Longleigh admired. How disappointed the duke must be to have sired a dandy in Joshua, a poet in himself, and a mathematical genius in Justinian besides the manly, adventurous James, his heir and favorite. Jason crossed his arms and put on his own Shawnee face to defy them. Let those fists pummel him black and blue, he would not reveal his sisters’ destination.

“You should have told us at once, Rick, and not allowed this farce to go on.” His mother appeared to be contemplating an assault on a bulging bicep with her fan, but she thwacked it against her palm instead.

“Oh, I had a desire to see how the drama played out and should not have indulged myself. When I first heard this preposterous story of the dying lieutenant, I thought my small sons concoct better tales to get out of their studies.”

That did it! Jason shot from his seat. "Do not deride my narrative abilities. I should call you out. I've met more fearsome men on the field of honor and prevailed with both sword and pistol."

The duchess's fan sliced into the space between the two men and with a tap to both broad chests made them move apart. "No duels among family. I am shocked to learn you have risked your life in such foolishness already, Jason. All of my sons are too beloved for me to lose."

"Simply angry husbands whose ire ruined their aim and their judgment. I confine myself to widows now, Mama. No one died. I acquitted myself very well."

"I paid the medical bills," the duke added.

"You knew and did not tell me?"

"Because of your tenderness for all your children, I wished to spare you, my darling."

"If he had died..."

"When a man makes a muck of things, he must own up to the consequences, dearest."

"Then I suggest you find a way to reconcile yourself to Phemie's marriage." The dainty duchess flounced from library, her huge husband right behind on her tiny heels.

"My guess is they are not heading for the bedchamber this time," the Earl of Danelagh said. "I ask your pardon for ridiculing your tale. I cannot rhyme two words together nor form a credible story myself. That is a special talent. Also, I admire your loyalty to your sisters, misplaced though it might be."

"Apology accepted. I suspect you are right. This argument will not be resolved upstairs."

~ * ~

At Battle Hill, all appeared very late for breakfast the following morning. None had slept well, if Jason could judge by the slamming doors, the footsteps pacing the hall, the voices raised and lowered in the family wing. He and Rick had made it up over a bottle of wine in the library where he proposed his idea for a great epic poem based on the exploits of the Danelagh ancestors—if his brother-in-law might consider paying the cost of publication.

"I concede Thalia thinks I do not support the arts sufficiently," the earl replied.

"Another way in which you and my father are alike. Let me fetch a few pages of my latest work in progress so you might judge the extent of my abilities with verse."

He'd gone upstairs to fetch his latest opus and heard the clamor his parents made, no straining bed ropes or cries of passion involved. Much as he thought his parents too attached, this did sadden him. Rick lasted through only twenty pages before falling into a doze, but Jason still considered his prospects good for a sponsorship. Going to his bed, he heard the duke and duchess still talking, their discussion reduced to a murmur.

Thalia seemed out of sorts as she crumbled more toast than she ate. He speculated she had less faith in his poetry than even Papa, but that was not the case. Rick appeared discomfited when he took his seat, and his spouse did not answer his "Good morning, my dear wife." The duke announced as they finished the meal that all but Thalia would sail to Inverness on a chartered vessel.

"If Mama goes, I do not see why I cannot," Thalia demanded.

"Because we have no notion of how long this mission will take, and the children have need of you," her husband answered.

"With so many in our nursery at Bellevue, I often had to forgo the excitement of accompanying your father on an adventure. Now, however, I am free to roam. Your time will come again," the duchess consoled.

The duke laced his tea heavily with cream and sugar, downed it in a few gulps and complimented his eldest daughter on the superb brew, but she continued to sulk. He tried a different argument. "There might be violence. Phemie claims this man is gentle, but we have no real idea of his true nature. Pandora is armed, and who knows whom she might shoot to protect Phemie."

"I am a Longleigh and not afraid of violence. How can you take Jason who betrayed you and not me?" She tossed those black curls she had in common with Phemie and flashed her dark eyes at her father.

Until this point, he'd had very little interest in another grueling pursuit with his father and would rather have stayed at Battle Hill to make a start on his Viking epic, but since no mention had been made of cutting off his allowance, Jason felt obliged to go. Now, however, he had to justify his being part of the group.

"The girls trust me. If an intermediary is needed, I am at your disposal."

His father had another notion. "Jason needs to atone for helping them escape, or he will have considerably less lace on his cuffs. On second thought, he shall remain behind to assist you in the absence of your husband. He is at your complete disposal. Do what you will with him."

Thalia gave her brother a sharp white smile, so amazingly feral against her dark complexion. He did not like it one bit. In fact, another jaunt to Scotland suddenly held great appeal. "I say, am I always to be left behind when adventure is at hand?"

"A man always has other opportunities!" Thalia claimed.

Jason cupped his ear. "Is that Pandora I hear speaking?" His eldest sister threw a crust at him. He waited for his mother's reprimand, but the duchess had been unusually silent during the breakfast table bickering. Jason thought her throat might be sore from last night's row, but that was not the case.

Pensively, she said, "I think this might be my fault—for constantly regaling my daughters with our adventures in America, for extolling my desire to have an adventurous life. How could they not want the same? Then, too, there is Snakeroot, the grandmother of the Shawnee warrior your father killed and scalped for my sake. She was thought to be a witch. We know she was a cannibal. Might she have cursed us to have trouble with all our children?"

"Nonsense, my dearest. She is long dead and gone. I paid her a generous reparation for Rattler's loss and that should have been the end of it. Considering I was the one raised among the Shawnee, you are showing yourself to be the more superstitious. As for being adventurous, the Longleighs cannot help themselves." The duke patted his wife's hand in reassurance, but still she shivered.

"You were not a slave to that old hag."

"All in the past. Finish eating. We leave for Hull to secure a vessel shortly. We might find a ship swift enough to overtake them before they reach Scotland."

Not likely, Jason figured. He'd given them enough of a lead that they must be past Edinburgh by now. Soon, Phemie would be in the arms of the man she loved.

Twenty-eight

Thank the good Lord their voyage would soon be concluded. Honestly, Pandora had done all she could to build Gladys's appeal to other men. When Miss Hotchkiss returned the two borrowed handkerchiefs washed and ironed by her own hands and now more neatly hemmed and embellished with the initials "PC," Pandora, forgetting her role, declared she could never have done such nice work and passed them around for all to see.

Her comment drew a giggle from Gladys, who asked, "Do you sew every often, Mr. Crowe?"

"Oh no, never. I have no interest in it. I only meant if I did sew, you would best me at it."

The rest of the men laughed heartily as well, and the widowed merchant remarked that a woman good with a needle would be an asset to any household, especially one with children who frequently tore their clothes. Pandora praised the girl's sweet, good nature over the port, but that only seemed to cement the notion that Mr. Crowe was courting Miss Hotchkiss. Formerly, she'd thought men had the easy part in gaining a wife. They made their choice and offered their proposal, most often to be accepted with joy. Now, she realized how a man might end up married through no intention of his own. Pitfalls lay everywhere, even at the dinner table where Gladys always sat next to Mr. Crowe. Pandora had not intended this to be a permanent arrangement.

Whenever she and Phemie strolled on the deck or went sightseeing along the way, she found Gladys hanging on her other arm with the reverend stomping behind, supported by that knob-headed cane so stout it could be used as a weapon. One wrong move and Pandora feared he would whip out his Bible and marry them on the spot.

They neared Inverness, thank God! While taking one of their constitutionals aboard, lacking the chaperonage of the grandfather for a change, Gladys asked, "Will you stay long in the city, Mr. Crowe?"

"Ah, no. I must scour the countryside for the best wool immediately before some other factor buys it up."

"Do they not shear in the springtime as we do in England?"

"I like to get an early start and judge the fleece while still on the animal. Must head out as soon as we reach port."

Disappointment descended heavily on Miss Hotchkiss, drooping her shoulders and making her steps lag. "I did ask Grandfather if you and Effie could reside with us at the parsonage while you were in town. If your sister and her fiancé have made no other plans, he could perform their marriage ceremony. He readily agreed. Could you not stay for a short time at least?"

"Well, you see, Effie's intended is not in Inverness proper. We are to join him at a place called Glenmoriston where there are sheep, lots of sheep."

Gladys gave a little bounce, which she often did when excited. "Oh, I know the place! I mean I have never been there, but a friend of my mother's visited recently to see the cave where Bonnie Prince Charlie took refuge. The novel, *Waverley*, inspired her travel to Scotland. Do you know it?

"Yes, the book is not to my taste."

"I have not put my mind to it yet, as it is very lengthy, but Mrs. Button assured me I would like Scotland when I removed there. She said the cave is now inhabited, not with thieves, but with a true

Scottish bard, who tells tales to the visitors in good, easily understood English."

Gladys hesitated a moment and glanced over her shoulder before saying, "He is a most striking figure with a beard of reddish gold and very long, well-formed limbs—of which he shows a great deal betwixt his kilt and his stockings. She also said that Scotsmen wear naught beneath their skirts. Have I shocked you? I should not have mentioned it. Grandfather would be very put out with me."

"Um, no. Being out and about the country, I am aware of what Scotsmen do not wear beneath their kilts, but I believe you have distressed my sister."

Phemie, hanging on her other arm, had suddenly tightened her grasp. Pandora led the women to a seat on one of the closed hatches with Gladys apologizing all the way.

"I am so sorry. What I said was most vulgar. I only meant to amuse. Please do forgive me."

Phemie hastened to reassure her. "No, your words do not upset me. You have just described Leonidas McLaughlin, my fiancé, perfectly. He is there waiting for me. He is truly there."

Wonder passed over Gladys's face. "You are to marry a kilted bard? From your elegant name and excellent manners, I thought he must be a very fine gentleman."

"Oh, he is a laird! And a physician and inventor of marvelous machines that will one day make him rich. Now I find he has a talent for tales, though I suppose I knew that already. I will never be bored with Leonidas because he is so many men in one."

Pandora spoke more seriously. "You had doubts he would be there?"

"There was always that chance, but I had to believe. Having Papa try to kill him must have been very discouraging."

"Oh," said Gladys. "I begin to understand. This is an elopement abetted by your kind and sympathetic brother. Never fear, I will not tell Grandfather. He would alert your family immediately. But I will help all I can. Please allow me to accompany you to Glenmoriston. I could be your bridesmaid, Effie."

Pandora saw the marital pit opening beneath her boots again. If she allowed Gladys to come with them without her grandfather's permission, they were as good as married. She put her foot down literally, thumping the deck with her rundown heel. "No. I would not jeopardize your reputation, Miss Hotchkiss."

"Then I shall ask Grandfather."

Speak of the Devil and here he came, brain-busting cane in hand. "What shall you ask me, child?"

"The Crowes are going on to visit the cave of the Seven Men in Glenmoriston. Might I go along with them?"

"Certainly not! I've barely gotten you home, and you want to traipse off into the countryside to visit a place that sheltered the papist prince."

Pandora breathed out with relief.

"To see more of Scotland before winter sets in. I will be safe in the company of Mr. Crowe." My, how the meek little girl could beg. Her misty blue eyes flooded with tears, a river about to run over.

Pandora had to act. "Only if you come as well, sir. I take it your family did not support Prince Charles Edward."

"We were for Protestant George." The reverend thumped his stick in emphasis.

"So you would have no interest in this historic place, not to mention the wear and tear on your rheumatic limbs to get there. Please do not endanger your health merely to allow us to enjoy your delightful granddaughter's company."

"Oh, you do not want me." The tears spilled, running like a rill in a Scottish glen and cascaded over Gladys's round cheeks. "I am so utterly foolish."

"No, no, not at all. I only meant to consider the reverend's indisposition. We might visit the parsonage on our return. That would be best for everyone."

Gladys groped for a hankie and found none. Pandora offered one the same young lady had embroidered with Mr. Crowe's initials. Gladys patted her face and offered a brave little smile.

"Do you promise? After all, you must come to retrieve your handkerchief. I shall have it all washed and ironed and could add further embellishments."

Panny felt a great urge to grab the hankie back, but it had already disappeared up Gladys's sleeve, probably to join her own. If she gave her word, it was the word of a Longleigh, and she would have to pay the visit, but this was a small pit, easy jumped before she returned home. One brief visit, then gone.

"I will see you before I leave Scotland, my word upon it."

Suddenly, she found her hand clasped top and bottom by Gladys' small, warm fingers. "I will wait for your coming as faithfully as Effie's intended." At a frown from her grandfather, Gladys broke the grip, but the promise had been made.

Twenty-nine

The oaks had lost their color and turned a drab brown. The winds of Glenmoriston plucked their leaves one by one and hurled them over the rocks like letters written to a long-lost love departed from this bleak and tragic world. Hunched before a small fire fueled by heather twigs, Leo shivered beneath his plaid and drew it up between his legs to staunch the draft on his privates. With his beard grown out, at least his cheeks and neck stayed warm. How much longer could he wait here for Phemie?

Brodie Urquhart said he'd guide the last of the tourists up the hill today. With inclement weather coming on, the trade would die down until spring brought the sightseers to Scotland again. God bless Mr. Scott for that. Now, the English could not get enough of the tartans and bagpipes their government had once banned. He'd provided Leo with a set of old pipes and suggested his bard give them a try to enhance the gratuities, but the noise conjured up only stirred the bats in the depths of the cave and distressed the lady visitors. Thinking with admiration of the piper who had performed at the handfasting, Leo realized producing Highland music amounted to more than simply fingering the chanter, blowing into the pipes and squeezing the bag.

He'd done better with a small goatskin drum called a bodhran that Brodie had off an Irishman and managed to produce a credible heartbeat rhythm with the double-headed beater as he practiced at night once the bats had gone out to feed. It passed the time. Mostly he used the drum to punctuate his stories at a dramatic moment, but Phemie would so admire his Celtic progress when she came—if she came. His wife claimed her father was not a tyrant, but most men of his status would have bought a more appropriate husband for his fallen daughter by now. Romantic as a meeting at the cavern might be, he would soon be forced off the mountain by the coming winter.

He heard the approach of the tourists. Female voices exclaimed over the briskness of the air and the magnificent view, just as they would go into raptures over his kilt and bare knees. Leo reluctantly left his fire and faded back into the dimmer recesses of the cavern to prepare for his dramatic entrance. As always, he strained to pick out one sweet voice amongst the others, the one that would tell him Phemie had arrived. Brodie's thick brogue overrode them all.

"Here ye come now to the famous Cave of the Seven Men of Glenmoriston, who sheltered Bonnie Prince Charlie in his time of greatest need. Could it be their spirits still lurk in its depths?"

Over the weeks, they had worked out this cue between them. Leo stepped forward in full regalia. On this gray day, the firelight provided the glint off the hilt of the *sgian-dubh* in his stocking, the claymore at his side and his red-gold beard. As usual, the women gasped. He spoke a much-rehearsed greeting.

"*Ceud mile failte*—one-hundred thousand welcomes. I am the Last Laird, and I have come to share with ye the tales of my clan from its founding to its demise at Culloden." Leo tapped his drum, ta-dum.

Toward the rear, a big blockish man, red-faced from the climb, remarked, "You did not tell me we would have to stand through a performance after hiking all the way up here."

"Do be quiet, Cecil. Let the man continue," his beguiled female companion said, never taking her eyes off Leo's bare knees.

He'd endured this reaction more than once, the jealous mockery of the males, the adoration of the females for all things Scottish. In the end, the men would open their purses and reward the bard generously at the urging of their wives and daughters. Once more, he reminded himself he did this for Phemie—to be here when she came. A cane of the sort usually hiding a sword thrust between the bickering couple.

"Make way, please. Allow this little lady a better vantage."

Jockeying for position was not unusual. By the time he made his way to the rock where he told his stories, he would be awash in women and none of them Phemie. Except for today. She eased through the ungraciously small gap the couple allowed and kept right on running. He dropped the bodhran and beater and opened his arms.

"*Mo ghra*, my love, I've saved those words for you and only you." He enfolded her against his chest.

"What happened to 'ye' is what I want to know," the blockish gentleman said.

"Hush, Cecil, this is part of the play. The Celts are a more passionate people than the British." His companion folded her hands across her flat bosom and sighed.

Another person, a dumpy man rather brown of skin and the owner of the cane, pushed between Cecil and his mate, widening the space with his arms. So this was the man the duke had chosen for Phemie over him. By the looks of his worn clothes, he had been cheaply purchased. Keeping his bright blue eyes on the sword cane, Leo's right hand found the hilt of his claymore. With nothing much else to do, he'd been practicing and had beheaded a great deal of the tall local heather that made its way to his hearth afterwards for want of any better opponent. He hoped his rival's skills were as shabby as his coat.

"Your husband?" he asked, still holding Phemie against his heart with his left hand.

"No," she laughed. "I would have no one but you, no matter what they did to me."

Leo absorbed the likeness to his small wife, the very dark eyes, intense and troubled, the sleek black hair and tinted skin. "One of your brothers, then, come to make you a widow?"

"No." She drew his head down and whispered in his ear. "My sister, Pandora, who helped me escape. My, how your beard tickles."

"You did say the Longleighs were an unusual family."

Brodie Urquhart cleared his throat in a most Scottish way that Leo had yet to master. "Have ye a tale to tell us, Last Laird?"

He did owe this man for food, shelter, and employment, such as it was. "I do. This is my dearest wife, parted from me after our handfasting by her father, a tyrannical English lord. I took to the heather the same as Bonnie Prince Charlie, but now we are reunited."

"Aaaah!" said Cecil's probable wife. Several other women, both young and old, echoed her exclamation. Cecil asked, "Exactly how long is this performance?"

With Phemie firmly tucked under his arm, Leo made his way to the rock where he usually sat to perform and placed Phemie at his side. The tubby, mannish woman handed him the fallen bodhran and beater. He gave the best performance of the season. Even Cecil appeared entranced once he got to Culloden. Exceptional gratuities followed, along with the picnic lunch.

The sky darkened from wooly gray to deep sable, and Brodie gathered his group. "Step ye right along and we'll be back at the inn before the foul weather arrives. Hurry now!" He urged them down the hill, sheep herded by a Border collie.

"I suppose ye'll be staying with the laird, missus?"

"Really, we should get a room at the inn, Phemie. A cold, damp cave is no place for you. It is not nearly as snug as our dungeon."

"Just one night, Leo. Then we will go out and face the world."

"And you, sir? Do you stay or leave?" Brodie asked of Pandora.

"A nice warm inn for me. I suspect I am not wanted, regardless."

Phemie managed to leave Leo's side for a moment and go to her sister. "Thank you, Panny, for all that you've done. I wish you the same—a great love."

"I'd settle for a great bowl of hot soup for dinner right now. Promise me you will come down early tomorrow, and we will see to getting you properly wed before Papa catches up with us."

"How could he know where we have gone?"

"Even if Jason has not told him, he will still find us. You know that, Phemie. Nothing deters him. Do not linger."

After a fond hug of her dearest sister, Pandora in a few long manly strides joined the flock of tourists still baaing over their extraordinary adventure. Urquhart called over his shoulder, "Don't ye forget, lad, part of that take is mine," and started back to the glen.

~ * ~

Leo settled Phemie on the bed of springy heather covered by his plaid and went to fetch more fuel from his store further back in the cave. He brought along the few precious sticks of oak Brodie allotted to him, a kettle, and a packet of tea. Filling the pot from the cavern's stream, Leo hung it from a goose-necked iron rod to boil. He lingered, stirring the fire and adding wood.

"There, we will be cozy in no time."

Phemie patted the place beside her on the plaid, making the heather beneath crackle. "Won't you sit by me, Leo? Aren't you glad to see me?"

"More than you will ever know. This was to be my last day in the cave, and I feared you might come and find me gone." He sat cross-legged beside his bride and very primly covered his knees with his kilt. "I dreamed of that happening—and of other things between us."

"Tell me about your dreams." Though his skin had reddened from an outdoor life, he still had the capacity to blush deeply. Phemie burrowed one small hand beneath the kilt and walked her fingers up his thigh. Both the hair on his legs and his prick stood on end, making a tent of the tartan. She reached the base of his cock and took the shaft in hand, smoothing it upwards and down. "You did miss me."

"I thought it might be ungentlemanly to jump upon ye the first moment we spent alone. We should talk first. Are there not things ye wish to tell me?

She withdrew her hand and watched disappointment possess his narrow, mobile lips half-hidden by his beard. Tugging the reddish-gold tufts on either side of his face, she drew Leo to her for a long, deep kiss. After releasing him, she said, "I have dreamt of doing this, too, only the man in my dreams was not quite so hairy."

"I can use the hot water to shave. I bought a razor, but Urquhart forbade me to use it. Part of the act, ye understand."

"How Scottish you have become with your beard and your 'ye'."

"Sorry, force of habit now. It won't take me long to return to my regular self."

"No, I like it. I would like something else as well."

"This?" Leo leaned over her, pressing her back into the bed of heather. He pushed up her skirts and covered her thighs with the flap of his kilt. Probing between her legs with his erection, he found the slit in her undergarments and sank into her warmth with a great shudder. Home at last. He tossed aside her bonnet and raked the pins from her hair with his fingers, freed her breasts from the long pelisse and gown and kept them warm with his kisses and his breath. Her hands went to his buttocks now and roved down to cup his balls. He thanked God for giving him a Longleigh woman.

"Say the words you saved for me, Leo. Say them."

"Mo ghra, mo leannan. My Phemie."

She urged him on with their want and their need so great, they kept at it until the water boiling over the fire turned to a warm mist in the cave. Beyond its mouth, the autumn rain sheeted down ensuring perfect solitude. When both had reached fulfillment, Leo lay by her side and made a study her of breasts, still stroking them gently. Phemie, eyes closed, made no move to cover them, but at last with reluctance, he replaced her gown and buttoned her coat.

"I would not want them to take a chill, not now, especially not now."

"You know?"

"I am a trained physician, a man midwife some would say. I know the signs. We will have a child in April. I shall deliver the baby. I trust no other."

"You are happy about it then. I did not want to tell you until we had renewed our love."

"I am. My guess is your father was not."

"He took it better than to be expected and devised a plan where my sister, Thalia, would claim to have given birth to the child and raise it as her own in a noble household. I was to be allowed visits as a favorite aunt. How could they possibly expect me to accept that?"

Leo brushed the black curls on her forehead with his lips. "Most women would abide by that decision and be grateful."

"Not a Longleigh woman."

"Aye, not a Longleigh nor a McLaughlin woman, either. Now I will make that tea. We have all night alone and together."

Thirty

Pandora paced the entry of the Glenmoriston inn. She caught a view of herself in the mirror set into the hat rack and realized she resembled a shorter, softer version of her father. The idea pleased her, and she expanded her smile into a huge, white grin of the type that should never be seen on the face of a well-bred lady. Pacing resumed, she wondered exactly how long it took for a young couple to become reacquainted. She must ask Phemie out of sheer curiosity. Still, half the morning gone and no sign of them. Did they not realize that Papa must be well on his way by now? She could feel the duke's approach on the back of her neck. Must she send the scrawny Scot who had led their tour up the mountain to fetch the heedless lovers?

Glancing out the window again, she finally spied Phemie, her elbow tightly clutched by Leonidas McLaughlin, mincing among the puddles on the street. By his solicitous care, she presumed her sister had told him about the baby. No help that Leo wore his Highland garb and drew the eye of every female or that Phemie, her curls free of their pins cascading out from under her bonnet and over her extremely wrinkled garments, looked as if she had slept in the heather. Every loiterer in town would remember the sight. Pandora went outside and beckoned them to hurry.

"Quickly, our hired carriage awaits to take us to Inverness. Our trunk is already aboard. As I have promised to visit Miss Hotchkiss, we might as well make use of her grandfather to see you properly wed."

On close inspection, Phemie's hair did contain small bits of herbage, but her face and eyes glowed as if her visage had been lacquered to a fine shine by a master painter. She supposed Leo was the artist who had brought that about and looked him up and down again.

"Pleased to meet you, also, Lady Pandora," he said, with not a trace of yesterday's brogue.

Pandora glanced quickly over her shoulder. "For now, I must remain Porteus Crowe."

"Of course. Allow me to settle up with Brodie Urquhart and return my costume. He will have to outfit another bard next season." He set down the medical kit he'd been carrying and hauled the knapsack from his shoulders. "I will need to change, but the tools of my profession can be loaded. I will not be long." Taking up the knapsack by its straps, Leo went inside to seek out his business partner.

"Just how long did you need up on the mountain? We should have been gone hours ago," Pandora growled at her favorite sister.

"Ah, Panny, when one is truly in love, one wishes to renew that love over and over, much like Mama and Papa."

Knowing a look of disgust showed on her face, Pandora quelled it and asked, "Have you eaten?"

"We toasted some bread over our fire of heather and finished the last of a pot of marmalade along with tea. The good news is that I kept it down entirely."

"Fine, then you are ready to travel? Why is he taking so long?"

"It has only been minutes. Do sit down, Panny." Phemie gestured to several rocking chairs on the porch of the inn, and Pandora flung herself into one.

"How dandy for you to be so collected. You've gotten what you want while I have Papa breathing down my neck on one side, and Gladys Hotchkiss to face with the other. What can I do to be rid of her?"

"Tell her the truth, but gently. Her life has been difficult since her mother died."

"Easier said than done."

They rocked in silence, Pandora, her leg crossed at her knee, more furiously than her sister, until Leo stepped outside again. He had resumed the drab, dark clothes of a physician but still bore the full beard and long hair of his masquerade that drew the eye like a house afire.

"Could you not shave?" Pandora demanded.

"If you will allow me the time, I would be happy to do so."

"No, we must leave at once. Up, up, Phemie."

Brodie Urquhart lingered in the doorway. "A peculiar young man, your brother-in-law, but such a wee, bonnie wife." He shook Leo's offered hand. "If ye decide to come back next summer, I would not chase ye away."

"Thank you, Brodie, but I hope to have my medical practice in Inverness well under way by then."

"Aye, most likely that earns a bit more, and ye do have a way with sprains and bumped noggins. I swear half those lady tourists slipped along the way simply to have ye minister to them. Word got round ye were a healer, too, after ye bound a few slim ankles."

"Yes, and one who would set a broken bone in exchange for a pot of mutton stew."

"What, ye say I dinna feed ye enough?"

"Living outdoors whets the appetite, my friend. You will always have a bed with us in Inverness."

Pandora tapped an impatient foot to hurry them along. Brodie held out a corked brown bottle he'd held at his side. "The finest Scotch whisky the inn has to offer to ease your travels, Leo. Think of me when ye take a dram." A manly embrace of shoulders and McLaughlin parted ways with Urquhart.

The travelers boarded the small, badly sprung hired carriage and rattled away with Pandora sitting on the coachman's side and Leo and Phemie facing forward to spare her sister any nausea. The couple gave no thought to her own nauseous feelings as they clung together with no space between them, hands clutched as if either one might fall out onto the road without hanging on to the other for dear life. Their tender kisses were more numerous than mile markers along the way. Finally, she'd had enough.

"Stop all that cooing. We need to consider how to approach the Reverend Mr. Hotchkiss. He is not likely to have any sympathy for runaway lovers. Miss Hotchkiss said so herself, but he still seems our best bet for quick wedding this side of Scotland."

"Never worry, Panny. I believe I know exactly how to handle him," Phemie stated.

"I doubt tear-filled eyes will have any effect on that codger. They never did his granddaughter any good."

"Not what I had in mind at all. My, I could use some rest," and without revealing any more of her plan, Phemie curled into Leo's shoulder and went to sleep in his embrace.

~ * ~

The reverend had been correct. His church was a landmark in Inverness and easily found. The visitors looked first within the solid red brick sanctuary totally free of popish fripperies: statues, stained glass, silver candlesticks, golden goblets, or pipe organ. A huge rugged cross loomed over the altar and gave the impression that Jesus Christ had just been taken down and hauled to his tomb to commit the Resurrection. Still, the goodly size of the edifice, and the worn places on the pews, told much about both the strength and length of the sermons given here. A number of iron stoves spaced along the walls possibly promoted winter attendance, and brass chandeliers aplenty hung low to illuminate hymnals during services.

The pastor was not within, and they turned to the parsonage next door, a substantial two-story building built of the same red brick and owning a stingy and unwelcoming stoop at the front door. A flutter of movement at a front window caught their eye and, in seconds, Gladys Hotchkiss hurried forth to greet them as if she had stood in that exact spot for days awaiting their arrival. With her brown hair arranged as Phemie had shown her, and topped by a small cap fluttering white ribbons, she wore a simple blue gown that brought more color to her misty eyes and a thick, woolen shawl of plain gray pinned with a small mourning broach containing a curl from a deceased loved one.

"Welcome, welcome. You have come at last!"

Phemie accepted a hug and Mr. Crowe a buoyant, bobbing curtsy. Gladys eyed Leo. "This must be your intended. My, what a fine figure of a man he is, Effie."

"I think so."

Pandora stifled a gag over the loving look her sister gave Leo. Very well, he had a fine male figure, better than hers all stuffed with pillows. If Phemie could have ordered a husband to her measure, it would be Leo, tall and striking but with none of the darkness of their brothers, a healer, a thinker rather than a man who took action without considering other means. She strove to be happy for Phemie, even if it meant she must part from her sister forever.

"Do come inside. I gave the order for tea and refreshments as soon as your carriage drew up outside. Of course, many visitors want to see the church first."

Pandora caught the disappointment in Gladys's voice that Mr. Crowe had not come to her side at once. "We sought your grandfather in order to ask him to wed Effie and Leo this very day."

"Just as I hoped! I will stand by your side as you say your vows, Effie. The reverend is in his study." Gladys led the way past a small sitting room with a meager fire and a threadbare upholstered chair by the window where a piece of sewing had been set aside and down a dim hallway. Pausing to knock timidly on a closed door before opening it a crack, she said, "Grandfather, look who has come to see us and wants a wedding performed."

"It had better be Porteus Crowe, the way he hung about you," the old man grumbled. "Come in and shut the door. Do not let the heat escape."

A coal fire big enough to stave off the rheumatism burned in the grate of the small room. Sweat trickled down their backs immediately upon entering. Religious tomes on dark oak shelving encircled the chamber. Reverend Hotchkiss worked on a sermon by the illumination of an oil lamp, the gray light from the single window not being sufficient for his aging eyes. He replaced his pen in the inkwell, steepled those knotted fingers, and eyed Leo.

"Who have we here besides Mr. Crowe and his sister?"

"Leonidas McLaughlin, M.D., Phemie, ah, Effie's fiancé. We have been parted for some time and want to marry as soon as possible. Today, this afternoon, right now. You see, we were hand-fasted previously but want a Christian blessing." Leo stumbled over his words in his urgency.

"Handfasting, a heathen custom, good enough I suppose, when roads and priests were few, but no excuse for it now. You are right to want a true marriage in the Christian church. I gather you have the permission of this young lady's father as she cannot be of age."

"She has my permission as her elder brother," Pandora said, seeking to leap the first stumbling block quickly.

"Then, I presume your father is deceased, Miss Crowe."

Both Pandora and Leo sucked in their breath, but Phemie answered calmly. "No indeed. He objects to my marrying a Scottish man because I wish to embrace his Presbyterian faith, and so I have run away to meet Leo here."

"You seek instruction in the true, unadorned word of the Lord, then. I will teach you our doctrine and then would be most happy to marry you in our church."

"I would like to marry first, as there is a small matter of urgency."

Phemie cast down her wide brown eyes and molded her hands over the very slight bump of her belly. The reverend caught her meaning without another word said. He had undoubtedly heard many such speeches before in this very study.

"This small urgent matter would be baptized in the Scottish Presbyterian faith."

"Certainly. My future husband insists."

Leo gaped and seemed as if he would protest. Pandora noted Phemie squeezed his hand hard enough to whiten her knuckles. The doctor wasn't a dim man, but most likely not religious either. He managed to say with some conviction, "Ah, yes. I was raised a Presbyterian and so shall my son be."

Phemie relaxed her grip and gave the reverend a grateful smile. "Another small matter. My true name is Euphemia Longleigh. I had to resort to some deception in order to leave England undetected."

"Longleigh, Longleigh." Hotchkiss stroked his long, hard jaw only slightly softened by wattles of aged flesh. "A very high and mighty family, if you are one of them. A Lady Thalia Longleigh married Lord Danelagh some years ago. Church of England, but very liberal, I have heard. Some say the Duke of Bellevue still practices the ways of Red Indians and rarely attends services."

"That is true, all of it. I am his youngest daughter and would not have my child influenced in such devilish ways. My mother was captured by the Shawnee and knew a Presbyterian minister who suffered martyrdom trying to bring the word of the Lord to the Indians and, in fact, married her to the duke. Even so, they embraced the Anglican Church after returning to England, but Papa has never been entirely civilized.

Pandora admired that Phemie managed her statement with a completely straight face and a great deal of sincerity. The Reverend Ewell Paulsen had been a Methodist and quite deranged, though the rest was true enough. Best to cleave as close to the truth as possible when lying. Who was the best actress now, her or Phemie?

A soft gasp from the shadows of the room reminded them all that Gladys was listening. "My best friend in the world is a duke's daughter, and you, Mr. Crowe, are Lord Longleigh." She dropped them both a deep curtsy so unlike her first greeting.

Pandora did not affirm or deny her statement, but Reverend Hotchkiss turned his blazing eyes on Porteus Crowe. "Not an honest wool factor then, but one of Bellevue's many younger sons who believe they can dally with a young woman's affections and pay no price."

"Not at all," Pandora asserted, though quivering inside. "Let us see my sister married, and then I would like to speak to Miss Hotchkiss in private."

"Gladys, see to the preparation of the church," the old man directed.

"Please come with me and take some tea while I make ready for your wedding. Lady Effie, you will have to pour."

Bobbing again as if she escorted the Prince Regent, Gladys took them to a front parlor where a stout-armed serving woman still strove with a bellows to bring a fire to life in the chilly room. However, the teapot steamed invitingly and the oatmeal scones, possibly made from the leftover breakfast meal, were fresh and studded with black currants. Another plate held squares of shortbread, each embossed with a thistle design.

"I know you are used to finer fare but do help yourselves."

Leo filled a plate before he took a seat on the black horsehair settee. "These look delectable to me, Miss Hotchkiss. No finer food than scones and shortbread."

"Yes, quite," Pandora managed to say. Her stomach had suddenly gone sour, but she took one of each and accepted tea from Phemie.

Gladys gave her a relieved smile. "I am glad the refreshments are to your liking, Lord Longleigh." She went to the fireplace where the servant had completed her work. "Mrs. Morris, hand down my two arrangements and come with me."

The woman filled her mistress's arms with two china vases painted with amateurish birds and stuffed with greenery and dried heather. They had flanked a painting of Jesus praying in Gethsemane, the scene of the Savior's betrayal. "You must have flowers, Effie, but the frost has browned even the chrysanthemums in the garden."

"I can think of nothing more appropriate than heather, Gladys."

The girl beamed at her best friend in the world and called to Mrs. Morris to follow her to the church. Once the two women had gone and shut the front door behind them, Leo grinned at Pandora over his cup.

"I would dearly love to know what you are going to say to Miss Hotchkiss after the wedding. That young lady seems to believe she is about to be engaged to a lord."

"Would that I knew, brother. Would that I knew."

~ * ~

With the aid of the brawny Mrs. Morris, Gladys had lowered every chandelier and lighted all the candles, mostly stubs left from the last service, and adorned the plain altar with her arrangements. The stoves nearest the front of the sanctuary glowed with the warmth of a good coal fire. The reverend entered wearing simple black and white vestments and beckoned Phemie, Leo, and Pandora to follow him down the aisle. Gladys darted forward and placed a nosegay of dried purple and white heather taken from the altar bouquets and bound by a white ribbon robbed from her cap into the bride's hand.

Phemie rewarded her with a sweet smile. "Thank you, dear friend."

Gladys stayed by her side, and Pandora stood up for Leo. Looking as pleased with the entertainment as a spectator at a Punch and Judy show, Mrs. Morris settled into a pew to watch the affair.

"Excessive use of candles and coal, child," the preacher muttered to his granddaughter.

"I am sorry, but I thought only of your condition and eyesight—and of making the occasion more festive."

"Marriage is not a festival, but a serious obligation. I find that when a young couple has put their passion before their vows, it is best to say a few words upon the matter first."

Hotchkiss placed himself behind a lectern with two fat wax candles in iron stands flaming on either side. The shadows deepened the crags in his face into chasms as the late afternoon progressed into darkness beyond the clear-paned windows. He glared at the bridal pair.

"Young man, if you should ever covet another woman in thought, word, or deed, you shall burn in hell. Young woman, if you should ever break your vows, neglect your marital duties, household, or children, you shall burn in hell." The rant continued for some time, listing all sorts of ways that Leo and Phemie might find themselves bound for eternal torment, among them not believing they were on the path of the damned.

Pandora stole a surreptitious glance at Jason's watch. Twenty minutes had passed, but the old man did seem to be winding down. Considering the confession that awaited her after the ceremony, she could have listened to fire and brimstone all day. In the end, the actual vows took only minutes. The bride and groom were not invited to seal them with a kiss. She signed the register as a witness with her initials,

P.J.B.W, for Pandora Jane Black Wing Longleigh, but the reverend need not know that.

Gladys added her name and marveled over the plethora of letters preceding the Longleigh name. "I suppose lords need more names than the rest of us."

Pandora smiled at the small jest, if it were one, and took the girl's arm for one last time as they followed Phemie and Leo from the church. Her reprieve had run its course. Time to be sentenced and hung for her crimes in the effigy of Porteus Crowe.

"We planned only cold mutton, this morning's bread, and some broth for supper, but we must have a nuptial feast. I will send Mrs. Morris to the chop house for something better. You will spend your wedding night here. The guestrooms have been made up for days and the sheets are scented with lavender." Gladys offered the bride and groom all in her power to provide despite an unhappy grunt from her grandfather.

"There is nothing wrong with bread and broth," the minister said.

Leo intervened. "No, indeed, but we have already taken rooms at an inn and must not impose on you any longer." He fished out enough of his gratuities to make a respectable contribution toward the work of the church and placed the money in the reverend's hands.

The gnarled fist closed over the offering and deposited it beneath the clerical robes. "I believe Longleigh needs to address my granddaughter before you leave the premises."

"Ah yes, we will wait in the carriage."

"Please stay, Effie," Gladys pleaded, already suspecting the worst.

"It will be all right in the long run," Phemie said. "We will talk tomorrow, I promise. Go with—ah—Porteus."

Pandora led the way into the parlor but remained standing by the fire even after Gladys shut the door and followed her across the room. "Please sit down, Miss Hotchkiss."

"I will if only you would call me Gladys," the young woman replied lightly. She took a seat on the horsehair settee and folded nervous hands in her lap.

Kinder to be swift in the delivery of the death blow, so the duke always said, but she could graciously accept this small intimacy before saying, "Gladys, I cannot marry you. I am sorry if I gave the wrong impression."

Hope could not have drained away faster from the girl's face if Pandora had stabbed her in the heart with the sword cane. Gladys studied her clasped hands.

"Of course, I am too far beneath the son of a duke and not nearly pretty or accomplished enough."

"No, no, not that." Pandora found herself on the settee chaffing those cold, little hands. The misty blue eyes brimmed over, and she learned that the tears of others could sting like acid.

"Effie told you I am not pure."

"What? No! She merely said your stepfather had made improper advances and you called your grandfather to come for you."

"He said I tempted him, and we were not father and daughter, no relation at all, so there was no sin in it. I tried to push him away, but was not strong enough. My fault, my fault that I did not leave sooner. I preferred the comforts of his home and lost my honor because of it." Her head sank again.

"Gladys, it is always the case that the man blames the woman. Never say this is your fault again! I do wish I could kill this villain for you. Has he left you in a family way?"

"Oh, no. He could not get a child on my mother in all the years they were together, and none will result from this attempt, either."

"Thank God. Now you must listen to me. Nothing is wrong with you. A woman does not become worthless the moment she loses her virginity. The sin is mine because I was deceitful. I told your grandfather a grievous lie aboard ship. The truth is I cannot perform my marital duties nor give you children."

"I—I don't think I would mind that at all. We could live side by side like loving brother and sister. Many children need homes, and..."

"Gladys, I am not Effie's brother but her sister."

The blue eyes widened. The trembling lips dropped open, but only for a moment. Gladys stiffened her spine and spoke. "I know you think me very uninformed, but I realize there are women like you who dress as men and act the part–and—and prefer to be with other women. My stepfather said I might be one of them when I did not welcome his affections. Perhaps I am. I would not object if only you would love me and take me from here." The small, cold hands clung tightly to Pandora's clenched fist.

"I am so sorry, but I am not one of Sappho's devotees."

"Sappho?"

"A Greek poetess who preferred women, my dear. She came from the isle of Lesbos, hence the term lesbian. We have her verses in translation at the Bellevue library. I am not sure Mama realizes, but perhaps she does, as they are quite sensuous and might be applied to any lovers. Regardless, I only assumed this guise to offer my sister escort to Leo. Not that there is anything wrong with my dressing this way. I believe firmly in the equity of women and comfortable clothes should be part of that."

"You could teach me so much if we stayed together."

"Not that! I do want to help you, Gladys, as I want to help all women escape male domination. Bide here awhile. Give me some time, and I will see what fortune and influence can contrive. I suspect the duke and duchess to be arriving shortly, and I will plead your case to my mother, who is very inventive. Now, no more tears. We will find a way for you. Here, wipe your eyes."

Pandora drew out one of the fine handkerchiefs she'd gotten off the little thief, but Gladys had her own in hand. She did not use it but traded it with her lost suitor.

"I added my initials in the other corner and hoped you would ask for it back. Please keep it in remembrance of me."

"Oh, Gladys, I am often told I would make a terrible wife and am quite sure I would fail badly as a husband, too. The world holds someone better for you, and we will find him, if that is what you wish. I must go. Stay well. Do not give up hope of leaving here." Pandora tucked the token away, pried her other hand lose from the girl's grip, and made for the door where the Reverend Hotchkiss waited beyond, knobbed cane in hand.

"And so, young man, are we to have another wedding?"

"She refused me. I am not good enough for her."

Pandora escaped immediately to the carriage where Phemie and Leo waited, passing time in a deep embrace. She tapped them with her cane. "Come up for air. I feel like such a cad, such a bounder. We must help her."

"We shall. You took long enough. We've been waiting to celebrate our wedding night," Phemie pouted.

"Looks to me like you have started already—and not for the first time."

Leo played the peacemaker. "Ladies, ladies, let me simply say I am grateful we are not staying here. If we had lodged beneath that roof, I doubt I could perform my husbandly duties for wondering if I enjoyed them too much, I might be on my way to hell."

Pandora gave him the amused smile he had earned, but as the carriage moved along the paved streets of Inverness, she peered out into the darkness. "Enjoy yourselves while you can. I tell you the duke is on his way."

Thirty-one

Impatiently waiting for the unloading of their baggage, the Duke of Bellevue paced along the dock at Inverness. Drat that women could not travel with only the clothes on their backs and a saddlebag full of the bare essentials. Early in their marriage, Flora knew how to travel light, but now boxes galore must be packed and dragged along, impeding them like General Bradford's wagon train. She claimed that, as a woman ages, she needs more devices to remain attractive, and since she had left her maid behind, she needed all the help she could get. Damnation, she would always be beautiful to him, always the love of his life.

He passed a post plastered with handbills touting the best inns and offering tours into the depths of the Highlands. One in particular caught his eye—as it was meant to do having been hand-colored by some poor woman in need of income. She had painted the hair and beard of the tall, fierce, heavily armed and kilted Scot a striking red-gold.

The bill read:

See the Cave of the Seven Men of Glenmoriston. Meet a Highland Laird, the last of his kind, and hear his stirring tales. Revel in the beauty of the Glen. Tours leaving daily from the Inn at Glenmoriston. Picnic box included. Fine accommodations. Reasonable prices.

Bellevue ripped the flyer from the post and carried it over to his wife like a hound delivering a trophy to its master. "This is him, Phemie's abductor, and this is where they are to meet. I am sure of it!"

"Nonsense, darling. I see only a stereotype of a Scotsman, the kind the British wished to destroy and now want back to amuse them, thanks to Mr. Scott." Lady Flora flicked his suggestion away with her fan.

"But the color of the hair, kidnapper's hair, is as Pandora described it. I caught a glimpse of it myself when he sailed away, the coward. Why would the colorist choose such a bright hue without special instructions to do so?"

"To draw your attention—as it did. You might as well begin referring to Leonidas McLaughlin as Phemie's husband because they are surely wed properly by now."

"Only because you took so long packing your bags, and now we must wait for the luggage. More delays. I suspect you are in sympathy with them."

"I will not deny it. Like Jason, I am all for love and always have been. Nor do I regard a man with the discretion to flee before your rage a coward. You seem quite ferocious to those who do not know you. I believe he made a very intelligent decision."

The duke wrinkled his broad nose, enhancing his bearish appearance. "Their scent is in the air, I tell you. Our daughters passed here."

"Of course, they did. All the passenger ships dock at this wharf. We should make inquiries about the *Selkie* and question its captain as to where the girls might have gone. Rick can begin a search of the better inns." She gestured to Danelagh, who waited patiently like a good son-in-law for Lord and Lady Bellevue to sort things out.

"I say we waste no time and leave immediately for Glenmoriston. What do you think, Danelagh?"

Rick bowed. "I am at your service, the both of you."

"Then we go to Glenmoriston. Ah, the baggage at last. Find us some transportation, son, if you wish to be useful."

The speed with which Danelagh left them to complete his errand indicated how little he relished being in the midst of their argument. Lady Flora flapped her fan again. "Very well, have it your way. We go on a wild goose chase. I tell you they are in Inverness."

For a moment, the duke's stubborn mien shifted. With Rick well out of hearing, he proposed, "Whoever is right gets to choose their favorite bed sports for the next week."

"They are all your favorites, but yes, I would enjoy having you at my mercy—providing only that you do not kill Phemie's husband once we find them. That would destroy my good mood."

"Oh, have it your way, then!"

"Excellent," said Lady Flora.

~ * ~

Upon pulling up before the inn at Glenmoriston, the duke left the carriage immediately, leaving Danelagh to hand down Lady Flora. By the time the two caught up with the forward charge, Bellevue was waving the handbill in the face of a wiry Scot and demanding he guide them to the cave at once.

Routed from his warm place on the settle and his afternoon pipe and pint, Brodie Urquhart replied, "Naught to see up there now but barren trees and brown heather. Tours have ended for the season."

"I seek this man."

"The tyrant lord," Urquhart muttered to himself.

"What did you say?"

"Just a turn of phrase our laird used in one of his tales. No insult intended. I do not even know ye, man. Leo got so good, he could tell the story of Culloden and the wounded warriors being slain by the redcoats on the battlefield that 'twould bring water even to this jaded eye." Brodie mimed blotting a tear. "He grew into a fine performer. Sorry ye missed him as he will not be back next summer."

"I am Pearce Longleigh, Duke of Bellevue, and you will tell where this man has gone." He loomed over Urquhart like a boulder about to roll over an ant.

"Weel, after his wee missus arrived..."

"She is not his missus. They are not wed."

"Handfasting is as good as marriage in the Highlands, and she seemed most eager to spend the night on the mountain with him. Why they came from the cave the next morning with her looking as pleased as a cat that upset the milk bucket, she greatly resembled the lady behind you in form and expression," the guide replied, as if he wanted to see how much more empurpled the tyrant lord's face could become.

Urquhart wiggled a finger over Bellevue's shoulder, and the duke heard his wife's light laughter. Placing his two broad thumbs on Brodie's windpipe, he seized the Scot by his scrawny neck and raised him off the broad pine boards of the inn's floor. "You will tell me where they have gone without any more blather."

"Inverness." Brodie took in a great gulp of air as his toes touched down again and the great hands loosened their grip. "The lad thought he could make a better living as a physician, and I will say he has the healing touch. Why, he delivered a barmaid having a breech birth by turning the babe ever so slowly as not to burst the womb and brought it safe into the world, fatherless though the bairn be. We took up a collection to buy him a round and had a little left over for his purse, we were that fond of Tess. A good man is Leo McLaughlin."

"Where in Inverness?" the duke said in a tone implying he was willing to choke off Urquhart's air again.

"Why, I dinna know. They were to seek lodgings there. The peculiar brother, Mr. Crowe, went with them."

Lady Flora laughter rang out once more. "As I said, dearest. Now, let us get a suite for the night if they have one available."

"No, we will trade the horses and set out for Inverness."

"Oh my, I am so fatigued I cannot go another mile." Flora yawned so immensely her dainty hand barely covered it.

"You seek to delay me again. Nap in the coach."

"But then, my love, I would not be able to collect my winnings, not with Rick riding along."

"We cannot play games at a public inn."

"Oh, I think 'tis been done before," Urquhart dared to say.

"I would not want to proclaim in front of this gentleman that the great Duke of Bellevue reneges on his bets." Lady Flora gave her husband a few light taps of her folded fan to emphasize her point.

"Very well, there is no torment a Shawnee warrior cannot endure in silence."

Her gray eyes lit with the challenge. "Really?" Flora led her husband aside out of the hearing of the inquisitive Urquhart and drew his ear to her lips with a tug on the lobe. "I choose the feather torture. You will only be bound by scarves, but you must stay still as if held by chains as I move the feather up your shaft and tickle its head, then down again across your balls and between your buttocks."

The duke caged his petite wife between his aroused body and the whitewashed wall. "Flora, you know how loudly I laugh."

"Deep and strong like your bellow, but so much richer. Think of the feather circling your nipples now and moving along your side." She slipped under the guard of his brawny arms and went to join her son-in-law.

The duke braced his hands hard on the wall and said without turning, "We stay the night, Danelagh. See to getting our chambers."

"I am sure ye will find the accommodations perfection, milord," Urquhart answered. "Come morning, may the hill rise behind ye, and may the mountain be always over the crest, and may the God that ye believe in hold ye in the palm of his hand, milady. Enjoy your evening's rest." With that, he returned to pint and pipe, clutching the coins the duchess had given him "for allowing my husband to abuse you so terribly without drawing the knife in your boot in return."

~ * ~

Rick clasped his pillows to either ear. Would the stentorian laughter in the adjoining room never cease? It reminded him sharply of his wife and the games she devised to keep him interested and content. Could it be she had learned of them from her mother? As far as he was concerned, they could snot get back to Battle Hill quickly enough with or without Euphemia Longleigh, he desired Thalia so. If they were not to raise Phemie's babe, time they started on their own.

Thirty-two

The duke and Lady Flora napped in the carriage next day, leaving Rick to direct the hired coachman regarding destination and stops along the way. His in-laws had come down late to breakfast and devoured more food than the innkeeper could possibly recoup for the price he charged for the meal. The stunned man merely watched aghast at the ravenous appetite of the tiny duchess and her massive husband. Too give them credit, they were so delighted with the evening spent at the inn in Glenmoriston, they did pay extra.

As for himself, Rick would have preferred several strong cups of coffee rather than the bracing pot of tea, but there was none to be had. Someone had to stay awake when they were on the march. When their group eventually reached Inverness again, he slipped the proprietor of a very fine lodging a banknote to house him on the other side of the establishment from his randy in-laws. He now understood better Thalia's objections to their great affection and surmised she had learned many of her tricks simply by overhearing them. Ah, the feather torture. He had fond memories of it and remained more than a little jealous this morning.

Dining that evening in a private room, the duke laid out their plans to search the city for Phemie, Pandora, and "that blasted physician who calls himself a laird." He intended personally to seek out the captain of the *Selkie* if still in port and learn what he could. To Rick, he delegated a search of inns and lodgings. Lady Flora received the gentlest task of taking the hired coach and going from church to church to inquire if any priest or pastor had wed their daughter to a Scotsman.

She did have one suggestion. "Rick, you do rather stand out in a crowd by height and breadth alone, but more so with your coloring. I shall give you some kohl to darken your brows and suggest you cover your hair and body with a hooded cloak. The weather is certainly nasty enough to warrant that."

Lady Flora gazed out the window at the steady flow of rain dripping off a streetlamp. "I fear if the girls recognize you, they will flee again before we can bring this adventure to a happy conclusion."

"There can be no happy ending," her morose husband said, having drunk a little more mulled wine than was good for him.

"Of course, there can! As I suggested the night in Glenmoriston when you lost your bet, accept Phemie's husband. Make him officially Laird of Castle Laughlin. His aunt and uncle grow too old to attend to all the details. Retire them and hand its responsibilities over to him. Allow him to work on his steam engine and this railroad idea. He could make you another fortune. Open your big arms and welcome another grandchild. You know you dote on them."

"And strip our eldest son of his estate and income? Never!"

"As a viscount, James far outranks a laird. He would retain his absentee ownership and the income from the flocks, fisheries and quarry, but Phemie and Leo will have a proper place to live and income from their stewardship."

"Woman, you befuddled me with your wiles in Glenmoriston, and now with wine and good sense. Let me sleep on it. Still, our search must continue in the morning, or we might never have our daughters back. What say you, Danelagh?"

"Again, I am at your service."

~ * ~

Pandora needed to get out of the quaint furnished cottage their pooled resources had rented for a month. Never had she suspected that Phemie so deeply resembled their mother. Yes, the physical appearance had always been there in the petite form and curly hair, but the likeness went so much deeper. With only two bedchambers side by side in the place, she had gotten little sleep. Had they any idea how loud their lovemaking became of an evening? Even the pounding of rain on the roof did not drown out the groans and sighs and shrieks.

The next morning, Phemie proudly presented her husband and sister with bowls of scorched oatmeal porridge made by her own hands over the fire Leo had stoked. Pandora did choke it down after submerging the gray mass speckled with burned bits in treacle and washing away the taste with weak tea. Leo ate the disgusting mess with gusto, as if nothing at all were wrong, not surprising given the man had recently lived in a cave. He did, however, remark that as soon as he'd established his medical practice, Phemie should have a scullery maid, indicating he did have some sense of self-preservation undimmed by love.

The tiny sitting room would have to serve as Leo's surgery and the equally small parlor as his waiting room. Phemie planned to make a place to sew by the window in the larger bedchamber. She intended to take in needlework to add to the household coffers, imagine that. The second smaller room would do for the baby when it came, and Pandora was back at Bellevue once more. All of which brought up another issue.

Here Lady Pandora Longleigh sat a plain wooden table with her legs stretched out crossed at the ankles, her waistcoat open and her shirt untucked into her breeches because she had not yet stuffed the gap beneath her breasts with a pillow. This seemed to unnerve Leo more than his bare knees had bothered women.

"We have enough food in the house to keep us until patients arrive, and I will hang out my shingle today. Please take what is left of our funds and buy a traveling dress to get you back to Bellevue," he begged.

"Yes, I think you should, Panny. Papa is likely to go easier on you if you are dressed like a lady. I suppose he will disown me and never speak my name again."

Pandora doubted that the bad oatmeal had caused the lump in Phemie's throat. Very well, if this small act would give her sister a little comfort, she would do it, loathe though she was to give up her comfortable breeches and be encumbered by skirts again.

"If I must endure a shopping expedition, won't you come with me?"

"No, Papa might have sent the Armstrong boys to search for us, but no one would suspect to find you dressed as a man. Imagine, you can hint that you are buying a gown for your mistress. I know that would make you smile."

"It would. Foul weather to go out, though, but how wonderful to stride along in boots, heedless of getting my hem wet. I will go in a hackney and make an umbrella my first purchase."

Leo rose. "Let me go out and find a vehicle. Phemie, you seem fatigued after the exertions of making breakfast. Why don't you lie down, and I will clean the pot and dishes?"

"Thank you, my dearest. I will do that."

Pandora tucked in her shirt, buttoned her waistcoat, stuffed the well-traveled pillow under it, and shrugged into her jacket. She seized her battered hat from a hook on the wall. "As I am still dressed like a man, I will find my own coach. Please, both of you get some rest while I am gone."

Certain they would be at it again as soon as she closed the front door, Pandora went out into the now light drizzle. With luck, they would be so worn out she might get some rest tonight. She progressed to a busy intersection and held up her hand to attract the attention of a passing hackney coach. How gratifying to do such things on her own with no man treating her as a delicate lily too weak to raise her arm and shout for a ride. The driver let her down in the shopping district as requested. Few were out in such poor weather.

Pandora strode along High Street heedless of the wet, with her hair still tight in its single braid and bound up behind beneath her disreputable hat. This hat did not deserve the protection of an umbrella. She searched for a dressmaker but came across a haberdashery with a window full of fine silk hats for men perched atop bald-headed forms.

How she would like one of those. Why, she could stick some jaunty black feathers in the band and add a short veil to the brim for use when she went riding. Perhaps she would set a new style...Pandora Longleigh who cared not for fashion. The thought made her grin and her reflection in the glass smiled back.

Behind her, a hulking form in a dark, hooded cloak drawn tight passed. She caught only a glimpse of bushy black brows and a pale, smudged face before the man abruptly skulked across the street. He could have been a character out of a gothic novel being so dramatic in his movements and dress. Pandora laughed at the thought. No timid maiden she to be kidnapped by a mad monk or evil lord, but to all appearances simply a pudgy gentleman. She entered the store and, after trying on several for size, purchased a top hat carefully stowed in a sturdy box and a black umbrella to protect it from the rain. Jason's castoff she did not care about at all.

Coming back out into the drizzle, she thought the cloaked man lingered in the deep arch of a doorway across the way, but could not quite make him out. If he planned to snatch her hatbox, he might be in for a surprise. Pandora gripped her sword cane tightly and regretted having left the pistol behind on a table by the door. Ah well, on such a damp day it might not fire. The sword would have to do if needed.

A short distance more along the way and a dressmaker offered her wares in a pretentious little shop named Madame Munro's Maison de Mode. Sighing, Pandora went inside and alerted the proprietor with the tinkling of a bell. She was greeted with a fake French accent and a fawning manner by the middle-aged and prosperously fleshy owner. There being no one else in the shop, she soon concluded her business. The dressmaker would alter a sample gray woolen, long-sleeved gown accented with black ribbons down the skirt and around the bodice for a lady about her client's height and full in the bosom to be ready on the morrow.

Now, Pandora supposed she would have to purchase a proper bonnet, too, though she'd spent far too much on the silk hat and funds ran low. Madame Munro suggested a hat shop not too far distant run by her cousin who would shave the price if the gentleman mentioned her name. Pandora thanked her and moved on to complete her purchases.

The cloaked man walked on the opposite side of the street, matching her stride for stride. She shivered and picked up her pace. He dropped behind as she reached the hat shop and took refuge there. Simply her imagination that the man stalked her. To all eyes, she was a none too prosperous gentleman, though she did possess a nice watch that she had checked once outside the dressmaker's shop. Perhaps that shiny object had attracted the rogue's attention. Pandora buried it deeper in her waistcoat.

To the disappointment of the dressmaker's cousin, the customer selected a very plain black bonnet without trim fit for a Quaker or a strict Presbyterian and ignored all offerings of fake fruit, silk flowers, and small, stuffed birds to enliven it. A second hatbox joined the first. The drizzle coalesced into rain as Pandora left the hatmaker's emporium with only small change jingling in her purse.

A coffeehouse beckoned on the opposite street corner in the triangular heart of the town and offered Pandora one last chance to stretch out her legs and read the current news over a hot, dark cup of brew before she resumed the garb of a lady. She seized that last chance. The cloaked man passed her in the crosswalk, his head turned away and bent down to keep the wind and rain from his face. He shouldered through the door of a tavern diagonally situated from the coffeehouse. Again, she experienced that frisson of fear a woman might feel about a male who could overpower her easily. Gladys Hotchkiss came to mind, along with a new burst of sympathy for the girl. But no, she acted the man and would not cower if he approached.

Placing her umbrella in a stand and her boxes on a chair, Pandora sat facing a window. She could at least be prepared if he approached, but the tavern's small, thick panes revealed no sign of her cloaked stalker. She ordered her coffee, a plate of shortbread, and a copy of the *London Times*. Stretching out her legs, she added cream and sugar to her beverage and buried her face in the paper. Hmmm, a steam-powered warship had been launched. Perhaps Phemie's husband was on to something, that Age of Steam he liked to babble about given half the chance. The Congress of Vienna had convened to carve up Napoleon's empire—interesting; Britain's victory about to yield an enormous profit for the empire. She would not allow an attack of feminine nerves to ruin this moment.

~ * ~

In the dark interior of the tavern, Rick threw back his hood, scattering droplets across sawdust-covered floor. The covering absorbed the water just as it did spilled drinks, blood, and all manner of other bodily fluids heavy drinkers were likely to expel. His black brows and white hair drew the interest of the barkeep, but when asked where he hailed from, he merely grunted in reply, ordered ale, and took his mug to a seat where he could watch the coffeehouse across the way without revealing his own form in the small-paned windows.

The duke would be pleased by his progress. Figuring the young lovers would not have the wherewithal to stay in the best establishments, he had concentrated on more modest inns. Not an hour ago, he'd found where Dr. and Mrs. Leonidas McLaughlin had spent their wedding night. Why, they hadn't even feigned a name on the register. Unfortunately, their stay had been short, and the innkeeper knew only that they had taken a small house somewhere in Inverness. A somewhat corpulent young man with a long, braided queue had traveled with them and signed as Porteus Crowe.

If that peculiar name and description had not been rattling around in his brain when he passed the haberdashery, Rick doubted if he would have noticed the slightly shabby gentleman perusing silk hats in the store window. Actually, the braided hair had caught his attention, black and shiny as a corbie's wing and so very out of style. Pandora, of course. He often found his sister-in-law strident and overly opinionated, but he had to admire her audacity. She possessed the spirit of the Longleigh women the same as Thalia, but remained ungentled by motherhood.

He could have tapped Pandora's shoulder, seized her arm and dragged her back to the duke, but he was only too aware that she had run off with a pistol possessing a hair trigger and leaned on Jason's walking stick, the one disguising a sword. Truly, he had no desire to be shot or skewered by a skittish woman convinced he was a footpad. His disguise certainly made him look like one. No, he would not approach but simply follow her to her destination and reveal that location to the duke at dinner.

Ah, here she came from the coffeehouse and searched the street for a hackney coach. Rick chuckled as Pandora awkwardly juggled her hatboxes and umbrella as she tried to free a hand to summon a ride. He doubted she realized how much she resembled a lady who had forgotten to bring her maid to carry her purchases as she waved with a flapping hand for a vehicle. A hackney bearing several other passengers on this miserable day stopped for her. She gave her destination and got inside, discommoding the other riders with her encumbrances.

Rick scanned the street and found no other vehicles taking on passengers. Well, if he could not follow Pandora, he would find her location another way. He retraced his steps to the shop of the dressmaker. At the tinkling of the bell, the owner came waltzing out with an ingratiating smile on her face from a curtained area in the rear.

"*Bienvenu a Madame Munro's Maison de Mode.*" She stopped so fast her notable jowls wobbled. "What—what is it you want?" The Scottish lilt to her voice banished any pretense of her being truly French.

"Madame." Rick bowed quickly to put her at ease. Evidently, having two men in a row enter her establishment had unsettled the poor old soul. "I merely wish to enquire about a previous customer, a young man, somewhat stout, braided black hair, and carrying a gentleman's hatbox. If you could give me his direction, I would be most obliged."

Somewhat lulled by his fine upper-class speech, Madame Munro momentarily remembered her professional ethics. "I am so sorry, but I could not divulge that information about a client even if I knew. Mr. Crowe indicated he would retrieve the dress himself tomorrow. He was willing to have one of our sample traveling gowns altered out of necessity for speed, truly only a matter of adding some length to the hem and expanding the bodice. With business slow on a day such as this, one of my girls is at work on it already."

"When do you expect him?"

"At noon, sir. He paid extra for expediency. If I might ask, why do you need to know?" Evidently, her desire for a choice piece of gossip overcame any lingering moral objections about speaking of a customer who intended to leave town very shortly.

"I suspect the gown is for a young lady who plans to run away with Mr. Crowe. It is in her best interests that she does not flee."

"Ah, impetuous youth, though I did not figure the gentleman to be a rake and a ruiner of maidens. He seemed very polite and soft-spoken."

Rick grinned at this description of Pandora, hardly the woman he knew. "Oh, Mr. Crowe has a hidden side you would never guess."

The dressmaker took a step back toward the curtain, almost tripping over her own trailing hem. Thalia had warned him his smiles often showed too many teeth and caused people to think of deadly predators. Quickly, he reached for his purse and offered a bribe. "I would appreciate if you would not mention our conversation to Mr. Crowe when he arrives."

She scuttled forward fast enough to take what was offered. "Whatever I can do to help save that innocent girl. Your sister?"

"Yes, my sister."

Rick returned to the street and now, of course, an unoccupied hackney waited at the curb for prospective customers, both horses' heads bowed in the rain, and the driver well-swaddled against the weather. At least he would be able to rejoin the duke and duchess promptly for dinner and deliver his news. He anticipated the hearty pat on the back from Bellevue already.

~ * ~

Cozily settled before a spitting fire, angry at every raindrop that found its way down the chimney, the duke and duchess sat in a private chamber where a generous dinner had been laid out on table covered with a clean white cloth. They were spitting angrily at each other as well when Rick entered the room and continued to argue as if he were invisible.

"To think I missed the *Selkie* by a day before she left port. What if the girls were aboard, disguised again?" The duke helped himself to a glass of wine from a bottle sitting between them.

"I told you not to waste time going to Glenmoriston, but did you listen?" Lady Flora held out her own glass and her husband poured.

"It was you who delayed me there. We might have made it back in time if we had returned at once."

Rick threw back his hood but before he could open his mouth, Lady Flora began to laugh and descended on him with a napkin in hand. Rising on her tiptoes, she scrubbed at his face.

"Rick, my dear boy, the kohl from your eyebrows has run all over your skin. You resemble a miner newly emerged from underground. Your visage is so forbidding I wonder any innkeeper spoke to you."

"They did and more. I suppose they were grateful I did not rob them." Rick seized the napkin to continue the cleaning and made use of a bowl of water set out for the washing of hands. As he scrubbed, he talked.

"I came across the place where our couple spent their bridal night, registering as Dr. and Mrs. Leonidas McLaughlin with no attempt at subterfuge."

The duke frowned into the glass of red wine. "A person may sign a ledger in any way they choose. It means nothing."

"True, I did not find any record of their marriage at either St. Andrew's or Old High Church, but still have innumerable sanctuaries and chapels to visit. The rectors simply would not allow me to go on my way without partaking of tea." Lady Flora sipped her wine as if grateful for the change.

"Ah, but the innkeeper said the young lady carried a bouquet of heather and declared she was newly wed, a radiant bride, his exact words."

"I am so happy for Phemie, that she has found the man she loves—as have I." The duchess patted the hand of her husband in a conciliatory way, even though it seemed he might snap the delicate stem of the wineglass at any moment. "Any news of Pandora? I hate to think of her returning to England alone."

"She remains with them in her guise as Mr. Crowe. I spotted her shopping along High Street still in her manly garb, but thought it best to find where the three of them hide rather than drag her back here bodily to interrogate."

"Yes, she would never tell. The girl has the fortitude of the virgin martyrs. But why do I find it more peculiar that she was shopping than that she still wears trousers?" the duchess pondered.

"We were lucky there. She ordered alterations to a traveling gown and will return for the dress tomorrow at noon. We have only to wait in the carriage and follow her back to their hideaway. Now, if you would pour me a glass of wine and order the soup to be served, I would be a very happy man."

Thirty-three

They hid in plain sight by sandwiching their hired carriage between two ordinary hackneys, both paid to keep their place in front and behind. As irate would-be passengers came and went on this far more clement day and each driver claimed to be waiting for ladies in the shops, the duke and duchess watched for sight of Pandora. The coachmen, given a description of Mr. Crowe, were to accept no other fare.

Wearing a new disguise of a many-caped coat, a tartan muffler drawn up around his face, and a low-crowned hat pulled over his brow, Rick hunched on the box of the carriage, ready to follow whatever vehicle his sister-in-law chose. By his posture and partially revealed white hair, he gave the appearance of an elderly coachman. The kohl had not entirely washed out of his eyebrows, thanks to the heavy application by the duchess, but he hoped Pandora would not notice if he kept very still and head down. He'd always delighted in the sport of coaching, but had done little tearing along roads with four in hand since his marriage. However, with the Longleighs, one never knew what skills would be called upon, and he could soon prove his worth to his wife's family again.

The tingle of an adventure about to begin made him twitch the ribbons and alert the horses, who jangled their harness and stamped in preparation. Rick soothed them with a few words and a loosening of the reins. Then, he saw her. Pandora made her way along the street much as she had yesterday, far less encumbered but much more nervous, glancing over her shoulder and into every dark doorway. Rick kicked the back of the driver's box to alert the duke and duchess. He heard them raise the window curtain and make a few quiet remarks.

"Would you look at her, our daughter, striding along with shoulders back and belly thrust out, swinging her cane good as any man," the duchess said to her spouse.

"Remarkable, our Pandora."

~ * ~

Porteus Crowe turned into the dressmaker's shop after taking one last glance at the street. Pandora did not see the hulking man who had spied upon her yesterday. For all she knew, he had seen through her guise and meant to punish her for wearing men's clothing as some bullies did to people of either sex they considered as unnatural. She had heard tales of English women snatched off the streets to be sold into foreign brothels as well. Whatever this culprit wanted of her, whether the gold watch or her honor, she had come prepared today with the pistol concealed about her person.

Madame Munro's demeanor had changed entirely toward her customer: no obsequies, curtsies, or faux French phrases today. The dressmaker had the garment bundled in brown paper and neatly tied with strong string. She turned it over as if she could not be rid of Mr. Crowe soon enough and counted every penny before Pandora had exited to the street. Maybe the woman had seen through her disguise, too, though it had worked well enough aboard ship.

She'd told Phemie, who fretted about her sister's safe return and her reception at home, that she intended to remain in Jason's clothes until she reached England. Afterward, she would assume the gown plain enough to be worn by a governess taking the coach to a new post. She had thought it through, no need to be accused of becoming too fond of male dress or any impetuous actions. Humpf...she prided herself on good sense and lack of romantic notions.

Luck being on her side, a hackney waited on the street for passengers. Pandora gave the driver her direction and got aboard. Surprising her, the coachman pulled out smartly without waiting for more fares. Ah well, she would be back at the cottage in plenty of time to endure another of Phemie's poorly cooked dinners. Wistfully, she looked out the window at the coffee house where she had spent such a pleasant interval and noted the carriage behind them had also turned across the road right behind, though no one had gotten into it.

The fine hairs on her neck rose. Having the hackney to herself, she changed positions to get a better look at the other coachman. For all his bent posture and white hair, he possessed strong, broad shoulders and large, competent gloved hands. Forbidding dark brows shaded his light eyes, though the tartan muffler obscured most of his face. The same man, the very same, who had followed her yesterday, Pandora was certain. Would he attempt to pass and block the hackney, pull her from within and thrust her into the other coach where, no doubt, his fellow villains waited to subdue her?

Carefully, she removed the pistol from its hiding place and laid it on the seat next to her. Preparing to fight, she loosened the sword from the cane, but the carriage merely followed closely. She would have no choice but to act without second thoughts when they reached the cottage. Small, pregnant Phemie stayed within, and Pandora would not allow the marauders to enter that house in pursuit. She would make her stand on the street. As the hackney approached her destination, she steeled her resolve, and took the pistol in one hand. The sword she held ready in the other, in case her shot failed to scare away the enemy.

Her coach stopped before the cottage with a newly hung shingle reading *Leonidas McLaughlin, M.D.* Pandora waited not a minute, but leapt out, very nearly tripping over her own feet. The huge driver of the following carriage whipped the reins around the brake and jumped from his box very nearly on top of her. She barely touched the trigger of her weapon and the ball blasted forth to lodge in the chest of her assailant. The tartan muffler fell away and the low-crowned hat pitched to the ground revealing the stricken face of Godric Erikson. He watched the bloom of blood on his coat before wavering backward only to be caught in the arms of an even larger man.

"Papa!" Pandora let the pistol slip from her fingers. Both men flinched as it hit the ground. The hackney driver whipped up his horses and fled from the scene of mayhem with the passenger door still wide open.

"Panny, you have killed me," Rick panted.

Bellevue lowered his son-in-law to the ground. "Oh God, I never meant for this to happen. What shall I tell Thalia?"

"That she is still perfection in my eyes. I love no other but her. Bellevue, you will raise my sons as warriors?"

"If you do not live to raise them yourself, my word upon it."

"No one is going to die," the duchess pronounced. "We stand before the house of a physician, and he comes to our aid. Dr. McLaughlin, I presume?" She addressed the tall man with reddish-gold hair who rushed, completely unarmed, to their assistance.

Leo executed a short bow. "Lady Flora, because you can be no other, my pleasure. We must bring him inside at once and lay him on my table, strip off his coat and shirt."

Giving a considering look at Rick's size, he seized the feet and nodded for the duke to lift the torso. Pandora watched, her entire body beginning to shake, as Leo transformed from a lovesick bard to an entirely competent and masterful physician. She had no great fondness for Rick and his towering masculinity, but she had not meant to slay him. Thalia would never forgive her for plunging her into early widowhood, nor would anyone else in the family.

"I thought he was a stranger who meant me harm, honestly I did."

Her mother's arms came round her, holding her close. "An accident, Panny." The duchess turned to her other daughter wringing her hands on the front step. "Phemie, do not stand there crying in the doorway. Boil water. Make tea. Bring out the whisky, if you have any. We all have need of it."

The duchess took Pandora's cold hand in hers and led her along, following the splotches of blood into the cottage. Rick lay on the old kitchen table which Pandora had helped haul into Leo's surgery yesterday as he prepared to open his practice with no regard as to where they would eat their dinner. That the Earl of Danelagh was to be his first customer went unremarked. With the duke holding Rick up, the doctor stripped off the coachman's coat and bloodied waistcoat, tossing them to the floor. The shirt he sliced away with a scalpel selected from his medical box and examined the broad, pale back of his patient.

"A pity the ball did not go all the way through. Now we must search for it." Leo probed the chest wound with a long finger. Rick groaned in so much pain the duchess attempted to herd her girls to the kitchen and away from the sight.

"Viewing such things is not good for your baby, Phemie. Shocks like this have been known to unseat an infant from the womb or mark the child forever. Come away now. Tell me, have you learned to boil water yet?"

"Yes, Mama."

Pandora would not be led anymore. Still shaking, she said, "I want to stay and be of service in any way I can."

Removing his scarlet finger from the hole in Rick's chest, Leo gave her a hard stare. "If you are given to fainting, we cannot use you."

"Not I. Direct me."

"Very well. The ball has gone deep and might have been deflected by the ribs. I can attempt to find it with a forceps or allow it to remain and simply bandage the wound tightly, letting it close on its own. Our friends, the French, have discovered this is often less damaging than the traditional removal of the shot and cauterization. What say you?" He directed his remarks to the duke, who still held Rick's shoulders.

"One cannot live full of lead. It must be removed, of course, but I would not expect a man midwife or an engineer to know that."

"In Glasgow, we studied all forms of medicine, and the anatomy of both male and female. Yes, I can deliver an infant into the world with no harm to mother or babe, but I can also suture a wound or remove a limb like the best of surgeons. As for being an engineer, the human body is naught but a complex machine with the heart its pump, the joints its pistons. Consider your choice again."

"The ball must come out," the duke replied stubbornly.

"Pandora, look in the bottom of my medical chest. Bring me the large, brown bottle you find there." She followed Leo's orders immediately.

"Now, hold it to the patient's lips and help him to drink half of it."

"What are you giving him, man?" the duke questioned, full of suspicion.

Rick, his Adam's apple bobbing in his thick neck, paused for a breath. He offered them a feeble grin. "Excellent Scotch whisky. Save some for later."

"Unfortunately, we will need the rest to wash the wound. Urquhart will never forgive the use of his parting gift, but I have nothing else at the moment. Now, Bellevue, hold his shoulders to the table. Pandora, keep his feet still while I search for the ball."

As Leo probed the chest cavity with his forceps, Rick's mouth opened wide, a rictus of agony so great it served as a silent scream. "Got it, but I pray I have not done more damage than the actual shot." He tossed the ball into the heap of bloody clothing on the floor. "I must lave the wound. This will hurt."

"No more than the last," Rick struggled to say, but his body bucked when the whisky hit the raw flesh and one booted foot threw Pandora clear across the small room.

Then suddenly, the patient went still. Leo put his fingers to pulse in his patient's neck. "As I feared, he is bleeding within now that the ball is removed."

"You should have had your cauterizing iron hot and ready!" the duke bellowed.

"I do not care if you are God himself, do not tell me my profession. The iron does still more damage. I will bind the vessels with ligatures."

Immediately, he went deep into the cavity, completing the delicate work with speed and skill, drawing up the severed veins with the hooked tenaculum and tying each one off efficiently. A splash more of alcohol, the vapors of a barroom, blood, and spirits, rising into the air and tickling their nostrils, he finished. Wetting a pad of lint with the last remains of Brodie's gift, Leo applied the compress to Danelagh's chest and bound it with a bandage.

"Pandora, if you are able to get up, find a bottle on the rack behind me labeled tincture of ergot and bring a teaspoon. It's one of Uncle Duncan's remedies. I've found it effective in stopping excessive bleeding after birth, and it will serve the same purpose here."

Pandora, still gasping for air, got to her knees and, using the whitewashed wall, managed to rise to her feet. Half hunched over, she found the bottle and spoon, delivering them into the physician's hands.

"Forgive me, but I must wake the patient." Leo administered two sharp slaps to Rick's pale cheeks. The earl's drowsy lids rose over glazed gray eyes. His mouth gaped, and Leo slid the teaspoonful of ergot between his lips and held his mouth shut. The patient gagged but got it down.

"Good, now he can rest. I'd rather not carry him up the stairs. We will arrange a pallet for him here before the fire. He must be kept perfectly quiet. When he wakes, he will receive more of the tincture and needs a strengthening stimulant, eggnog perhaps, if any of the ladies can prepare it." Leo looked ruefully at the empty whisky bottle. "We are out of this particular remedy."

The duke, very quiet now, said, "My wife has some knowledge of care for the sick. I shall send out for the best spirits available."

"I commend you, sir, on your concern for your servants. Many of your rank would not have bothered to show a coachman so much care."

"Your Grace," the duke corrected, demanding his honorific title.

Leo stared him in the face. "I am a laird in my own right, and my clan once owned the lands you now possess. I shall not bow and scrape before you."

The duke's face spread with one of those white grins that could be interpreted as a deadly threat or vast amusement. "I like you. You are not the coward I supposed and seem a very useful sort, which is more than I can say for most of the aristocracy. This fellow on the table I love like my own sons. He is Thalia's husband, the Earl of Danelagh." The duke delivered one of his friendly blows to Leo's back and shook droplets of blood from the surgeon's fingertips.

"Could you send for that whisky now?" Leo requested, his hands so strong and sure in surgery Pandora wondered that they trembled slightly now.

Holding her bruised stomach, she laughed, and then grimaced with discomfort. "I believe he will live, Leo. A man who kicks that hard must be difficult to kill."

"I should examine you as well, sister. He might have done you internal harm with that blow."

"I will be fine." She withdrew the pillow that created her fake belly. "Thank heaven for this or I might have taken more injury than a boot-shaped bruise. Here." She handed it to her father. "You can use it to cushion Rick's head. I will not be in need of it anymore."

Thirty-four

The Longleighs gathered in Phemie's tiny parlor with the duke's size and Leo's length making the room seem even smaller and very, very crowded. Pandora, in the spirit of atonement, had scrubbed the surgery table and mopped its floor once Rick was removed to the mattress from her bed and laid before the fire with the pillow from her waistcoat cushioning his head. Still, no one suggested the table be returned to the kitchen for the serving of dinner, and they partook of the stew Phemie had concocted by bending over small bowls and spooning it up where they sat. A loaf from the baker and a crock of butter sat on the low tea table for all to share.

Out of his mouth, Leo removed a small bone from the badly dressed hare that served as the base for the meal and set it aside. The duke in a conciliatory spirit said, "Reminiscent of Shawnee cookery."

"Yes," the duchess agreed. "They used little salt. I was once chastised by old Snakeroot for adding too much of it to a venison and cornmeal stew that I believe I could still make today if need be."

"Salt! Oh, that is what I have forgotten. Let me fetch it." Phemie rushed to the kitchen.

Pandora grumbled, "If only she could bring some savory herbs and less mushy potatoes, too."

Her mother gave her a quelling look. "She will learn, if she must, but I do not think that will be necessary. Will it, my dearest?" This last remark she addressed to her husband. "You do recall our discussion at Glenmoriston and last evening, the simple solution to this situation."

Why the duke went redder in the face, only Rick tucked away in the surgery would know. He cleared his throat. "Your Mama does know how to get a point across."

Phemie returned holding out the saltcellar first to her father. The duke took the small spoon between his large fingers and sprinkled his stew, all the while gazing on the face of his most beloved daughter, his Little Dove. At her anxious look, he tasted his dinner again.

"Better?" she asked.

"Yes. So much like your mother—and her first efforts at cooking."

Phemie carried the dish of salt to her husband and held it out. "Thank you, my love, but I have finished already."

"Should I bring you more?" Phemie asked eagerly.

"Och, no. I will be sitting up with my patient tonight and do not want to overfeed lest I sleep."

The duke appraised his unwanted son-in-law, Leo's tender glance at Phemie, the young man's unwillingness to hurt her feelings. Before he could speak, Pandora did.

"I want to sit the night with Rick. Doctor, you have earned your rest and I have not done enough to make up for my violence." She waved away an offer of salt, set down her half-eaten stew, and crossed her trousered legs at the knees. "I would not want to overfeed either."

The duchess raised her eyebrows at Panny's casual manly stance, but the gentlemen appeared or pretended not to notice. Instead, Leo took up her offer.

"Thank you. He will be feverish. It is always so with gunshot wounds. Make sure he stays still. You may put cool cloths on his brow. Call me if he becomes delirious, and I will administer a febrifuge made from willow bark that my uncle swears by."

The duke coughed hard into his hand as if some object had lodged in his throat. Alarm crossed Leo's face. "Do you choke on a rabbit bone, sir? Nod if you need my assistance."

"No, I am well. I never thought to say these words, but I offer you the lairdship of Castle Laughlin."

Leo's posture went from one of preparing for immediate action to a sudden stiffening of the spine. "It is not yours to offer as I am already the laird, though I thought nothing of it before meeting your daughter, my Lady McLaughlin."

Phemie laid a softening hand on her husband's shoulder, again so like her mother, and betrayed herself with a small gasp when her father said, "I retract the offer."

"Pearce!" the duchess admonished with all the anguish of seeing her careful plans for her daughter's happiness go helter-skelter again because of the stubbornness of men showing on her face.

Bellevue inhaled, expanding his great chest. "I meant to say, I want you and Phemie to oversee the castle and properties for Viscount Laughlin. You shall have a share of the profits from the grazing rights, quarry, and fisheries, though James will retain the greater amount to fund his expeditions. I will also finance this steam engine of yours as an investment. Do not fail me."

"No, no! I shall not. Phemie, we are going home to Castle Laughlin."

"And we will not live in the dungeon!"

"Marvelous, all is settled then." The duchess set aside her stew. "Now, I shall need a dozen eggs, sugar, both milk and cream, and a nutmeg to make a strengthening posset for Rick. Will you see to obtaining some Jamaica rum and a bottle of brandy for the receipt, my dearest?"

From across the hall, the Earl of Danelagh called out in a voice already regaining its strength, "Just bring me the bourbon and rum and leave out the insipid ingredients."

"He mends," replied the duchess, raising her voice. "He will drink every bit of my posset. But if he is feeling well enough in the morning, the ladies shall go back to Madame Munro's Maison de Mode and outfit Pandora with some proper clothes for our return to Bellevue Hall."

Pandora groaned and flung herself back in her chair, her legs sprawled forward. "Can we not simply find that cowardly blackguard of a hackney driver and retrieve the traveling gown and the lower half of Jason's cane?"

"I will set your father to that task, but oh, what fun we shall have. First, we must wash and dress your hair. You will need slippers and undergarments as well, not to mention a becoming bonnet."

Pandora dropped her head into her hands. "Why did not God make me a man with all their rights and freedoms and none of their vices?"

The duchess gave serious consideration to that question and answered, "Because someday you shall meet a man who will make you rejoice in your womanhood, Pandora Jane Black Wing Longleigh."

"Unlikely, very unlikely, and I would make a wager to that effect." She allowed herself one last languorous stretch of her limbs before her mother hurried her back into petticoats.

The duke held up a cautionary finger. "I warn you, never bet against your mother. She is always right in the end.

Epilogue

Bellevue Hall, Christmas, 1814

The Longleigh grandchildren, and there were many, gathered around the oval table and vied for a turn to push the tiny smoking steam engine and its six-wheeled oar carts filled with pebbles, sand, and chips of coal around on its rails. The engine made frequent stops to offload its cargo in little heaps and pick up its burdens on the next trip round.

"My turn, my turn to push," young Piers Erikson shouted.

Helena, his baby sister, wormed her way through Aunt Clio's and Aunt Callie's children, two sets of twins born within a day of each other, two boys and two girls, and between Piers and Axel. "No, mine! My doggie wants to ride." She held out the tiny figurine of a spaniel she'd found in the toe of her stocking hung on the bedpost for St. Nicholas to fill with treats and toys and placed it on the platform car as Axel slowed the train for the new passenger.

A recent addition to the railroad, the canopied platform car outfitted with miniature chairs, waggled along at the rear. The little girls loved this feature best because miniature dolls greatly resembling

261

their grandparents in splendid dress rode there. The real Duke of Bellevue swore he would ride the L & M Railroad from the quarry to the sea on its first run, no matter what the danger, as simple incentive to build a safe invention. Lady Flora insisted she would die by his side.

"No one will die on Leo's contraption, Mama. I still say we must arrange to have toys made from the plans. By next Christmas, every child will want one." Charmingly round in her fifth month of pregnancy, Phemie gave Leo's arm a proud and possessive squeeze.

"I agree. Our son-to-be must have one," said Joshua's wife, Kate, also pleasantly full-bellied with child. The gold flecks in her brown eyes sparkled with her joy.

"Are you so sure of a boy, then?" the duchess asked.

Kate nodded. "At times, I still hear from Fair Annet, and she assures me I will bear the next in line of Longleigh male heirs."

"You would take the word of a ghost?" Pandora sneered, clearly indicating she thought Kate still addled from her past ordeal when she had conjured a ghost for company.

"Only the ghost who helped me to find her," Joshua Longleigh, as tall and darkly handsome as all the Longleigh men, but far more fashionably dressed in a red and gold waistcoat for the holiday than the rest of them. He kissed his wife's hand.

"Did Fair Annet say anything about my child?" Phemie asked, more willing to believe in fairy tales since her abduction by Leo.

Kate smiled with Madonna-like serenity. "Only that Leo is no longer the Last Laird of Laughlin."

"A boy, my dearest, we are to have a son!"

Leo humored his little wife. "While I've found there is no sure way to guess or guarantee the sex of a child, I will take Fair Annet's word on it."

Jason wandered over to their group and gave Pandora a peck on the cheek. "Thank you for the new silk hat. The sword cane is even more splendid than my old one."

"Well, Mama would not allow me to keep the hat and said I owed you a new cane. Put them to good use," she replied ungraciously.

A maid offering small cups of eggnog on her tray passed among the family members. Sitting by the fire, Rick shooed her away. "I've had enough of that invalid's drink to last me a lifetime. Haven't we anything stronger?"

Sitting at his side, Thalia took two glasses. "You are not fully recovered as yet, no matter what you say. But you still have a lifetime ahead, thanks to Leo and none to Pandora. Drink it. Drink it for me, dearest." She held his gray glance with her dark one and raised the cup to his mouth. Rick downed the eggnog and licked the foam from his lips, never breaking their intense stare.

The duchess observed to those around her, "Nothing like nearly losing your love to fan the flames of passion. We shall have another grandchild on the way by spring, I'd wager.

"No one will take that bet," her husband answered.

"Look over there in the corner. Another of my successful matches. How Bertie does dote on Miss Hotchkiss. I merely had to mention that Gladys had been ill-used and needed only gentle words and a good heart in a husband rather than grace on the dance floor or a glib tongue. She shows good judgment in preferring a man who is more kind, even if chubby, than handsome and dashing. Now if only we could get him to take her to *his* father's home. The both of them have been visiting overlong."

"His interest peaked after you supplied her with a suitable dowry, but I suppose Butterworth's heir will do for Gladys. He is good-natured and not too proud being the son of a baker's daughter," Pandora remarked. "She might have done even better if you had given her half my dowry, as I suggested."

"That baker you spoke of supplied most of London with bread and dominated the fancy pastry trade as well. Lady Butterworth was a substantial heiress. Too big a dowry can be just as bad as none, since it will draw fortune hunters. You must beware of that type during your next season, Panny."

"Why must I have a next season?"

"Because I want you to be happy, Pandora Jane!"

Pandora's identical twin sisters, Clio and Calliope, curly-haired, shorter and five years her elder, approached and bracketed her arms on either side. "Come, don't be sour. Do sit and tell us of your adventures dressed as a man," Clio said.

Pandora's dark face brightened. "You have no idea of the freedoms denied the female sex, even in matters of dress."

Callie lowered her voice to a whisper. "We heard you nearly became engaged to Miss Hotchkiss."

Leo blinked as if seeing double. His gaze cut across the room to their identical twin husbands leaning casually against the holly and evergreen bedecked mantle and conversing with Rick. Clearly overwhelmed by the numerous and complex Longleigh family, not an unusual reaction in new members, his brothers-in-law had assured him, he excused himself.

"I believe I would like to walk in the conservatory for a while. Phemie, would you care for a stroll?"

"Not now, dearest. I must be sure Panny does not exaggerate our adventures."

"As if anyone could."

Leo left the crowded drawing room, noisy with the high-pitched voices of children, the chatter of women, and basso of men, and walked the halls to the duchess's pride and joy, her collection of rare and exotic plants, all of them maintained by his Uncle Duncan. He entered the glass-walled chamber where moisture slid down the windows like perspiration on an overheated face. The gravel of the path through the tropical foliage crunched beneath his shoes as he made his way by the cold moonlight reflected off the exterior snow to a fountain where a statue of a naked nymph poured water into a basin. She reminded him of Phemie, with her curls and dainty smallness, and of how lucky he was to have her, even with all the Longleighs in tow.

A dark shadow stole across the nymph like the approach of a satyr about to steal her away. Leo twirled and sought the small knife carried in his boot, a Scottish habit the duke seemed to approve. He did not have to draw it.

His uncle Duncan stood before him holding out a dusty bottle. "I waited for ye to come away from the others. On wintry nights, I often sleep here to be sure the heating doesna fail. The duchess appreciates that, but truth be told, I sling my hammock between two trees and dream I live on a tropic isle the likes of which I will never see. Here, a wee bit o' Christmas cheer, well-aged Scotch whisky left over from your last visit here."

"No drugs or herbs in it?"

"Ye wound me, lad. None at all, but if ye be needing any help in the bedchamber, come by my cottage tomorrow and I will see what I can do."

"No, thank you. My bride is already pregnant."

"Aye, with the next laird. The curse is broken. Ye will have a long life now, Leo, and the treasures of the earth will open to ye."

"Phemie is my treasure. I need nothing more."

"Then, we will disregard holding the castle again, getting a share of the profits from the sheep, quarry, and fisheries, and gaining financial backing for the steam engine. Instead, we toast Lady McLaughlin." Duncan cracked open the bottle and took a swig. He wiped the lip and passed it on to his nephew.

"To my beloved wife." Leo took a sip. "And to Uncle Duncan, who brought all this about, no matter how." He drank again. "I am sorry we had to pledge not to reveal that Phemie's husband is the gardener's great-nephew. The Longleighs are liberal and I am not ashamed of our connection, but they don't want any vicious gossip to wound their daughter. Marrying a laird is falling low enough for a duke's offspring."

"Och, laddie, anyone I care about knows already. As for the rest, I dinna mind. I keep my position and my cottage. The duke has an understanding of clans from his years with the Shawnee and knows I would never betray him again, now that we are united by marriage and soon by blood when the wee bairn arrives."

The sound of the conservatory door opening, and the light tread of slippers on the path ended their private conversation. Leo marveled that, after so short a marriage, he recognized her footsteps. As Phemie emerged from the leaf-dappled shadows, Duncan stepped behind a man-sized potted palm.

"There you are and all alone. Believe me, I know how overbearing my family can be. We need some time together without them." Her big brown eyes assessed the size and strength of a nearby bench. Her fine-boned hands reached up and tugged on his red-gold side whiskers, the remains of the once impressive beard. He'd left them at her request and not argued that a clean-shaven face was more sanitary for a physician.

"My lion in the heather." She drew his mouth to hers.

The old head gardener emerged, doffing his cap and doing his bob. "Your pardon, Lady Euphemia, I was on my way back to the cottage after checking the conservatory temperature. Aye, it is hot enough in here, and I will go."

Phemie dropped her arms and, instead, delivered her kiss to Duncan's whiskery cheek. "Merry Christmas, Uncle."

"Now, now, lass, I mean to keep my word and know my place. I will celebrate Boxing Day tomorrow with the rest of the servants."

"In private, you will be my dear Uncle Duncan, to whom I owe all my happiness."

"Thank ye, child. May the blessings of the season be upon ye, Leo, and the babe to come." He left, trudging along the gravel walk in his heavy brogans loud enough for them to know when he had reached the door.

"I believe we are free of members from both sides of the family now." Leo bent his head to claim the kiss delayed.

Phemie reached for his whiskers again. "Now, my love, shall we play lion in the hothouse?"

Meet Lynn Shurr

Lynn Shurr grew up in Pennsylvania Dutch country, but left to wander the world shortly after getting a degree in English literature. After living in several states and Europe, she picked up a degree in librarianship. Her first reference job brought her to the Cajun Country of Louisiana. Eventually, she became director of a library system. For her the old saying, "Once you've tasted bayou water, you will always remain here," came true. She raised three children near the banks of the Bayou Teche and lives there still with her astronomer husband, where she writes, paints, studies history, and roots for the LSU Tigers and the New Orleans Saints.

Other Works From The Pen Of
Lynn Shurr

Lady Flora's Rescue: Book One of the Longleigh Chronicles – Lady Flora follows the man she loves into the American wilderness not knowing he plans to remain there. Will he choose love over his own liberty?

***The Perfect Daughter**: Book Two of the Longleigh Chronicles* – When a fascinating gentleman rejects perfection, what must a young lady do to gain his love? Perhaps seduction.

Daughter of the Rainbow: Book Three of the Longleigh Chronicles – Shy but lovely Iris Longleigh is passionate about only two things—painting and Lord Valls, who will not marry her due to a secret he harbors.

The Double Dilemma: Book Four of the Longleigh Chronicles – The Longleigh twins wish to marry only twins and find them in an isolated castle on a forbidding coast. The adventure begins!

The Greatest Prize: Book Five of the Longleigh Chronicles – Jilted by the man she was supposed to marry, Kate sets out to prove she can win a greater prize.

A Taste of Bayou Water – a prequel to *Blessings and Curses*. When Celine Landry refuses to leave Cajun Country to marry billionaire Jonathan Hartz, what else can a brilliant techno-geek do but try to become Cajun?

Blessings and Curses – Adrienne and Pete—is their love real or are they the victims of an old traiteur's love potion?

The Courville Rose – Can four souls find love in two bodies?

A Place Apart – A wounded warrior and a society girl both seek seclusion on the same deserted island. Sparks fly!

Letter to Our Readers

Enjoy this book?

You can make a difference

As an independent publisher, Wings ePress, Inc. does not have the financial clout of the large New York Publishers. We can't afford large magazine spreads or subway posters to tell people about our quality books.

But, we do have something much more effective and powerful than ads. We have a large base of loyal readers.

Honest Reviews help bring the attention of new readers to our books.

If you enjoyed this book, we would appreciate it if you would spend a few minutes posting a review on the site where you purchased this book or on the Wings ePress, Inc. webpages at:

https://wingsepress.com/

Thank You

Visit Our Website

For The Full Inventory
Of Quality Books:

Wings ePress.Inc
https://winasepress.com/

Quality trade paperbacks and downloads
in multiple formats,
in genres ranging from light romantic comedy
to general fiction and horror.
Wings has something for every reader's taste.
Visit the website, then bookmark it.
We add new titles each month!

Wings ePress Inc.
3000 N. Rock Road
Newton, KS 67114

www.ingramcontent.com/pod-product-compliance
Lightning Source LLC
Chambersburg PA
CBHW070629100726
47907CB00007B/1916